BT
3/5/10
27.95

D1126125

HEART OF STONE

HEART OF STONE

Jane Jackson

This first world edition published 2009
in Great Britain and 2010 in the USA by
SEVERN HOUSE PUBLISHERS LTD of
9–15 High Street, Sutton, Surrey, England, SM1 1DF.

British Library Cataloguing in Publication Data

Jackson, Jane, 1944–
    Heart of Stone.
    1. Single mothers – England – Cornwall (County) – History –
    19th century – Fiction. 2. Quarries and quarrying –
    England – Cornwall (County) – History – 19th century –
    Fiction. 3. Veterans – Wounds and injuries – Fiction.
    4. Cornwall (England: County) – Social conditions – 19th
    century – Fiction. 5. Love stories.
    I. Title
    823.9'14–dc22

ISBN-13: 978-0-7278-6825-1   (cased)

All Severn House titles are printed on acid-free paper.

Severn House Publishers support The Forest Stewardship Council [FSC],
the leading international forest certification organisation. All our titles that
are printed on Greenpeace-approved FSC-certified paper carry the FSC logo.

Mixed Sources
Product group from well-managed
forests and other controlled sources
www.fsc.org Cert no. SA-COC-1565
© 1996 Forest Stewardship Council

Typeset by Palimpsest Book Production Ltd.,
Grangemouth, Stirlingshire, Scotland.
Printed and bound in Great Britain by
MPG Books Ltd., Bodmin, Cornwall.

To Mike, as always, with love

One

One

Sarah Govier hurried along the deeply rutted dirt road towards the quarry. Mud squelched around her leather half-boots and caked the hem of her skirt and petticoats. A wet April meant a good wheat harvest and it was now mid-May. With the sun shining in a cloudless sky the colour of bluebells, surely the ground would begin drying soon.

The gusty breeze had a sharp edge that made her glad of her navy wool cloak with its red worsted lining.

Why hadn't Jeb come and told her himself? She shouldn't have had to discover it from Becky.

As she neared the quarry, she could hear the rhythmic clanging of sledgehammers hitting a steel-tipped borer. Her heartbeat quickened as she reached the top of the slight incline. Ahead of her, anchored by eight stout chains, she saw the upright mast and angled jib of the wooden crane. Stone lay in untidy waste heaps amid the furze, bracken and coarse grass that surrounded the gaping hole. As she walked into the quarry, down along the broad shallow slope used by heavy wagons to carry the stone down to the town quay, she saw two men working on a huge block of granite and another three examining the new face revealed by the recent blasting. As they caught sight of her, hammers were lowered and all five snatched off their caps as they exchanged glances.

Guilt tempered her anger. Why hadn't they come to her? 'A word if you please, Jeb?'

He scrambled down, crossing the dusty rock-strewn floor towards her, 'Miss.'

'Mr Flynn is not here?'

'No, Miss.'

'Have you seen him at all today?'

Jeb shook his head. 'No, Miss. Nor yesterday.'

Hot and bright as a flame, renewed rage flared inside her and, with it, remorse. Yes, she had been frantic with worry about her son. But that was no excuse.

'I understand the men have not been paid for several weeks. Is this true?'

After a moment's hesitation, Jeb nodded, twisting his cap. 'Yes, Miss.'

'Why didn't you come and tell me?'

'Flynn said you knew.'

Shock rocked her. 'What?'

'Anyhow, we didn't want to give you no more trouble, what with your boy being ill and all.'

Her heart clenched in to a fist inside her chest and shame burned her cheeks. 'I didn't know, Jeb. I would never have allowed . . .' She shook her head. Now was not the time. 'How have you managed?'

'Gived us credit, didn't he,' Jeb said grimly.

'*Credit?*'

His weathered face darkened. No longer silenced by the ganger's lies, or by concern for her, words poured out of him.

'Flynn own a bakehouse in Penryn, see? He said we could have what we wanted and put it on the slate. Not just bread, neither. He's in with other gangers who work for Kinser Landry. They got shares in a grocery shop, an ironmongers and the Black Bull Inn. Trouble is, all of 'em do charge higher prices than the other shops. But having no money, we couldn't go nowhere else.'

'So now you're in debt?' Sarah asked quietly. He nodded.

It was pointless telling Jeb he should not have believed Flynn; he should have come straight to her.

'And the other men?'

''Tis the same for all of us, Miss.'

'How long is it since you were paid?'

'Be seven weeks come Friday,' Jeb said, then lowered his voice. 'Arthur's in some state, what with Mary about to have their third. See, even if Flynn do pay'n what he's owed, once Arthur have settled with the bakehouse and grocer and paid his rent, he won't have enough to live on till next payday.'

Sarah wanted to shake him. How could Jeb have believed that she would have any part in such a wicked scheme? He had worked at Talvan quarry for nearly thirty years. Even her father had never been able to read granite the way Jeb Mundy could. After her father's death, she had offered Jeb the position of ganger. But he had turned it down, saying he hadn't the heart for hiring and firing men he'd known all his life. She knew other quarry owners and granite merchants had tried to entice him away with the promise of higher wages. But Jeb was loyal. How could she berate him for wanting to spare her worry?

'How much do they owe?'

Jeb scratched his head. 'I aren't rightly sure.' He hesitated. 'I reckon we're all afeared of finding out.'

Sarah nodded. 'I understand. But we have to put a stop to this now. Flynn had no right to withhold your money. Tell the men when they finish work this afternoon they are to go to each of the shops where they owe money and ask for a settlement figure.'

'*A settlement figure,*' the quarryman repeated, frowning.

'That's right. Ask for it to be written down on a piece of paper. You do the same. Don't be put off. You might have to wait a few minutes, but all shopkeepers keep records. They'll have everything written down. All they have to do is open the account book and find each man's name. You bring those figures to me first thing tomorrow.'

Raising a knuckle to his forehead, he nodded. 'Right you are, Miss. Boy coming on all right, is he?'

Sarah smiled and felt some of the tension ease from her shoulders. 'He's much better, thank you.'

''Tis some nasty, that scarlet fever. Still, if he's on the mend, he'll be dripping on 'bout being bored.'

Sarah laughed. 'We've heard little else from him all this week.'

'Wrap 'n up warm and send 'n out in the fresh air,' Jeb advised. 'Tire 'n out and you won't have no trouble getting 'n up over stairs of a night.'

'He went into Penryn with Becky today.' She hadn't wanted him to, sure that it was too soon. But Becky had said they would take the donkey shay so he wouldn't have to walk. He had been fine, just as Becky promised. Jeb had raised three sons to adulthood and spoke from experience. But Jory was only six years old. And the terrible days and nights when she feared she would lose him were still painfully fresh in her mind.

'I'll see you in the morning. And Jeb, please tell the men that Flynn lied: I didn't know.'

''Glad to hear it, Miss. I did wonder.' Replacing his cap, Jeb touched the brim in salute and turned back to the waiting men.

Wondered, but didn't come and ask me, which would have spared us all this trouble. With the sinking sun at her back and the breeze urging her along, Sarah headed home.

Facing south, the long, low cottage was actually two dwellings. The larger of the two had two downstairs rooms, two bedrooms and a scullery containing the copper at the back. Adjoining it under the same slate roof, with an entrance at the side, the smaller dwelling had a single living room/kitchen with a bedroom over it and a lean-to washhouse.

Thick cob walls gleamed white under their coating of lime wash. Smoke curled from two chimneys, and six small-paned sash windows sparkled in the afternoon sunshine.

Closing the garden gate, Sarah walked up the path and through the open door to the kitchen, inhaling the sweet fragrance of the candied-peel and raisin-stuffed *hevva* cake Becky was sliding from the baking iron and on to a cooling rack.

Jory looked up from the slate on which he was carefully chalking letters, flashed her a beaming smile and turned the slate around so that she could see.

'Look, Ma. I can write.'

Her son: the joy of her life. Philip had forfeited so much. Six years had dulled the pain of his brutal betrayal, and now he rarely crossed her mind. When he did, she thought of all that he was missing. But he had made his choice.

'You're a clever boy.' Shaking her head, she sent Jory a mock glare. 'And a very grubby one.'

His grin widened. 'I been busy.'

'You have? I want to hear all about it.'

'Later,' Becky intervened. 'Right now your ma look like she need a cup o' tea.' She turned to Sarah. 'The kettle have just boiled. Come and sit down.'

Unfastening her cloak, Sarah hung it on the wooden peg beside the door, dropped a kiss on her son's curly-haired head and came closer to the fire.

'Was it right, what I heard?' Becky asked softly.

Sarah nodded. 'I should have known . . .'

'Oh yes? Got the second sight, have you?' Becky had set out plates, cups and saucers, buttered bread, fresh scones cut in half, a dish of jam and another of clotted cream. Setting a glass of milk in front of Jory, she filled two cups with tea and pushed one towards Sarah. 'Come on, my bird. You'll feel better for something to eat.'

As Sarah drew out a chair, Becky sat down opposite. 'You'll never guess who I seen in town this morning.' She didn't wait for a response. 'That man Crago, from Jericho Farm? Great long streak, he is.'

Sarah's lips twitched. Becky was five feet high and the same around. Compared to her, everyone was tall.

'Got some thatch of black curly hair. Don't look like he been near a scissors since he come back. Folk was staring something awful, poor soul. He was in front of me, so I couldn't see his face. No wonder he don't go out much. More than two year since he moved into the place, but Ivy reckons he haven't been in town above twice.'

Sarah cradled her cup. 'Who can blame him?'

'Still, he's doing some lovely job on the farmhouse.'

'Has Ivy seen it?'

Becky shook her head. 'No. But with Noah working up there, she do hear all about it. Mister's grandpa owned the farm. I remember him before he shut his self away and let the place go to rack and ruin. Slates gone, roof leaking, plaster falling off, hall floor rotted away. Since Mister came back, he's spent a cartload of money on it. Told Noah he wanted only the best of craftsmen and materials. Going to be 'andsome when 'tis finished.'

'Let's hope he lives long enough to enjoy it.' As Becky's eyebrows rose, Sarah rubbed her forehead where she could feel an ache forming. 'I'm sorry. I shouldn't have . . .'

'Is he going to die, Ma?' Jory piped up.

Becky clicked her tongue, muttering, 'I tell you, that child is sharp as a tack. He don't miss a thing.'

'No, my love. It's just – Mr Crago owns a gunpowder mill and that's a very dangerous place.'

'Will it blow up?'

'I hope not.'

'Grampa blowed up, didn't he? In the quarry?'

Sarah's eyes met Becky's. The blasting accident had killed her father and Becky's husband; a shared loss that had drawn the two women even closer.

'Yes, but—'

'You going to eat that scone, boy?' Becky interrupted. ''Cause if you aren't—'

'I am! I am!' Jory said quickly and took a huge mouthful that left smears of jam and cream around his mouth. Sarah picked up his slate and diverted his attention by writing his name for him to copy.

When they had finished eating, Becky washed up. Drying the dishes, Sarah returned them to the dresser and gave in to Jory's pleas to be allowed to go and lock up the chickens for the night.

Becky wiped the table. 'The boy didn't mean nothing by it, my bird.'

'I know,' Sarah hung the dish cloth over the clothes-drying rack. 'Children are so open, aren't they? Saying whatever comes into their heads. Father would have been the first to laugh. Oh, Becky, I do miss him. Jeb admitted that they're all in debt. No ganger would have dared take advantage if—'

'If your father was still living, you wouldn't have needed no ganger. When you took Flynn on, you done what you b'lieved was best for the men and the quarry. 'T'idn your fault that he turned out bad. Now, leave it go. If you're up half the night fretting, you'll be no use to man nor beast.'

'You're right.' Sarah sighed, pressing the heels of her hands to her eyes. 'Becky, I don't know what I'd do without you.'

'Get on,' Becky snorted. 'Right, I'm gone. You mind what I say. You done your best.' As the door opened and Jory came in, Becky bent, caught his face in her hands and gave him a noisy kiss. 'G'night, my 'andsome. Sleep tight.'

'Mind the bugs don't bite,' Jory grinned back at her and scampered away as she pretended to chase him.

'Goodnight, Becky,' Sarah said. 'And thank you.'

With a dismissive wave, Becky closed the door behind her.

Her best? Sarah had believed so. But it wasn't enough.

Half an hour later, she had Jory stripped and standing in the big enamel basin in front of the fire while she soaped him down.

'Ma? Now I'm better, can I go with Uncle Noah again? I like it with the men.'

'I'll ask him.' Kneeling, she scooped water over him to rinse off the soap. Looking at his pale skin, gilded by the firelight, she recalled the livid rash and high fever that had terrified her.

'Promise?'

'I promise.' Sarah wrapped him in the towel and lifted him out, on to the rug. 'Foot.'

He rested his small hand on her shoulder and lifted his foot so she could wipe it. 'When I was in town, I saw Micky Keast. He said you were a horse.'

For a moment Sarah was baffled. 'Did he? I wonder why.'

Jory shrugged and changed feet. 'Aunty Beck heard him and her face went all red. She said he was a wicked boy and stung his legs. He ran away then. I don't like him.'

As she realized what Micky Keast had really said, Sarah held her son's small body close, her heart raging. It was not against the skinny, ferret-faced child with two older brothers and a mother clearly terrified of her husband. The focus of her fury was Micky's father, Nathan Keast, an arrogant flirt with a reputation for bedding any woman he set his sights on.

Ever since Jory's birth, she had been a target. But having known Nathan since they were children, she was unimpressed by either his looks or his slick charm. Realizing that he counted any re-action – even disgust – as a victory, she simply ignored him, responding neither to greetings nor comments, and continued on her way as if he didn't exist.

In calling her a whore, Micky had been prompted by his father. Becky had not mentioned it. Sarah guessed there were many such incidents that Becky had chosen not to mention, believing 'least said, soonest mended'. That Jory had misheard was a blessing. But how much longer would she be able to protect him?

'Ma? Why did Aunty Beck smack him?'

Dropping the towel, she slipped the warmed nightshirt over her son's head. 'Because it's rude and unkind to call people names.' She kissed his soft cheek and shooed him away. 'Go on now, up to bed.'

'Will you read me a story?'

Sarah pretended to consider.

'Please, Ma? *Please?*'

Helpless against his pleading grin, she nodded. 'All right. Only for a few minutes, mind. Which would you like?'

'*Ivanhoe,*' he said at once.

'Again? Go on, then. I'll count to five. One,' she clapped her hands. Giggling, he scampered up the wooden staircase.

Two

Each morning upon waking, James Crago walked through the bare echoing house and opened every window, for Sam had warned against painting until the fresh plaster had had time to dry out. The rising sun beamed pale light in to rooms that were as empty as his soul.

Leaving the master bedroom, he crossed the landing to a wide, shallow staircase that curved down to a generously proportioned hall. Beneath his palm, the new balustrade was satin-smooth.

The new floorboards were dusty and bore traces of mud, but soon they would gleam with varnish. Doors had been taken down, the old paint and door furniture removed, new applied and fitted, then rehung. Rotted and rat-gnawed panelling had been replaced, the upper walls replastered. It was nearly finished. But what then?

Despair yawned in front of him, a vast black pit that terrified and enticed. He blinked, breathed deeply, then thrust it back, locking it away. Then? Then he would unpack the cases he'd brought back from India, bring the few good pieces that had belonged to his grandfather out of storage, buy whatever was lacking and furnish the house. After that – he would not think beyond that.

Back in the kitchen, he folded the blankets, laying them neatly on top of the wood-and-canvas folding bed that currently occupied one corner and part of the inner wall. At its foot stood a large dresser. Between shelves above and cupboards beneath, the broad surface was covered with neat piles of invoices, bills, orders and other paperwork, each pile held in place by a glittering lump of granite he had picked up off the moor.

To the right of the kitchen window, a pump supplied fresh water from the well. Beneath an oblong brown stone sink on brick pillars with a draining board alongside were two buckets, a dustpan and brush and a wooden box containing rags, boot-blacking and brushes. Alongside the back door, another door led into a scullery.

A large oblong table of sycamore wood occupied the centre of the kitchen with a single chair tucked beneath. A wheelbacked armchair with a flattened cushion on the seat stood beside the range. Draped over a drying rack suspended from the ceiling above the mantelpiece by a pulley, were shirts, socks and several towels.

Crago straightened, arching his back and flexing his shoulders. He had forgotten what it felt like to sleep in a proper bed. But the new one was almost finished: a spacious rectangular frame that would accommodate his six-foot-plus length in comfort. Noah Hichens had made a superb job of the oak headboard and footboard. On the new range, a monster of black iron and polished brass that drew the workmen's gaze every time they entered, a large copper kettle – dented and green with verdigris – heated for the second time.

Washed and shaved, Crago spooned tea from a metal caddy into the blue and white teapot. Putting the tin back on the mantelpiece and using a scorched pan-holder, he poured water on the tea leaves and replaced the lid. A smile briefly lifted one corner of his mouth as he fitted the thick-knitted tea cosy. A few weeks ago Noah Hichens had tossed it on to the table and said that his wife hoped it might be useful: a small act of kindness, unexpected and appreciated.

Since his return to Cornwall, Crago had deliberately limited his contact with people. He saw Zack, Nessa and his team of workmen. That was enough.

After long years of neglect, the house was nearly ready. Confident in Sam and his team, he had set up his business a quarter of a mile away in a steep-sided valley that marked the edge of his land.

After diverting the small river into a leat to drive a waterwheel, he had hired Noah Hichens' cousin Joe and his apprentice to build several sheds. His instructions, to make one side of each shed deliberately weak, had been met first with bemusement, then with startled realization. Once the sheds were finished, Joe and his lad had joined the team working on the house.

The isolated position of the farmhouse meant that on wet mornings, men arrived soaked. Crago knew all too well what that felt like. In India during the monsoon he had spent more time wet than dry. Boots and clothes had sprouted mildew overnight.

Riding the two miles into Falmouth, his hat pulled down over his forehead, he had bought a tea service of blue and white willow patterned china with an additional set of cups and saucers, paying extra for immediate delivery.

Two days later, on a cold, rainy October morning, he had brewed a fresh pot of tea, refilled the kettle and milk jug and set out every one of his new cups and saucers. First to arrive as usual, Sam Venner had paused on the threshold to shake the rain off his coat. Stepping into the kitchen, he had glanced at the table.

'Help yourself,' Crago said mildly. 'It's just been made.'

'Never expected this.'

'I know,' Crago said.

'The lads'll take it kindly.'

With a nod, Crago had shrugged on his coat, picked up his hat and left the house.

When he returned that evening, the men had already gone. The cups were set neatly at one end of the table, washed and dried. From that day on, every man arrived ten minutes early.

Hearing footsteps and voices, Crago lifted his hand to loosen the cord that held back his hair while he washed and shaved. He shook his head so that it tumbled forward, half-masking his face.

The voices grew louder. There was a brisk knock and immediately the back door opened. Sam led the way in, with Noah close behind.

'Morning,' Sam said.

'Another lovely day,' Noah added.

'Good morning,' Crago nodded. Of all the men currently employed in the house, only Sam and Noah ever met his gaze directly, though never for long. He knew it wasn't disgust that made them avert their eyes, but sympathy. He wasn't sure which was worse.

Dropping the basket containing his croust and pasty dinner on the flagstone floor, Noah crossed to the table and then paused, glancing up. 'All right if I . . .?'

Crago gestured for him to go ahead. Noah began pouring the tea. A few moments later more footsteps announced the rest of the team's arrival. With nods and murmured greetings, they gathered around the table to pick up filled cups, then gravitated towards the new range, with its black iron and gleaming brass. Beneath the rectangular hotplate, small doors stood open, revealing glowing coals behind black retaining bars and a tray to catch the ash underneath.

'Some great slab that is.'

'My missus would dearly love that there oven alongside the fire.'

'Look at that! If you took hold of they knobs and brung that there slatted shelf down lower, there's space on 'n for pots and pans.'

'Dear life, if my missus seen this, I wouldn't know a minute's peace till she 'ad one.'

Listening to the men talk, Crago knew that, although the range was new and had cost more than some of these men earned in six months, they were looking at the future. He would buy a set of plans from the manufacturer in Camborne and commission Dickie Dunstan, a blacksmith in Penryn, to make up a couple. He'd sell them at cost plus fifteen percent: ten for Dickie, five for him. As word got around, demand would soar. It would be an excellent investment.

'Mister?' Sam said, cradling his cup between scarred and calloused hands. 'Listen, about that there hedge you want put up out the back. The stone id'n no problem. We can get that easy from Talvan quarry. It's handy by, and Noah says we can get all the granite we need from the spoil heaps, so it won't cost much.' Beside him, Noah nodded.

'But?' Crago asked.

'Well, see, that hedge will take a good few weeks to build and there's still two bedrooms need skimming, and the dairy to be plastered.'

'You want additional masons?'

Sam nodded. 'The word is that Kinser Landry's looking to buy Govier's quarry.' When Noah frowned, Sam shrugged. 'That's what I heard.' He turned back to Crago. 'I know two of the men working at Talvan. Skilled stonemasons they are, and worth their wages. Landry won't want them. His gangers like to hire their own labour. So, what do 'ee think? Ask 'em to come and see you, shall I?'

Crago shook his head. 'No. If you recommend them, offer them the job.'

With a swift grin, Sam raised a hand in a gesture that was both salute and acknowledgment. Noah did the same. Then both men drained their cups and replaced them carefully on the table.

'Come on, lads,' Sam raised his voice over the buzz of chatter and laughter. 'Drink up. We're burning daylight here.'

Three

Sarah was up even earlier than usual. With both Jeb and Flynn expected, she wanted time to deal with her chores and prepare for what was likely to be a difficult discussion.

Jory chattered all through breakfast. She turned from hanging the big black kettle on the hook above the fire, about to scold him. But as he looked up at her, his scrubbed face shining and his toffee-coloured curls neatly brushed, her heart brimmed with love.

The quarry was his inheritance. Somehow she had to keep it open and productive. The first step was to get rid of Flynn.

With her usual quick knock, Becky poked her head round the door. 'I'm going over to see my sister-in-law . . .'

'Can I come, Aunty Beck?' Jory turned beseeching eyes towards his mother. 'Can I, Ma? Please? Aunty Ivy likes to see me. She said so.'

'And you hope to see Uncle Noah so you can persuade him to let you carry his tools.'

'Go on, Ma. Please?'

'It's all right, maid,' Becky said. 'He won't be no bother. You'll get on better without little ears flapping.' As Sarah shot her a look of gratitude, Becky lifted Jory's coat from the peg. 'C'mon, boy. And before you ask, yes, you do have to wear it. Don't want to be ill again, do you?'

Shaking his head, he pushed his arms into the coat that Becky held out for him, while Sarah knelt to tie the laces of his leather boots.

'Mind you be good, now.' She said, and kissed him, cupping his small face.

A grin split his face. ''Course.'

Becky shooed him out.

Sarah made the beds, washed and dried the dishes, wiped the table, took the rugs out and shook them and swept the floor, moving briskly from job to job, telling herself that she had everything under control. But it wasn't true. How could it be when she'd known nothing of Flynn's actions?

Jeb arrived and handed her several crumpled scraps of paper with figures scrawled on them. Assuring her that the men had at least another two days' work, he left for the quarry.

Sitting down at the scrubbed table, Sarah opened the ledgers and, with a pencil and fresh sheet of paper, started working through the figures.

A brisk rap on the door brought her head up and she saw that an hour had passed. Rising from her chair, she crossed to the door, paused to take a steadying breath and then opened it. 'Mr Flynn,' she said before he could speak. 'Please come in.' She indicated a wooden chair. 'Sit down.'

'With respect, Miss, I don't have time . . .'

From the far side of the table, Sarah eyed him levelly. 'Yes, you do. You weren't at the quarry yesterday, or the day before, and I doubt you've been there this morning. So please, sit down.'

She waited while he scraped the chair over the flagstone floor. Then, resuming her seat, she folded her hands on the paper in front of her. 'You have withheld money from my men. We both know you had no authority to do such a thing. How much do you owe them in unpaid wages?'

Shock flashed across his face. Then his gaze slid away and he tapped the fingers of one hand on the table. 'You can't expect me to carry all the figures in my head—'

'Oh, come now,' Sarah made no effort to disguise either her scorn or disbelief as she cut him short. 'You know how many weeks it is since you paid them. You will have a record of exactly how much each of them owes you for goods purchased in your bakehouse. Goods they were forced to buy at an inflated price.'

'I don't see that's any of your business—'

'When one of my men is being threatened with eviction because he can't pay his rent, and the reason he can't pay it is because you have withheld money he has worked for, it's very much my business,' Sarah retorted. 'I will allow you twenty-four hours to produce the figures.'

He rose. 'If your father—'

'My father would wonder why I haven't already reported you to the magistrate, an action I am seriously considering. But he is not here. I am. The quarry is mine, Mr Flynn.' She closed the ledger and stood up. 'I am responsible for the men working there, and I will not have them cheated.' Crossing to the door, she held it open. 'Until tomorrow.'

'I'll need time—'

'Take the rest of the day. The men have work and do not require your supervision. Which is just as well, as I understand it is several days since you were last at the quarry.' As he passed her, she added, 'Just so we understand each other, Mr Flynn, I have the men's accounts of what you held back and what they owe you and your friends.'

His mouth twisted in a sneer. 'You believe them?'

'I have known those men most of my life. They have never given my father, or me, cause to doubt their honesty. I cannot say the same of you. Until tomorrow, Mr Flynn.'

He glared at her, his mouth a thin, angry line as he strode out.

Closing the door, Sarah leaned against it. Taking several deep breaths, she relaxed her taut shoulders and allowed herself to shake.

Returning to the table, she sat down and spent the next two hours going through the ledger in which all the quarry receipts and expenses were listed, as well as the file of orders and correspondence.

Rumour had it that Kinser Landry's quarries were inundated with work. Yet Talvan had received no new orders for weeks. As well as supervising the quarrymen, Flynn should have been nego-tiating contracts with merchants and shippers. Clearly, he had not been doing so. But why hadn't he?

Though she intended to retrieve every penny of the money that Flynn had stolen, it might take time. Meanwhile, her workmen had to be paid and their debts settled so they could shop where they chose. The money would have to come out of her funds, and these were dangerously low.

She picked up the letter from Kinser Landry. He wanted Talvan quarry to add to his expanding business and sought a meeting in order to discuss terms. Though it had arrived two weeks ago, she had not yet replied. Even before the shock discovery of Flynn's activities, Sarah had been concerned about the quarry's future.

During the winter, nearly every week one or another of the men had been laid up through sickness or injury. When she had questioned Flynn about the decline in orders, he had told her not to worry, it was just a seasonal slump and things would pick up again after the turn of the year. But they hadn't.

In March she and Becky had spent two weeks spring cleaning. They had replaced heavy winter curtains with light summer ones and brought down the feather mattresses and hung them over the line to air. After the curtains and blankets had been washed, ironed and put away with lavender bags, the chimneys had been swept. Every surface had been washed, walls inside and out had been painted with fresh lime wash, floors scrubbed, then carpets and rugs beaten until the two women's arms ached.

They had just finished when the April rains set in and Jory collapsed with scarlet fever. For nearly a month Sarah had devoted every waking moment to nursing him.

With her son now fully recovered, she knew decisions had to be made. According to Jeb, Flynn shared business interests with Landry's gangers. Was it possible that Flynn had an even closer connection with Landry himself?

Goviers had owned and run Talvan since her grandfather's time. Her father had enlarged and developed the quarry. His untimely death had forced her to take over, and she had done her best. But while her heart demanded that she turn down Landry's offer, her head knew that things could not continue as they were.

Philip Ansell stopped a short distance from the bed, keeping his breathing shallow, trying not to inhale the sickening odour: a combination of rose water, sweet-sour perspiration and the metallic stench of blood.

He could not bring himself to sit, or to take the trembling hand that Margaret held out to him. Looking at it, he saw a tentacle that, if touched, would coil like a snake around his arm, drawing him closer and closer until he was trapped amongst the lace edged frills and that gut-churning smell.

'I'm so sorry,' she whispered, her hand dropping on to the coverlet. Her fair hair, damp with sweat, lay tangled on the pillow. Her sunken eyes swam with tears that spilled over and slid down her temples. 'Please don't be cross, Philip.'

'I'm not cross,' he lied.

'Next time will be different. I promise.'

Promise? How could she promise? 'Hush.' He spoke softly, hoping he sounded sympathetic. 'Don't worry about that now. You need to rest and rebuild your strength.'

'You're really not angry?' Her gaze begged for reassurance.

'For heaven's sake!' he snapped, making her flinch. Quickly, he forced a smile. 'Naturally I'm disappointed, as I know you must be.' *Disappointed* did not even begin to describe his fury and frustration.

She stifled a sob. 'I know how much it meant to you.'

'Margaret, this does no good.'

She wiped her nose, her mouth quivering. 'Please be patient, Philip. I shall soon be strong again. Then everything will be different.'

You said that last time, and the time before, he wanted to shout. 'Let us hope so.' His face ached with the effort of maintaining a smile.

She lifted her hand from the coverlet, palm out, a silent plea for him to stay. He had liked her better when she did not cling.

Seven years ago his father had told him that it was time he married. 'We need investment.'

'We need customers,' Philip had responded, thinking of Sarah, who excited him and believed that he loved her. Marrying her was out of the question, but he wasn't ready to give her up.

'Listen to me, boy. Ansell's has been moving cargo for over a hundred years. Though the slump of the last few years has cost us, it's your future. Do you want to see it fail?'

'Of course not. So who do you have in mind for me?'

'Margaret Tregenza. Her father made a fortune from leasing mineral rights on land he inherited at Carnmenellis and Carnkie. And he has a thriving chandlery business down on Commercial Road. They're our neighbours . . .'

'Not so you'd notice,' Philip had said drily. 'In fact, Horace Tregenza has planted so many trees and shrubs in those acres of garden, you can barely see the house from the road.'

'That's what money can do. We might not have as much land, but we share a common boundary.' He rubbed his hands together. 'Margaret is their only child and will inherit a considerable fortune one day. If you can't see the advantages for yourself, you're no son of mine.'

He had seen Margaret at church and at various social events: a young woman of middling height with a full figure, fair hair and unremarkable features. But his thoughts skipped back to Sarah. Dark-haired, slender, vibrant Sarah, who stirred his blood and whose inheritance would consist only of moorland scrub and an ill-paying quarry. He sighed. 'If I must.'

Wooing Margaret had proved surprisingly easy and he'd been flattered by her eager response. Winning over her father would have been considerably more difficult, but again Margaret had helped, convincing her parents, used to indulging their only child, that her entire future happiness depended on marrying him.

Aware that he must play the devoted husband, and knowing that Sarah would send him packing if she knew his plans, he decided not to tell her. Her passionate nature inflamed him. He knew that she loved him and believed he loved her. He had to marry Margaret. But first, he wanted Sarah.

Arranging to meet her out on the moor, he had tumbled her into long grass in a hollow among huge granite boulders. In warm summer sunshine fragrant with gorse, he had ambushed her with kisses and caresses. Using every trick he'd been taught by Sally Jenkins, he had roused her to flushed, sleepy-eyed desire, then taken his pleasure.

Leaving her had been necessary. But putting her out of his mind had been a lot harder than he'd anticipated. And recently, he had found himself thinking of her ever more often.

'Philip?' Margaret pleaded. 'Please, will you hold me?'

His stomach heaved and he swallowed hard. 'My dear, like most men, I am neither comfortable nor of use in a sickroom. What you need now is rest. Indeed, the doctor insisted I must not tire you.'

Her eyes brimmed again and her mouth quivered. 'But I shall have all night to sleep.'

'Your mother is waiting downstairs. She's most anxious to see you.' He turned towards the door.

'Have you spoken to the doctor? How soon can we—'

'Hush now.' Glancing back, he avoided her eyes. He knew that she was crying; knew that he should show sympathy. But what he felt was rage: rage, revulsion and bitter disappointment. He took a careful breath and slipped into the role of concerned husband, one perfected by too much practice. 'Now is not the time for such discussion.' He opened the door.

'Will you come up again later?'

'Provided you do as the doctor says and rest.' He closed the door and stood on the landing, trembling with anger and frustration. She had produced two daughters with no trouble at all. But in the past twenty-four months, she had miscarried three boys.

What was wrong with her? Why could she not give him a son? Damn it, he needed an heir. He didn't entirely trust his father-in-law and sensed that the feeling was mutual. The birth of a grandson might make all the difference.

Descending the stairs, he saw the front door standing open, glimpsed the doctor leaving and saw Mary Tregenza come inside. She closed the door before catching sight of him and hurrying forward to lay her hand on his arm.

'My dear Philip.' Her eyes filled. 'What can I say? This is devastating, just devastating.'

He nodded. 'I think Margaret would welcome your company. I . . .' he allowed his voice to hitch. 'I don't know what to say to her. She needs the understanding and comfort only another woman can offer. Who better than her mother?'

She squeezed his arm. 'I shall go to her at once.' Grasping her full skirts, she hurried up the staircase.

Philip entered the small room he liked to call his study and closed the door. Crossing to a side table on which stood a polished silver tray – a wedding present from one of Margaret's wealthy relatives – he poured whisky from a crystal decanter – another gift – into a tumbler. Swallowing in three gulps, he grimaced as the spirit burned its way down and then curled, hot and smoky in his stomach. He refilled the glass, then dropped into a leather armchair, recalling the doctor's warning.

Margaret needed at least a year to allow her body to recover from the stress of three miscarriages. Did he understand? Of course he understood. He was being told to stay out of the marital bed. Not that he had ever found much pleasure there. Margaret's rapt attention, the flirting that had led him to believe – to anticipate – had all been a sham. He scowled, embittered by false promises.

He had hoped to find in her the same joy, the same passion, he had discovered with Sarah. Sarah: who had been so warm and affectionate, who had loved him. If Sarah had come from money rather than being the daughter of an impoverished quarry owner, he would not be in this wretched situation.

He drank again, remembering his wedding night. Lying on her back, shrouded from chin to ankle in a voluminous nightgown, Margaret had announced in a voice trembling with nerves that he might do as he wished. Her mother had informed her that men had certain needs and it was a wife's duty to oblige her husband.

That joyless description – making him wonder about his father-in-law's domestic arrangements – had come close to unmanning him. But by closing his eyes and thinking of Sarah, he had been able to achieve consummation. Afterwards, Margaret had wiped her eyes and, trying unsuccessfully to mask her shock and dismay, told him she was sure that she would grow used to it.

During the day she was her usual sociable self, entertaining friends in the small house that her father had given them as a wedding gift. Indeed, in all other respects she seemed very contented and managed the household admirably. The birth of her first child had imbued her with new radiance. She adored their little daughter. The enthusiasm with which she embraced even the most demanding aspects of motherhood had kindled in him both relief and jealousy.

The congratulations and celebrations that greeted the safe arrival of their second daughter were accompanied by reassurances that the next child was bound to be a boy. It was early days. They had plenty of time.

But as one year passed, then two, without the birth of a longed-for son, her confidence began to wane and his patience to grow short. Each month her moods swung between feverish hope and desperate disappointment.

If it was difficult for her, it was even harder for him. To get the son that he wanted, he had to lie with her. But the business was conducted in joyless silence and with tightly closed eyes. Only by allowing his imagination full rein was he able to perform at all.

Today, informed that three miscarriages had sapped his wife's strength to such an extent that were another pregnancy to occur, she might lose not only the child, but her own life, he realized that he did not care. He supposed that he should. But he was tired of a wife who, at not yet thirty, had lost her looks.

She had spent nearly two years suffering either the ailments of early pregnancy or the repercussions of its loss. He knew, regardless of advice or warnings, that she would not stop. Nor would she be willing to wait a full twelve months.

Curled up in agony on their bed while waiting for the doctor, her tears mixed with the sweat beading her ashen face, she had demanded his promise that they would try again. But if the doctor was correct, next time might be the last.

He played with the thought. Obviously the girls would miss

their mother. But they had two sets of doting grandparents. Then, after a decent interval, he could remarry.

Of course, he would have to bide his time. No doubt her parents had questioned the doctor, and it wouldn't be wise to give her father cause for suspicion. But with the prospect of an end to his unsatisfactory marriage – an end, moreover, that would win him sympathy – he could be patient. In three months, four at most, Margaret would be begging him to return to her bed. Until then, he would be a model of consideration.

Four

The following morning, after seeing Jory off with Noah, Sarah hurried upstairs to change. First, she pinned her hair in to a coil on the nape of her neck. Then, she stepped into a second stiffened petticoat and fastened it over her flannel one.

In the haberdashery shop a few weeks earlier she had overheard Miss Nicholls telling a customer about a new stiffened petticoat made of horsehair. It would, Miss Nicholls had assured, be a relief for the many ladies who had felt obliged to wear up to six petticoats in order to ensure that their gown was supported to the width dictated by current fashion.

Shaking down the skirt of her green checked gown, Sarah sighed as she fastened the buttons. Stiffened horsehair did not sound very comfortable. But she no longer even possessed six petticoats, having sacrificed two in order to make underdrawers and nightshirts for Jory.

She checked her reflection in the long glass. Despite less than voluminous skirts, she looked both elegant and demure. Through the open window she heard the garden gate open.

Glancing out, she saw the ganger walking up the path. She descended the stairs, stopped at the bottom and inhaled deeply. The unnecessarily loud rapping made her flinch. Annoyed at her own reaction, she opened the door.

After checking Flynn's figures against those she had calculated from the ledger and the slips that Jeb had given her, she opened the metal cash box, counted out a small pile of coins and pushed them across the kitchen table.

'What's this?' the ganger demanded.

'The total owed to you.'

Flynn raised angry eyes. 'That's not nearly enough.'

'It's all you're getting. You kept their wages, Mr Flynn. Money the men had worked for. You forced them into debt. That money is the difference between what you withheld from them and the debts they incurred in your shop. Neither they, nor I, owe you another penny.'

'I'm not having that. I'll—'

'Go to the magistrate?' Sarah asked coolly while her heart drummed. 'You do that. I'd be very interested to hear his opinion of your actions. In the meantime, as of this moment you are free to seek employment elsewhere.'

'What?' He started to bluster. 'You can't—'

'Yes, I can,' Sarah interrupted. 'I'm dispensing with your services, such as they were. You no longer work for me, Mr Flynn. So you have no reason to go anywhere near Talvan quarry.' Crossing to the door, she opened it and stood to one side, her hand on the latch. 'I don't want to see or hear of you on my property again.'

Snatching the coins from the table, he stuffed them into his pocket and marched out, pausing on the threshold. 'You haven't heard the last of this.'

'Good day to you, Mr Flynn.' As he stomped down the path, she closed the door and released a trembling breath. She had been dreading the meeting, but it was over now. As for his threats, they were only to be expected. She already had enough to worry about.

Carrying a sack containing his special boots and a cloth-wrapped pasty baked by Sam Venner's wife, Crago started along the track leading to the valley. Then, remembering that he'd promised Noah a decision about wood for a wardrobe to match the bed, he turned back. Just as he reached the yard, a small figure shot out of the barn.

'Uncle Noah, I found it!' the figure shouted, clutching a wooden plane to his small chest. Upon seeing Crago, he skidded to a stop, pride fading to uncertainty.

Crago saw a small boy wearing trousers tucked into scuffed lace-up boots and a jacket buttoned over his woollen shirt.

''Morning,' the boy said and, to Crago's surprise, snatched off his cap. But instilled manners were no match for curiosity as he stared openly at Crago's face. 'Does it hurt?'

'Sometimes.'

'I fell out of an apple tree in our garden,' the boy confided. 'There was lots of blood, but I didn't cry. Well,' he admitted with touching honesty, 'I did, but nobody saw. I've got a white mark.' He drew a grubby forefinger under his knee. 'It's not big like yours. But it doesn't hurt now. I 'spec' yours will feel better soon.'

Crago nodded. 'I hope so. What's your name?'

'Jory Govier. I know who you are. You're Mr Crago. That's your house.' He pointed. 'You make gunpowder. My grampy got blowed up in his quarry.'

'I'm sorry to hear that.' He realized now who the child was. He had overheard Sam Venner snap at one of his labourers, telling the man that Sarah Govier was no cheap tart and if he couldn't keep a civil tongue in his head, he'd better find another job. *No cheap tart?* A girl who had conceived a child out of wedlock, then defied gossip and convention to keep him? What, then, was she?

'What are you doing here?' Crago enquired.

'Helping Uncle Noah. He's a carpenter and he—'

'Jory! 'Tis in the big box . . .' Noah rounded the corner. Seeing Crago and the boy, his stride faltered.

'I found it, Uncle Noah!' Jory shouted, holding up the plane, then he turned to Crago. 'Can I go now?'

Crago nodded. 'Take the plane inside.' He watched the boy scamper away and then turned to Noah. 'Rather young for an apprentice, isn't he?' He raised a hand before Noah could speak. 'Since you started bringing him here – and I'm thinking this isn't the first time – has he suffered any injury? Cuts? A fall?'

Noah was instantly affronted. 'No!' He shifted uncomfortably as Crago raised one dark brow. 'No,' he repeated quietly. 'That's God's own truth. He knows never to touch the saws. But I do send him to fetch tools for me sometimes. Sharp as a tack, he is. Knows the difference between a jackplane and a smoothing plane. He had the scarlet fever last month. Sick for weeks, he was. I didn't think it would do no harm to bring him along with me, give his mother time to . . . See, since her father – well, it isn't for me to say . . .' He broke off. 'P'raps I shouldn't ought to have brung him. But he's good as gold. He jest like to watch.'

'And fetch tools,' Crago said drily. 'Oh, the reason I came back. The oak you asked me about yesterday? Order it.'

Noah beamed. 'Handsome!' With a brief salute, he hurried back into the house.

Sarah pulled gently on the reins. 'Whoa now.' Sliding from the seat, she lifted the reins over the donkey's head and tied them to an iron ring in the granite wall. Adjusting her straw bonnet and dark green hip-length cape, she reached into the small cart for her basket, then turned to wait for a gap in the traffic.

Mid-morning was always a busy time. Amid the farmers' carts, delivery vans and little donkey shays, heavy wagons hauled by teams of oxen or horses lumbered along the main street, coming from or returning to various Landry quarries. Each laden wagon carried a single enormous block of granite known as a dimension stone. Once they reached the quay, the stone was offloaded on to a waiting ship.

The animals knew the route so well that in the evenings it was common to see four or five teams plodding along the road out of town, their drivers sprawled out on the bed of the last wagon, roaring drunk.

She had never expected to compete with Landry to supply the dimension stones needed for new dockyards and pier extensions. But there were other markets: slabs for monumental masonry; setts for roads and kerbs; scalpings for drainage and road bases; and gravel. These had been the main outlets for Talvan granite. With the market for granite buoyant and expanding, she did not understand what had happened. For, not only were there no new enquiries, this morning she had received a letter cancelling a regular order.

Spotting a gap in traffic, she seized her chance and hurried across the street, heading for Miss Nicholls' Haberdashery. Jory had put his foot through one of the sheets: it was not his fault, for constant laundering had worn it thin. She had been meaning to go through the linen cupboard anyway. It was yet one more job she hadn't got to. The torn sheet could be set aside for bandages and dusters. Others with worn centres – and she was bound to find some – could be turned ends to middles.

Two men were unloading a brewer's dray, rolling the barrels down sloping planks and in to the hotel's cellar. Passing Mitchell's Shoemaker and Repairs, she saw old Mr Mitchell sitting in his window, wearing a leather apron with a row of tacks in his mouth. Returning his friendly nod, she marvelled at the speed with which he whipped the tiny tingle nails one at a time from between his lips and hammered them into the sole of the boot on the metal last between his knees.

'Well, if it isn't sweet Sarah, the light of my life. Looking more beautiful than ever.'

Hearing the hated voice behind her, Sarah's stomach clenched. Resisting the urge to turn and face Nathan Keast, she continued walking.

He followed. 'Come into town to find me, did you? Well, here I am, ready and waiting. Want to take a walk up to College Woods?'

Furious at his harassment and her inability to prevent it, she tried to shut him out.

'Must be lonely living out at Talvan.' He was relentless. 'Tell you what, how about one night I come to visit—'

Sarah swung round so quickly, she had the fleeting pleasure of seeing him start. Though fury burned in her cheeks, her voice was icy. 'Set one foot on my land, Nathan Keast, and I'll report you to the magistrate for trespass and harassment.'

His brows shot up and his expression was one of hurt innocence. But his eyes betrayed him. Beneath his glee at having goaded her into responding, she glimpsed raw lust.

'Dear life, maid. No need for that. Just being friendly is all.' His grin was feral. 'You look like you need—'

Turning her back, she pushed open the door of Miss Nicholls' shop, relieved that his parting words were drowned by the tinkle of the bell above the door. Vaguely aware of two other customers, she closed the door firmly, then fought for calm as she crossed a rainbow-hued display of reels of cotton and skeins of embroidery silks.

She heard the crackle of folding paper of a parcel being wrapped, the clink of coins and a drawer opened then closed. One of the customers turned from the counter and paused on her way to the door.

'Morning, Miss Govier. How's your boy? Better, is he?'

Turning, Sarah saw a tentative smile and faded blue eyes full of concern. 'He's fine again, Mrs Tallack. Thank you for asking.' Hearing a loud sniff, Sarah glanced up. Miss Nicholls' neat head with its centre parting and tidy bun was bent over a bolt of material she was unfolding for the remaining customer, whose face was concealed by the long poke bonnet.

'Must have been some worry for you,' Mrs Tallack shook her head and pulled her wool shawl closer. 'My cousin's boy had the scarlet fever, then she caught it. The boy wasn' too bad, bless'n. But poor Maggie, all her joints swelled up. I never seen nothing like it. In some state, she was.'

'I'm sorry to hear that.'

'She's all right again now, dear of her. But 't was some nasty business. So you mind yourself. You don't want nothing like that. Awful, it is.'

'I'll be careful,' Sarah smiled. 'Becky tells me your father's been ill. I hope it's nothing serious?'

'Only his chest again. But he's coming on now.' Mrs Tallack nodded. 'I'm going up the butcher's to get a bit of liver. He said he fancied it with onions.'

'He hasn't lost his appetite, then.'

Mrs Tallack gave a wry smile and rolled her eyes. 'See us all out, he will.'

As the door closed, Sarah picked up three reels of white cotton and carried them to the counter. The remaining customer turned, revealing sharp features framed by the frilled cap inside her bonnet. Sarah's heart sank, but she nodded politely. 'Good morning, Mrs Rogers.'

'Don't you speak to me!' the woman hissed, narrowing her eyes in to slits. 'Shameless, you are. I saw you, making up to Nathan Keast. I don't know how you dare show your face. You ought to be ashamed, flaunting yourself around the town. Your father should have had you put away.'

Miss Nicholls gasped.

Her face burning, Sarah stared into a face tight with malice. Spittle flecked the thin, bitter mouth.

'What you saw, Mrs Rogers,' Sarah said, tilting her head, 'was me telling Nathan Keast that if he sets one foot on my land, I will report him to the magistrate.'

'Huh! So *you* say.'

'Indeed,' Sarah nodded. 'And as you have raised the subject of troublesome men, I'd like to make something clear concerning your husband. I am an occasional customer in his shop, nothing more. I did not seek, nor do I welcome, his attentions. They are as much an insult to me as they are to you. So instead of holding *me* responsible for his behaviour, I suggest you place the blame where it belongs, on him.' Sarah paused, then added, 'You could also ask yourself why he feels the need to look outside his own home for comfort, companionship, or whatever else he is seeking. But I doubt you will. Good day.'

As Mrs Rogers' eyes bulged and her mouth opened and closed with no sound, Sarah turned to Miss Nicholls and placed the reels on the varnished wooden counter with trembling hands. 'How much do I owe you?'

The door slammed on Mrs Rogers' departing figure.

Miss Nicholls took the money, closed the cash drawer and looked directly into Sarah's eyes. ''Tis time she was took down a peg or two. She could strip paint with that tongue. No wonder Henry . . .' She broke off, flustered. 'He don't mean no harm.'

'Perhaps not, but he's causing it just the same. Good day, Miss Nicholls.' Sarah put the cotton in her basket and crossed to the door. She did not regret speaking out, but wished it hadn't been necessary.

Occupying an elegant Queen Anne building at the lower end of Bohill, stood Ansell's Cargo Brokerage. It was just a short distance from the quays and warehouses that lined the river upstream of the swing bridge carrying traffic from Commercial Road towards the port of Falmouth.

During office hours the black-painted front door stood wide open, held back by an iron ingot. A boot-scraper beside the step and a thick bristle mat kept the tiled passage relatively mud-free.

Philip crossed the passage to his father's office. George Ansell was seated at his desk with an open folder in front of him. A large seascape hung above the empty fireplace. Light glanced off a glass-fronted bookcase and, on either side of the window, shelves held the last five years' worth of files and ledgers. Those from earlier years were stored in dusty rooms upstairs.

Philip waited until his father looked up from the papers he was holding. 'Yes?'

'Joseph Peters. His account is three months overdue.'

'Is Mr Scoble aware of any—?'

'Nothing of use to us. I think perhaps I should have a word with Mr Peters.' Anticipation surged through him, tightening his muscles, causing him to clench then flex his hands.

Laying the papers carefully down, his father sat back, doubt and unease apparent on his face. 'I will not countenance violence, Philip. We have never resorted—'

'Exactly.' Philip felt heat climb his throat. 'Which is why men like Peters laugh behind our backs. He needs a lesson. One he won't forget.' His father was studying him, a frown drawing his brows together.

'In all the years he's used us, Peters has never paid on time. But he always settles in the end. Don't play me for a fool, boy. It's this business with Margaret. You're mad as fire and looking for someone to take it out on. You have my sympathy.'

Philip snorted. Sympathy, a lot of use that was.

'But,' his father warned, 'your domestic problems have no place in this office. You hear me? We cannot afford the kind of repercussions—'

'I'll tell you what we can't afford,' Philip snarled. 'We can't afford to have ship-owners refusing to carry our cargoes. Which is what will happen if we can't pay them because our customers haven't paid us.'

'I don't need you to tell me that. Nor have I any objection to you making clear to Peters that if he doesn't settle within a week, we will resort to law. But you're not to lay a finger on him. I'm telling you, Philip. Horace Tregenza would not take kindly to his son-in-law being hauled before the magistrate for assault.' Shaking his head, he sighed. 'Listen, boy—'

'No,' Philip interrupted, pleased at the shock on his father's face. 'No lectures. I'm in no mood to listen to homilies from the man responsible for this mess.'

'Mess? What—?'

'My marriage, Father. The marriage you were so determined upon.'

'Philip, wait, I—'

Closing the door behind him, Philip pressed a fist to his raw stomach where fury and frustration burned.

He left the office, walking up the hill towards Broad Street and Simmons' Hotel. The coffee room was a popular meeting place, where local businessmen and visiting ship's masters could catch up with national and foreign events from the newspapers and periodicals purchased by the landlord or talk business over a drink or a meal.

Philip found it the ideal place to make discreet enquiries regarding the financial stability of potential new clients, or to discover whether whispers of a company or individual in trouble were simply gossip-based rumour or verifiable fact.

Five

As she emerged from the shop, Sarah saw Kinser Landry approaching, his portly figure immaculate in a flatteringly cut blue frock coat, dove-grey trousers and patterned silk waistcoat.

'Good day to you, Miss Govier. This is indeed a fortunate encounter.' Inclining his head, he raised the silver knob of his ebony cane to the brim of his top hat.

Noting the minor courtesy, Sarah knew it was offered only because she was in possession of something he wanted. She mirrored it, also inclining her head. 'Mr Landry.'

'You received my letter?'

'I did.'

'Yet you have not replied. Perhaps you have been busy.' Irritation made his smile brief and insincere.

'I have.' She owed him no explanation and would not be bullied into offering one.

After waiting a moment, he continued, 'My offer is very fair, considering your granite is of poor quality and fit for little other than road stone.' Small and dark, his eyes reminded her of raisins embedded in dough.

'Forgive me, but I don't understand.' Sarah regarded him with puzzlement. 'If Talvan granite is as poor as you suggest—'

'Oh, there is no doubt of it. The survey shows—'

'You surveyed my land?' Her cool interruption threw him for an instant.

'No, I did not. I understand the survey was carried out by a geologist several years ago, your father would have known. But perhaps he did not consider it necessary to inform you.'

Recognizing the snub, Sarah maintained her composure. She neither liked nor trusted Kinser Landry. But he had surmised correctly. Her father had not informed her.

Although after Jory's birth she had begun assisting with correspondence and bookkeeping, it would not have occurred to her father to discuss practicalities with her. After his death she had had to learn a large amount very quickly. No doubt along the way she may have missed or overlooked certain things.

'Then why do you want to buy it?'

'I have acquired a number of quarries on the eastern side of the road, and another at Longdowns.' His tone boasted and his manner patronized. 'As a result, I need somewhere to tip the over-burden and waste stone.'

'I see,' Sarah nodded. 'Thank you for explaining.'

'So, do we have an agreement?'

'You must excuse me, Mr Landry. I am not used to discussing business in the street. But I will give the matter my attention and write to you shortly.'

Frustration and annoyance darkened his face. This time he did not touch his hat, instead merely nodding. 'I look forward to receiving your letter. You would be wise to accept, Miss Govier. You will not receive a better offer.'

Reaching the junction, Philip paused while a loaded wagon pulled by two heavy horses rumbled up from the town quay. As it passed, he looked across the road and saw Sarah. His heart gave an uncom-fortable thud. She was talking to his uncle. What could they possibly have to discuss?

Green suited her. Straight-backed, her chin high, she looked . . . *strong, proud* and infinitely desirable. As he watched, she dipped her head and then walked briskly up the street, leaving his uncle glowering after her.

This glimpse of her was an acute reminder of what he had lost. For an instant, he contemplated following. He even took a step forward, then stopped. What would he say? It had been years since their paths had even crossed. It had occurred just up the street. She'd been walking with an older woman and had looked right through him, as if he wasn't there. For a moment he'd thought she hadn't seen him, but she must have.

It still rankled. He was somebody in this town. One day she would look at him again. He'd find a way to make her take notice. Meanwhile, what business did his uncle have with her? After a quick look in each direction, he crossed the rutted, muddy road.

'Good morning, Uncle.'

'Philip.' Kinser Landry said absently, then he turned from his frowning study of the retreating figure to face his young relation. 'I heard about Margaret. It's a shame about the child. But—'

'Don't.' Philip warned, anger leaping with bared teeth. Was he supposed to listen in respectful silence while a man with two healthy adult sons proffered sympathy and advice? It was too much. 'No doubt you mean well. So, I'm sure, do all those who tell me God moves in mysterious ways. Or that we are still young. Or that, blessed with two healthy daughters, we should be grateful. So if you were about to offer such *comfort*,' his tone was bitter, 'I beg you will not bother. I have heard every banality and am sick to death of them all.'

Landry snorted. 'Had you waited, you would have heard me say that I always had doubts about the match. I told your father as much. But he was determined on it. And there are none so deaf as those who refuse to hear. Still, you may take some comfort in the knowledge that the weakness – whatever it is – lies with the Tregenza family.'

'I don't fol—' Philip said, confused.

'Sons,' Landry said succinctly. 'You already have one. Even if he was born on the wrong side of the blanket and you chose not to acknowledge him.'

As Philip felt his eyes widen, his uncle gave a harsh bark of laughter. 'You thought I didn't know?'

'No. I mean, no, that wasn't what I—'

'Yes, yes, all right.' Landry cut in testily, then looked up the street once more. 'That young woman is the most . . .' he stopped, shaking his head.

Following his glance, Philip glimpsed dark green and a straw bonnet vanishing in to the crowd.

'Sarah Govier?'

'Indeed.' Landry's frown deepened with annoyance. 'The impertinence! Who does she think she is, keeping me waiting. Three weeks she's had that letter, and not even the courtesy of an acknowledgement, let alone a reply. Seeing her today I thought . . . All she had to do was agree. The contracts are drawn up and ready to sign. But no, she has the impudence, the temerity, to announce that she will not discuss business in the street.' He was quivering with rage. 'I did not want a discussion, just a simple yes.'

'To what, Uncle?'

'Talvan. I want her quarry.'

And I want her. Philip could barely keep pace with the thoughts and possibilities streaking through his mind like rockets. His earlier rage had dissolved, vanquished by an idea so bold yet so simple that he could barely contain his excitement.

'Uncle, we've both had a difficult morning. What do you say to coffee and brandy at Simmons'?'

As she rode home, Sarah considered her options. Landry wanted to buy. She had no idea if the sum he was offering was fair or not, but she could take advice on that. And selling would give her money now when she so badly needed it. But once that money was gone, what then?

What if, instead of selling, she leased the quarry to another stone merchant? He would pay all the costs involved in extracting and transporting the stone, set the selling price and keep all the profit. Though she would make very little out of the arrangement, at least she would retain ownership. The quarry would remain hers in trust for her son.

But if her granite were fit only for road stone, margins would be small. That meant no merchant would be willing to pay more than a minimal amount for the lease. It was all very well to plan for the future, but she needed money now.

The following evening, with the supper dishes washed and put away and Jory in bed sound asleep, Sarah and Becky sat on either side of the fire, a lamp on the table casting light over their sewing.

Becky leaned forward. 'All right, you've talked about everything but what's really on your mind. Someone upset you, have they?'

Ready to deny it before seeing Becky's warning frown, Sarah dropped her hands to her lap. 'Ellen Rogers.'

'I should have guessed.' Becky clicked her tongue. 'Sour as lemons, she is.'

'She was in Miss Nicholls' shop and saw Nathan Keast following me—'

Becky straightened. 'I hope you told him—'

'I warned him if he set one foot on my property, I'd report him to the magistrate.'

'About time, too.' Becky gave a decisive nod. 'That will have given him a shock. So what did Ellen say? Something spiteful, I'll be bound.'

'She accused me of encouraging him.'

'She never did!'

'She called me shameless, said I flaunted myself and that Father should have had me put away.' Six and a half years of being stared at, whispered about and shunned by people she had known all her life and previously thought of as friends had taught her what to expect. She had sinned and must be made to suffer for it. For many, that meant treating her as if she carried some foul contagion. Each time she ventured into town she braced herself in preparation. But some remarks could still cut deep.

Becky's eyes glinted in the firelight as she nodded. 'Oh, so that's the way of it. She seen Henry sniffing round you again.'

Sarah sighed. 'He's such a sad little man, and always polite. But I wish he'd stop trying to give me little extras for Jory. Or offering to deliver the groceries. He says it would save me the journey into town.'

'It would, too.' Becky looked up. 'So why do you turn him down?'

Sarah shrugged. 'Two reasons. I don't enjoy going into town, but I'm not going to let anyone stop me. I refuse to spend the rest of my life hiding. That might suit people like Mrs Rogers who point their fingers at *me*. Yet all the while *their* husbands are visiting Sally Jenkins round the back of the Three Tuns.'

Becky's eyes widened. 'How . . .? Who told . . .? You're not supposed to know about such things.'

Sarah laid a gentle hand on Becky's knee. 'Becky, there are many who think I'm no better. I've heard the gossip. Besides, the way Sally dresses, she might just as well carry a sign.'

Once, when they passed in the street, Sally had startled Sarah by winking, as if they shared a secret.

Becky shook her head. 'She love bright colours, that's for sure. Never mind her. What's the other reason?'

'I just sense − I might be doing him a grave injustice, but even when he smiles, there's something desperate . . .' She shook her head. 'I don't want him coming here.'

'If that's what you feel, bird, you done right to say no. If he won't take a hint, you'll have to speak plain. And if it do sound rude, 'tis his own fault.'

'Yes, but *I'll* be blamed. I don't *want* to be rude to anyone, not Nathan Keast or Henry Rogers. Do you know what really infuriates me?'

'What, my 'andsome?'

'That *I'm* supposed to feel guilty when *they* are the pursuers.'

'That's the way of it, bird. I did warn you, so did your father. A child and no wedding band,' she shook her head. 'You chose a hard path.'

'I couldn't have given him up.'

'I know that.' Patting Sarah's hand, Becky smiled. 'No more'n I could have turned from you.'

The night her mother and newborn brother had died, five-year-old Sarah had, in every way that counted, also lost her father. Unreachable in his grief, he had buried his wife and son in the churchyard and himself in work, leaving his daughter to be cared for by his foreman's wife.

With no children of her own, Becky had taken the bewildered child in to her generous heart. When Sarah wanted to talk about her mother, she asked Becky. Becky had helped her through the pains of growing up. It was Becky who had held her while she wept anguished tears over Philip's betrayal. And it was Becky to whom she turned when she realized that she was pregnant.

Her father had been furious. Listening in silence to his tirade, she had waited for him to run out of breath. Then, with the spirit that she knew he admired and deprecated in equal measure, she had answered.

'I did not make this child all by myself. Philip is equally responsible.'

Her father's response had been blunt. 'Philip Ansell has put himself well out of reach. You're alone, Sarah. He'll want nothing to do with you, or the bastard he's fathered.'

That was what had cut the deepest. Philip had made her believe that he loved her. Then, without a backward glance, he had walked away.

Philip was the first man she had kissed: the first to awaken emotions and sensations that had startled and then swept her along like a river in flood while he coaxed, urged, begged her to prove her love. Believing, trusting, committed, she had given herself to him. Then, just three weeks later, to her stunned disbelief and despite all his promises, he had married someone else. She had learned of it from a white-faced Becky.

For weeks she had lurched between bewildered grief and shattering self-doubt, wondering what was wrong with her that he could have treated her so. Then one day Becky had gripped her shoulders and shaken her hard.

'There id'n nothing wrong with *you*! 'Tis him. Weak, greedy and selfish, he is. And a bloody fool. Him marrying Margaret Tregenza was George Ansell's doing, and hers. Margaret wanted a husband. Philip will enjoy her money right enough, but he won't find happiness. I doubt there's enough love in him to fill a thimble.'

Pulling Sarah close, Becky had rocked her like a child. 'But you, my bird, you got a heart bigger'n Talvan. Right now you're hurting and you don't want to hear me. But you're better off without him, and that's the truth. He served you ill. But he'll pay dearly for it. You wait and see.'

Sarah lifted her sewing and then dropped it again, remembering. 'Father called me wanton and foolish.'

'He didn't mean it, bird. It was the shock.'

'He meant it, Becky.' Maybe he'd been right. That afternoon with Philip she had discovered a sensual side to her nature that she had not known she possessed. Caught up in the moment, she had stopped thinking altogether. In that single hour of passionate abandon they had made a child. She glanced up. 'I'll always be grateful for the way you stood up for me, telling Father a child was a precious gift, not a sin.'

Masking an ocean of heartache at her own barrenness, Becky's anger had been spectacular.

'Certainly shut him up, didn't it?' Becky shook her head. 'I surprised meself. But I wasn't having you sent away. I told him straight. If you went, I'd go, too. He'd 'ave been in some mess then.' Her mouth curved. 'Remember the night Jory was born? Dear life, he was in some hurry. We never even had time to send for the midwife.'

Sarah nodded. Her labour had been short and excruciating. But the moment Becky had laid the warm, wet little body on her stomach, Sarah had been engulfed by a love so fierce and powerful that it erased all memory of the pain. As she gently stroked the pink, downy cheek, marvelled at dark hair so like her own and listened to kitten-like cries from tiny lungs, she had let go of the past, briefly sad that Philip would never know nor share what she was feeling. But that was his choice, his loss.

'I was ready to fight the world.'

Becky smiled. 'You didn't need to. When that babby caught hold his finger,' she shook her head, 'your father's face was a picture. For weeks I never heard him say two words together without a mention of his grandson, dear of him. I won't deny he was angry. But I reckon half of it was grief that you'd lost any chance of marrying well. Still, he stood by you. And he loved that boy.'

Sarah nodded. Jory's birth had given her father an heir. He had planned to teach his grandson everything he knew, intending that Jory would one day take over the quarry business. But the accident had changed everything. Her father was dead and she was alone. Though she had done her best, it wasn't enough. She was being deliberately undermined. Despite the bright flames and the room's cosy warmth, Sarah shivered.

Six

Despite living as a virtual recluse, Crago had heard of Sarah Govier. Local opinion was as sharply divided about her as it was about her efforts to keep Talvan Quarry running. Tart or not, she had done a good job with her son. He had hoped to have children. Had even allowed himself to entertain the possibility that he and Anjuli . . . He shook his head, an abrupt and deliberate shut-off.

But instead of the piercing sense of grief that for almost two years had been his constant companion, what he now felt was sadness. Young and lovely, she had been a pawn in the hands of her relatives and murdered in the name of honour. Her father had called him friend, and also arranged his death. *Had Sawyer not been with him . . .* He caught himself. The past could not be undone, only lived with.

He entered the wooded valley. Sycamore, oak, ash and willow unfurled young leaves in varying shades of pale green. Below the narrow path bluebells spilled in a fragrant cascade down the slope, swirling round trees and bushes. Pigeons cooed, blackbirds whistled, and he could hear the creak of the waterwheel and the river tumbling over stones in the bottom of the valley.

Spring, a time of new beginnings, of hope. For others, perhaps. Yet he should not complain. Since setting up the mill, Crago had swiftly established a considerable business. Not only was he sending regular orders of gunpowder to Carnkie mine and to two local quarries, he had successfully negotiated a contract to supply fine-grade powder to Bickford's safety-fuse factory at Tuckingmill. He had achieved an astonishing amount in a relatively short time. Yet that was scarcely remarkable when his every waking moment was devoted to work.

He shook his head in irritation. He should be pleased and proud. Part of him was. But the rest . . . What *did* he want? He was no longer sure.

When he had first come back, his face barely healed and his heart a raw wound, all he had wanted was to be left alone. Work had been his salvation, and there had been plenty of it. To restore the house, he had sought craftsmen who shared his vision and didn't require constant supervision.

While the succession of small sheds was being built in the valley, he had ordered purified sulphur from a refinery in Marseilles and saltpetre from a supplier in India. Then he had walked every inch of his valley, seeking willow and dogwood, for they would provide the very best quality charcoal.

He had spent weeks felling and then chopping the wood into three-foot lengths, finding an escape from nightmarish memories in hard physical labour. Stripping the bark, he had stacked the wood and left it to season, buying in what he needed for that first year. Down in the valley bottom, in the wide spaces between the sheds, he had planted new stands of willow.

Enquiries for a charcoal burner brought him Zack Bottrell. With Zack had come Nessa. Thirty years old and profoundly deaf following childhood measles, her quick intelligence and careful hands had proved invaluable at the mill.

He had buried himself in work, rising before daybreak and falling on to his cot in the kitchen when exhaustion made it impossible to keep his eyes open.

The shocked stares and remarks provoked by his scarred face ensured that he ventured into Penryn or Falmouth only when necessity demanded. But solitude no longer offered the escape that it once had. Reluctant to acknowledge what he considered a weakness, he knew what was wrong. He was lonely.

A twig cracked beneath his feet as he approached the clearing. In the centre, Zack was packing ashes and earth over the bracken that surrounded the large cone of carefully stacked willow logs to form a clamp. Crago opened his mouth to call a greeting, but before he could speak, Zack looked over his shoulder.

'Heard you coming.'

Crago wondered if Zack's acute awareness had been honed by the need to protect his daughter from dangers she was unable to hear for herself.

'All well?' Crago glanced across the clearing towards the two red-painted wooden wagons with curved roofs and large yellow wheels. A short distance from the wagons a fire burned merrily within a ring of stones. Steam rose from a large iron pot suspended over the fire on a wooden tripod. Clean washing was pegged to a line strung between two trees.

Zack nodded, patting the clamp. 'I'll have it lit directly.'

'Nessa?'

'Gone for water.' As he spoke, a short, wiry woman appeared at the edge of the clearing carrying two large pitchers. Silver threads streaked nut-brown hair braided into a thick plait that hung down her back. Her face was lined, her complexion rosy and weathered. She wore a faded print bodice with the sleeves pushed up to reveal sinewy brown forearms, a thick skirt of brown wool and a coarse hessian apron tied around her waist.

Seeing Crago, she smiled and set both pitchers down beside the wheel of the front wagon. The sounds she made were unintelligible, but as she tapped her chest and then pointed down the slope raising her brows, Crago nodded, glancing automatically at her feet. She was wearing the boots that he'd had made for her. As his gaze met hers, she wagged a finger at him. Laughing, he sat on a log, pulled off his black topboots and replaced them with the ones in his sack, securing them with strips of soft leather.

Leaving a hole in the top of the clamp through which he would set light to the wood, Zack dusted off his hands and crossed to the fire. 'You mind her, now.'

'I will, don't worry. She's worth two men to me.'

'Worth more to me. Men don't cook,' Zack retorted.

'Have you told Jeb yet?' Becky asked, exchanging the cool flat iron for the hot one on the hearth.

'Told him what?' Sarah glanced up from folding the washing she had just brought in from the line.

'That you've got rid of Flynn.'

'Not yet. I meant to walk across to the quarry yesterday, but—'

'You'd best get on over there now and tell him. He'll only fret else, wondering why Flynn haven't been round, and did he ought to tell you.'

'I can't leave you with all this,' Sarah objected, indicating the pile of folded laundry.

'Don't you worry about that. Anyhow, some of it's mine. I brung it in so I could do the lot together. Go on.' She didn't give Sarah a chance to interrupt. 'Do you good to get out in the fresh air.'

'Becky, I was in town just two days ago.'

'Yes, and in a right old state when you come back. Get on out, girl. Unless you don't trust me to do a proper job.' She cocked one eyebrow.

'You know that's not . . .' Sarah threw up her hands in surrender. 'All right, I'm going.'

'Take your time. 'Tis a lovely day and you was stuck in here weeks while the boy was sick.'

Leaving Becky to the ironing, Sarah slung her father's cloak over her cream calico bodice and blue serge skirt. Though the sun was shining, it invariably felt two coats colder up on the moor. But the cloak and a brisk walk would keep her warm.

By the time she reached Talvan, her cheeks were glowing and the exercise had dissolved the tension weighing heavily on her shoulders. For the first time in days she felt cautiously happy. But as she walked down the slope into the quarry, she realized that two men were missing.

Seeing her, Jeb jumped down off the granite shelf and hurried forward.

'Afternoon, Miss,' he raised a forefinger to his ancient peaked cap. 'If you're looking for Flynn, I haven't seen hide nor hair of him since—'

'I'm glad to hear it, Jeb. I dismissed him and told him to stay away from Talvan.'

'You did? Well, I can't say I'm sorry, Miss. He didn't belong here.'

I wouldn't have hired him in the first place if you had been willing to accept the responsibility, Sarah thought.But that wasn't fair and she should not blame him. He had been honest with her, confessing his limitations. Shading her eyes, she tipped her head to look up at the men working on the shelf.

'Jeb, you're two men short.' Immediately, she felt a tightening at the back of her neck. 'There hasn't been an accident, has there?'

'No, Miss. Nothing like that. They've gone to work for that Mr Crago up Jericho Farm.'

'What?' This was their thanks after she had helped them out of their troubles with Flynn and his cronies?

'I don't hold with them leaving like that, Miss,' Jeb said. 'It isn't right nor proper, not after all you done for them. But see, truth is, the wages he's paying – well, they got growing families.' He shrugged, visibly torn by conflicting loyalties.

'What about you, Jeb? Will you be next?' Hurt fired the words out of her mouth. But seeing him flinch, she instantly wished them unsaid.

'No, Miss,' he said with a dignity that shamed her. 'I started here with your father, God rest him, and I'll never leave unless you tell me to go.'

'Jeb, I'm sorry. I should not have spoken so. We both know I couldn't manage without you.'

'That's all right, Miss. But truth is, the way orders have dropped off, we'll be hard pressed to keep going much longer.'

'I know. I really hoped it wouldn't come to this.' She took a deep breath. 'Kinser Landry has offered to buy Talvan. He wants the land for dumping overburden and waste stone.'

Jeb's bewilderment was plain. 'He don't want the granite?'

Sarah shook her head. 'He says the survey shows it's poor quality, fit only for setts or road stone. But even those—'

'What survey?' Jeb broke in.

Sarah gestured helplessly. 'Apparently it was done some time ago. He says my father knew about it. Anyway, the point is—'

'Pack of lies, that is,' Jeb said, anger crossing his face. 'Your father never said a word to me about no survey, which he would've done. Trusted me, he did. I might not have book learning, but I know granite. 'Tis true what we been getting out this year is poor stuff. But a month ago when we blasted, I seen a change in the stone. I didn't want to say nothing to you then in case it come to nothing. Blasted three times since then, we have.'

'I heard it yesterday afternoon,' Sarah said.

'That's how I had to wait till this morning before I could go down and have a proper look.' Jeb grinned, his eyes shining. 'There isn't no doubt, Miss. We got it.'

'Got what?'

'Only the finest granite I ever seen.'

Sarah stared at him. 'Here, in Talvan?'

Jeb nodded. 'True as I'm stood here, Miss. That's why Landry want your quarry.'

'But how would he know about it?' Even as the question left her lips, Sarah knew the answer.

'Flynn.' They said together.

Her mind raced. 'Jeb, what would it be worth?'

'Top price, Miss,' he replied instantly. ''Tis a good few year since

Talvan produced dimension stone. But demand is going up every day. I reckon we could be up along with the best.'

Ruthlessly suppressing the excitement that bubbled through her fury at the ganger's duplicity, Sarah nodded. 'But before we can sell it we have to get it out.'

'Yes, and that's going to cost,' Jeb warned.

'What would you need?'

Scratching his head while he thought, he settled his cap firmly in place and ticked off the items on his fingers. 'Blasting powder and fuses, a blacksmith on-site to keep the borers sharpened, labour to work the crane and winches, more masons to scapple the blocks to the right size and wagons to shift the stone down to the quay.'

Sarah nodded. She hadn't enough money to pay for any of it. But she knew someone who did.

Telling Jeb not to worry, and not to say anything to the others yet, Sarah sent him back to work. She left the quarry and walked quickly back the way she had come. But when she reached the crossroads, instead of heading home, she turned right.

As she approached Jericho Farm, her anger at the man who had deliberately enticed away her stonemasons was tempered by curiosity. Her steps slowed as she drew level with a new wooden gate that opened on to the short drive.

The last time she had seen the farmhouse, one end was a ruin and the rest hidden beneath rampant ivy and old man's beard. But even in so sorry a state, the pleasing proportions and solidity of the building had been undeniable.

It looked very different now with all the tangled growth stripped off to reveal stone walls with granite quoins, tall chimneys, wide windows and a pillared porch. Through the open windows she could hear hammering and the sound of male voices. Jory was in there somewhere with Noah.

Not wishing to be seen peering at the place like one of the town gossips, she hurried on.

More familiar with the wide skies, rugged moorland and a panoramic view over small fields and copses, she was surprised by the quiet beauty of the steep valley. She wondered why he had based his business in so inaccessible a place. The answer occurred almost at once, and with it, a shiver that tightened her skin. In the event of an explosion the steep valley sides would contain the blast, minimizing the danger to anyone else.

Soothed by the subtle shades of green and dappled sunlight, she breathed in scents of moist earth, bluebells and wild garlic.

Up on the moor the ever-present wind often carried the mewing call of soaring buzzards, a curlew's plaintive cry or the harsh croaking of crows as they wheeled and swooped to warn of wind or rain.

But here in the woods, the air was soft, still and filled with bird-song. She fancied she caught a hint of wood smoke. She could definitely hear the river.

As she picked her way carefully along a faint narrow badger trail, the sound of tumbling water grew louder, and with it, a rhythmic creaking. She stopped, suddenly nervous. Was this really a good idea? What was her alternative? Do nothing and allow Flynn and Landry to cheat her out of Talvan and deprive Jory of his inheritance?

She had faced worse than this and survived. Iron forged in fire became steel. She was stronger than she looked. A fact that James Crago was about to discover.

Walking further down the gently sloping trail, she saw three small buildings. Beyond was a further row of sheds, widely separated and interspersed with thickly planted willow, meandering along beside the river. A leat diverted from the river powered a large waterwheel that creaked as it turned, spilling water in a gush. Moored to wooden stakes in the riverbank, tubs floated like tiny boats.

As she watched, a woman emerged from the end building carrying what looked like a large wooden bowl with a lid on it. Crouching at the river's edge, she placed the bowl in one of the little tubs attached to a rope. She pulled on the rope so that the tub floated down the river and stopped outside the first of the long line of sheds.

Straightening up, she saw Sarah. Her eyes rounded in panic, she ran forward, waving her hands. The strange, unintelligible noises emerging from her mouth startled Sarah, who froze. The woman disappeared in to the middle building.

A man strode out of the shed, pausing as he spotted her. His black brows met in a frown.

'Stay exactly where you are.' Both his deep voice and tense posture radiated anger. 'Don't move.'

Though her temper flared, she stood perfectly still, instinctively responding to a tone and manner that commanded instant and unquestioning obedience. She watched him reassure the woman, his hands gentle on her shoulders. Then he urged her back towards the trio of small buildings. As she went, she glanced over her shoulder. Her pursed mouth and shaking head made Sarah feel guilty of something very foolish. But what? What had she done?

Crago came towards her, his soft boots silent on the beaten earth. His black hair was thick and shaggy and clearly needed the attention of a barber. As he approached through a shaft of sunlight, she realized why.

Warned what to expect, she had believed herself prepared. But for once, rumour and gossip fell short of reality. The white scar crossed his sun-browned face like jagged lightning. Struggling to hide her shock, she felt unexpected and wrenching sympathy.

How many times must he have met quickly averted gazes or horror-filled stares, awed whispers, children pointing? Good manners demanded that she look away so as not to embarrass him. But she was all too familiar with turned backs and cold shoulders. She would not do to someone else what caused pain in her.

Looking beyond his disfigurement, she saw a well-proportioned face with a broad forehead, strong jaw and a wide mouth with chiselled lips. It was a face that would have been called handsome before his nose was broken and puckered white flesh angled from beneath his left eye to the lower edge of his right cheek. What had caused such a terrible wound?

A muscle pulsed in his jaw and his lips tightened. Beneath black brows his eyes were the same colour as the surrounding bluebells and as cold as a quarry lake. He had seen her reaction, must have observed it countless times on other faces. He lifted his chin: the small movement a declaration that he despised her shock and rejected her pity.

It stung, but she understood. Did she not meet rejection and contempt every time she ventured into town? Becky's description of him as 'some great streak' was fairly accurate. But what she had failed to mention was the impact of his physical presence.

Over six feet tall, wearing a workman's check shirt and coarse dark trousers tucked into the strangest boots she had ever seen, he had the powerful shoulders, deep chest and muscular build of a man familiar with hard manual labour. Yet the rumours declared him wealthy, and they had to be true. For without money, how would he have been able to restore the house or establish his business?

'Well?' he snapped. 'What do you want?'

Seven

Sarah stiffened. 'Such rudeness does you no credit, Mr Crago.'

'I owe you no courtesy, madam. Not only are you trespassing on private property, your presence here is a danger to us all.'

'I *beg* your pardon?' As he came steadily towards her, only pride and his command that she stand still stopped her backing away. 'I don't—'

'This,' he interrupted coldly, his gesture encompassing the sheds, river and waterwheel, 'is a gunpowder mill.' He stopped a yard from her, *too close*, and glared down. 'All it takes to set off an explosion is a single spark. A shoe nail strikes against a stone and *BOOM.*' His sudden, expansive gesture made her flinch. 'That is why I told you to stand still.'

'I–I'm sorry. I didn't—'

'Think?' His contempt struck like a whiplash. 'Lift your feet so I can see the soles.'

Her face burning, Sarah braced herself with one hand against a tree and raised each foot in turn. *I should have realized, should have thought.* The fact that the soles of her boots were stitched and not tacked made her feel a little better. Now she understood the woman's panic, his sharpness and the unusual footwear they both wore. She had seen pictures of Red Indians wearing similar boots of soft leather fastened with thong bindings.

'Is there any metal in your clothing? A belt buckle, for instance?'

Her fingers flew to the large button that fastened her cloak and felt the smooth surface of horn. 'No.'

'Well, then? Why are you here?'

Her anger flooded back. 'You stole two of my stonemasons.'

His expression remained stony but his gaze betrayed surprise. 'You must be Miss Govier.'

Her chin rose a fraction. 'That is correct.'

'Sam Venner told me he'd heard you were selling your quarry. As I need two masons and yours would have been out of work, I told him to offer them a job.'

'Mr Venner is mistaken. I am *not* selling.'

'If your masons were aware of that, they could have refused my offer.'

Sarah fought chagrin as she recognized the truth in his words. For months the men had been working on poor-quality stone, and they knew it. No doubt Flynn had dripped his own brand of poison in their ears; doubts about the quarry's survival, hints that she might be ready to sell. Yet, though she understood their reasons for leaving, it still felt like disloyalty and it hurt. 'I can only assume that they, and Sam, were taken in by rumours put about by Kinser Landry with the assistance of Paddy Flynn, my ganger. Though Flynn no longer works for me as I dismissed him.'

One corner of his mouth twitched. It might have been amusement. It could equally have been irritation. She had no way of knowing.

'Landry wants your quarry?'

She nodded.

'Why?'

She opened her mouth to tell him and then quickly closed it again. What was she doing? This man was a total stranger. For all she knew, he could be a friend of Landry's. Though somehow, she didn't think so. But what did she know? She had trusted Philip, believed Philip. She looked away, startled and unsettled. What had that to do with this?

'That is not your concern.' She hadn't intended to sound so curt. But the ground seemed to be shifting beneath her feet. Now she did take a deliberate step backward, relieved to feel the firmness of hard-packed earth.

'Miss Govier, you arrive here uninvited and accuse me of stealing your masons. That makes it my concern.'

Though she bitterly resented the fact, he had a point. 'Very well, then. A few weeks ago Kinser Landry wrote to me saying he wanted to buy my quarry. He claimed my granite is poor and therefore worth very little. He said he planned to use the land for waste stone.'

'But you declined his offer.'

She shook her head. 'Not yet. Though I intend to. I admit that recently there have been problems at Talvan, situations I was unaware of. My son was ill and . . .' she broke off as heat coloured her face. 'But that is by the by.' The reality was that the quarry had been in trouble long before that: starting when her father's death had plunged her into a situation for which she was untrained and ill-equipped. 'The point is, regardless of what Mr Landry chooses to believe, I am not selling.'

His eyes narrowed. 'Then I understand your anger at losing your masons.'

'Believe me, Mr Crago, losing my masons is only part of it.'

'Oh?' He waited.

'The stone taken out these past months is indeed of limited use,' Sarah allowed. 'But behind it is granite of very high quality. Though I only learned of this today.'

'How? I mean, who told you?'

'From Jeb Mundy, my foreman. He—'

'I know who he is. You think Landry knew about this quality stone when he wrote to you?'

Sarah nodded. 'I believe my ganger told him. He – Flynn – had already withheld wages from my workmen, forcing them to buy on credit from shops in which he and his friends have a financial interest. Such a man would not hesitate to pass on information, especially to someone willing to pay.' Indignation scalded her cheeks. 'Small wonder Mr Landry was so anxious to secure my agreement to sell.'

'Miss Govier, I assure you I knew nothing of this when I told Sam to engage your masons.'

She believed him. And was startled by her relief. She didn't want him to be like the Landrys, Flynns and Nathan Keasts. Why should it matter? Because in him she sensed a kindred spirit. Yet if her experience with Philip had taught her anything, it was to be wary.

'So, did you come here merely to scold me?'

Her nerve wavered. But the spirit that had survived betrayal, denial and ostracism drove her on. 'No.' She paused, her mouth suddenly dry. Everything depended on the next few moments and her own courage. Trying to ignore the flush that made her aware of her high colour and her clinging shift, she forced the words out.

'Talvan quarry contains granite of superior quality. However, I can't sell it unless – until – it is extracted. In order to achieve that I need . . .' She counted out on her fingers and repeated the list that Jeb had rattled off earlier. 'Though if I can agree a contract with a granite merchant who wants dimension stone for one of the big breakwater or harbour projects, I intend to negotiate shared costs for the wagons.'

'I wish you success.'

Unable to read anything from his tone or expression, she clasped her hands together tightly. 'My difficulty is that I do not have enough . . .' She stopped. Landry had lied. She would not. 'I do not have *any* money to pay for it.' She met his eyes. Brilliantly blue, they gave nothing away.

'And you are telling me this because . . .?'

'You took my masons,' she blurted. 'Naturally they would not turn down the wages you can offer. Wages higher than I can afford. But I can't manage without them. So I think that under the circumstances you owe me compensation.'

His brows climbed. 'Miss Govier, am I to take it that you wish *me* to fund this enterprise?'

She nodded. Her throat was so dry that it hurt to swallow. 'Yes. It is hardly a huge amount to someone in your position.'

'What do you know of my position?'

'Only that you'd have to be a man of means in order to set up this business and employ all the men currently working on the farmhouse. I'll pay you back as soon as the stone is sold. With interest,' she added, desperation making her reckless. 'You can draw up an agreement . . .' She stopped as he looked away.

She'd heard people talk about a *sinking heart*. Feeling the dragging weight in her chest, she knew what they meant. But she could not regret trying. Perhaps he was thinking that it served her right. That she deserved no better for her temerity in taking her father's place. In daring to think that she could successfully run a quarry.

She caught herself. Jory's illness and her fear of losing him had pushed all thoughts of Talvan from her mind. She had no right to blame this man or anyone else for her failings. But unless she could come up with another plan – tears blurred her vision. *What other plan?* Tipping her head, she took a deep breath, determined to extricate herself with some semblance of dignity.

'Very well,' he said.

As her head jerked up, a single tear spilled over her lashes and on to her cheek. Ashamed at betraying weakness, she flicked it away. She had little patience or sympathy with feminine tears, knowing them too often manufactured and manipulative.

'You mean it?'

He looked down his broken nose at her. 'I'm not in the habit of saying things I don't mean.' Before she could apologize, he continued, 'I'll supply everything you've asked for. As for the stonemasons, Sam will arrange their work so they will be available when needed at the quarry.'

Gratitude welled inside her. And was shredded by cold claws of suspicion. *Please don't let him be like the others.* 'This may sound . . . I do not intend to be impolite. But why?'

He regarded her in silence. She knew it was ridiculous to imagine that he could read her thoughts. She wanted to look away from that steady blue gaze. But pride and her obligation to him would not allow it. Anyway, how would she know if he lied? Brutal disfigurement would have taught him that survival lay behind a mask of impassivity.

'Why? First, I consider Landry's methods contemptible. Second, Jeb Mundy is known as one of the best granite men in Cornwall. If he says the granite is of high quality, then my investment is safe. Third, getting the stone out will allow me an opportunity to test a new blend of blasting powder. So it is in all respects an excellent business proposition.' He raised one dark brow. 'Does that reassure you, Miss Govier?'

Though his manner was coolly polite, she sensed rebuke, even mockery. And realized that in fearing he might want something personal from her, she was guilty of terrible conceit. What right had she to assume he was any less discriminating than she was herself? She knew she was not ill-looking. But even the most pleasing appearance could never compensate for a shattered reputation.

'It does. Thank you.' Fighting the confusion he had stirred, she gestured. 'May I ask why there are so many sheds?'

'The three small ones at the end are separate stores for the ingredients that make gunpowder. Each of these alongside the river has its own special function.' He pointed. 'Mixing house and powder mill. The others are where the powder is pressed, corned, glazed, then packed. Each stage is kept separate to minimize risk of explosion or fire.'

Sarah nodded. It made perfect sense. 'But where are all your workers?'

'Apart from Zack Bottrell, my charcoal burner, and his daughter Nessa, whom you met earlier, I work alone. It is safer. Now you must excuse me.' He nodded formally.

'Good day, Mr Crago. And thank you.' She turned to leave.

'Miss Govier?'

She glanced back. 'Yes?'

'I met your son this morning.'

Suddenly still, she made him think of a deer sensing a tiger, poised to flee but uncertain where safety lay.

'He is a credit to you.'

Her quick smile betrayed love, pride and visible relief, reminding him that she would have spent the boy's entire life protecting him from snubs, slights and the cruelty of those who would blame a child for its parents' actions.

'Thank you,' she said simply.

He paused outside the glazing house, watching as she followed the path that angled up the hillside, and was irritated by his own confusion. There was no doubting her courage. But after asking for and receiving his promise of help, she had suspected him of wanting payment in kind. She hadn't actually said so, but the implication had been there. Though his answer had set her mind at rest, it was less than the whole truth. For he was indeed attracted to her.

Her hairstyle was simple, her clothes unremarkable. Yet there was something compelling about her. It – like she – had taken him by surprise. Despite her initial shock, she had continued to look directly into his face. Briefly suspecting boldness, even bravado, he had recognized something more unsettling: *empathy*.

He guessed that she was constantly fending off unwanted attentions from men who considered her fair game. That alone was reason enough for her suspicion. She did not know him, had no idea if he could be trusted.

Why had she kept the child? Such situations were usually dealt with by removal to a distant relative until after the confinement and the child offered for adoption or placed in a foundling's home. The girl then returns home with no one outside the family any the wiser.

So why had she defied respectability and common sense by keeping her son? Who was the boy's father? Why had he not married her? *She's no cheap tart.* An ardent Methodist like Sam Venner would not have defended her had the man been already married. Her choice to keep her son had not merely ruined her reputation, it had wrecked her chance of marrying. A widow and child inspired sympathy. An unmarried mother provoked doubt and distrust.

She didn't remember him. Why would she? She had been a little girl, not much older than her son was now, when he had come to live with his grandfather after his parents died from influenza within days of each other.

Solitary since losing his wife to the same illness and unwilling to take on the role of parent, his grandfather had sent him to school in Truro. On his eighteenth birthday, he had brought home a copy of an advertising poster offering adventure and advancement for spirited young men in the East India Company's army.

His grandfather had read it and nodded. 'You'll do well.'

At the Company's orderly room in 35 Soho Square his application had been accepted. Two months later he was on his way to India, teaching himself Hindustani on the voyage.

During the next fourteen years he developed a cast-iron stomach and a constitution able to cope with intense heat, endless dust, cold nights and monsoon rains. He journeyed across wide plains to cool foothills. He learned the science of warfare, how fireworks were made and that when dealing with the warrior castes of the Ganges valley, courtesy produced better results than the arrogance and bullying too often employed by his superiors.

He took part in bloody battles, learned everything he could about the manufacture of gunpowder, joined a small elite band sent to explore unknown territories and discovered the difference between *thagi*, with their religious traditions, and the roaming bands of armed *dakaiti* robbers whose preferred method of torture involved fire.

From Laswari in the north, he eventually reached Pondicherry on the south-east coast. From Tanjore, he had crossed to Kodagu. There he met Anjuli.

Jerking himself out of the past, he focused on the retreating figure. Each piece of information, each snippet of gossip, had piqued his curiosity. The dimly remembered child was now a stranger, a wary and attractive young woman. Not at all the person that gossip had led him to expect.

He had seen the shock in her eyes, and a brief flash of pity, but no revulsion. She had not turned aside. For those few minutes he fancied she had looked beyond his wrecked features to the man inside.

What self-indulgent foolishness was this? She had come here because she wanted something. Of course she would make an effort, hide her disgust. And it had worked. He had agreed to help her with money and workmen.

Because it was a good investment. That was incontrovertible fact. But not the whole truth. She was the first woman who had looked directly into his face, into his eyes. Used to reading nuances of movement, the sideways glance that rendered polite words a lie, he had looked at her and recognized shared experience.

In a small Cornish town where everyone knew everyone else and many were related, she would have – must have – suffered for what she'd done. By keeping the boy, she had defied convention. For that alone the old townsfolk would make her pay. Had she loved her son's father? Did she love him still?

Why should he care? Her personal life was no concern of his. So why was he thinking about her? Raking a hand through his hair as if to erase these unsettling thoughts, he turned abruptly towards the glazing shed.

Eight

'So what did he say?' Becky leaned forward, her plate of mutton and barley stew momentarily forgotten as Sarah related the morning's events.

'For one awful minute I thought he was going to refuse. I don't know what I'd have done.' She shook her head, recalling her apprehension. 'But I told him I would pay back every penny once the granite was sold, so there was no way he could lose. Becky, he's agreed. He'll pay for everything we need to get the granite out.'

'He will? What does he want in return?'

'I told you. I'll repay him the money as soon as—'

'That's not what I mean and you know it.' Becky scooped up a mouthful with her fork. 'Come on, my bird. This is me you're talking to.'

Setting down her knife and fork, Sarah sat back. 'I did wonder if there would . . . if he might . . .' She met Becky's gaze, reluctant to admit even to this dearest and most treasured friend the depth of her fear that his offer had been conditional. That he was like the others. 'So I asked him right out *why* he was willing to help. And for my suspicion I was put firmly in my place.' She pressed one palm to her hot cheek as she recalled the flash of irony in his cool gaze.

'He said Jeb's reputation made it a good investment. Also, he was glad of the opportunity to test some new blasting powder. He made me feel my doubts were foolish and I should be ashamed of having them.'

'You was just being careful.' Pushing back her chair, Becky gathered up the plates and took them to the sink while Sarah cut into a rhubarb tart and lifted slices carefully into two bowls.

'He's different, Becky.'

'He surely is.'

'You know I don't just mean his face.'

'No more do I. That wound will have changed more than his looks.' Resuming her seat, Becky spooned up clotted cream from a glass dish and dropped it on to her tart. 'Listen, bird. He may well be different. But think a minute. When you knew Talvan was in trouble, why didn't you go to other men for help? Men who had known your father?'

'You know why. Because they would have told me to sell: if not to them, then to Kinser Landry. None of them would have offered assistance so I could keep Talvan going myself. They would prefer me out of sight and out of mind.'

Becky nodded. 'See, that's what I mean. People believe a woman's place is in the home, raising a family. Not running a business.' She raised a hand before Sarah could speak. 'We both know there's any number of women in Penryn and Falmouth that own shops, inns, hotels, even breweries. But they either took over after their husband died, or they've never been wed. But you, you broke the rules and they don't like it.'

'Something else we both know is that I couldn't have managed without your help.'

'Glad to do it. And I'm glad Mr Crago have offered the help you need.' Leaning across the table, she patted Sarah's hand. 'I hope he's everything you wish.'

As Sarah tilted her head to hide a betraying flush, Becky went on. 'Just remember, whatever happened to him, that scar is only part of it. 'Tis the wounds inside, the ones you can't see, that are slowest to heal. If he's willing to use his money to get that there stone out all in the name of good business, then who am I to argue against it? It's what you need, and you'd be mad to turn him down. But whatever reasons he's given you, they won't be the *only* ones.'

'How can you know that?'

Becky shrugged. 'Because I've lived a lot longer than you. And because he's a man. Men do keep more inside. Now stop playing with that tart and finish it up. You need your strength.'

With her head and newly awakened heart at war, Sarah obeyed. She had a business arrangement with Mr Crago, one that bene-fited them both. He deserved her gratitude.

By the time they had washed up, saving the rest of the stew and tart for Jory's meal that evening, it had begun to rain. Too restless to sit and sew, Sarah decided to turn out the cupboards under the dresser, a task postponed by her son's illness.

Piling the contents of both cupboards on to the kitchen table, she washed and dried the shelves, then sorted through what was to be kept and what could be passed on or thrown away.

Becky sat by the fire, busy with her needle, as she relayed bits of news and gossip passed on by her sister-in-law, who was very much involved with the chapel.

Sarah sensed her occasional glances and was reminded of a mother hen with a chick. Her thoughts were confused, her feelings even more so. She looked up to find Becky watching her.

'I'm fine!' Sarah threw up her hands in exasperation.

'I never said a word.'

'You were thinking very loudly.'

Laying her sewing on the table, Becky nodded at the cupboard. 'That's a good job done. I'll put the kettle on, then I'm off. Jory will be home d'rectly. I love that boy dearly, but he do talk your ear off.'

The following morning Sarah drew back the curtains and opened her bedroom window. The overnight rain had passed, leaving the air fresh and crystal-clear.

In the distance, the Carrick Roads glittered like polished silver in early morning sun that lit the sails of anchored schooners, brigs and barques. The ships reminded her of what she had to do that morning, and she pressed a hand to her stomach to try and still the nervous flutter.

While Jory washed his face, she prepared his breakfast and then wrapped up bread and cheese, a scone with butter and jam and a bottle of lemonade, packing them in to a canvas bag with a long strap. After brushing his hair and buttoning his coat, she set his cap over his curls.

'Mind you do what Uncle Noah tells you.'

''Course,' he grinned, lifting his arm so she could settle the bag behind him, leaving his hands free. 'Bye, Ma.'

Bending, she cupped his face and kissed him. 'Bye, my love.'

He raced out of the door and down the path. Standing in the doorway, her arms folded over a flower-patterned bodice faded from laundering, she watched him greet Noah, returned Noah's reassuring wave and went back inside.

By nine thirty the dishes were put away and the beds made. It was time to get ready. After giving her hair a thorough brushing, she swept it back, twisting it into a neat coil anchored with pins.

The latest fashion for a centre parting with bunches of ringlets on either side of the face was for ladies who had a fleet of maids and endless spare time.

Gazing at her reflection, she assessed her features: dark brown hair with a natural wave that made curling irons and rags unnecessary. Eyes that were neither green nor brown, but a mixture of both. A clear complexion. But the pink in her cheeks denied her the fashionable look of pale fragility. Daily walks and the physical demands of housework had kept her waist trim. But the once-slender girl had matured into a woman.

She blew out a sigh. Her birth and breeding equalled the best in Penryn, and eight years ago she had possessed an extensive wardrobe. Taught by Becky how to cook, sew and manage the household, her skill at budgeting and neat handwriting had persuaded her father to delegate quarry paperwork to her. He had paid her a small wage which she usually spent on her fast-growing son.

But she and Becky had managed to meet the challenge of each season's innovations by adding new trim to a skirt or bodice, decorating a bonnet with fresh ribbons and altering the cut of a sleeve.

Current fashion might dictate floor-length skirts, but as she regularly walked over the moor to the quarry, or down into town along muddy roads, so common sense required she keep hers a couple of inches shorter.

Over her shift and boned stays she wore a flannel petticoat, with another of stiffened tarlatan to support the full skirt of her emerald shot-silk gown. The sleeves had been altered from billowing fullness to a closer fit, and she had added a white lace collar to the neckline. Though eight years old, it was her best dress.

Her short cape was the wrong green, and the occasion called for something more feminine than her father's cloak.

Opening a drawer, she took out a large shawl with a pinecone pattern of emerald, turquoise and cream that smelled sweetly of lavender. Folding it diagonally, she swung it about her shoulders. Then, tying the emerald ribbons of a small bonnet that framed her face, she picked up her gloves, checked her appearance one last time and walked downstairs, just as Becky opened the back door.

'My dear soul! A proper picture, you are. Want me to walk down with you? I don't mind.'

'I thought you were baking this morning.'

'Well, I was. But I can do that later.'

'It's kind of you, Becky. And I appreciate the offer—'

'But you'll go quicker on your own.'

'It's not that.' Though they both knew it was. 'While I'm walking, I shall practise what I'm going to say.' The exercise would also, she hoped, get rid of the butterflies dancing beneath her ribs. 'I should be back by twelve.'

'I'll have the kettle on, bird.'

Sarah walked down Helston Road into Lower Street. Passing the new clock tower and the Town Hall that formed an island dividing the road, she turned left down the steep slope of St Thomas Street.

At the bottom, crossing the open area in front of the Chough Inn, she reached Thomas Trenery's yard.

Two huge solid wooden gates were fastened back to allow easy access for carts and wagons. One heavy wagon was drawn up on the quay. The team of four horses stood placidly, while behind them chains rattled, winches squealed, seagulls shrieked and half a dozen men shouted to each other as they helped the crane operator manoeuvre a huge block of granite into the hold of a ship moored to the quay.

The tide was out and the pungent smells of mud, fish, tar, seaweed and sewage were strong. Further down the quay crates and sacks were being carried from a warehouse to another coastal schooner.

Lifting her skirts, Sarah picked her way around puddles as she crossed the uneven ground, glad she had worn her boots. She headed purposefully towards a stone building with a large wooden sign attached to the side: THOS. TRENERY. GRANITE MERCHANT.

Reaching the open front door, she took a deep breath and walked in. Behind a second half-open door on her right, she could hear male voices. She knocked, then pushed the door open wider.

The man standing behind a large paper-cluttered table turned his head, frowning at the interruption. Upon seeing her, his expression softened to surprise.

Of stocky build with big hands and a weathered face, his brown cutaway coat, yellow-check waistcoat, fawn trousers and dark cravat neatly knotted over stiff shirt points, bespoke a man of wealth and substance. But the ledgers, letters and invoices on the table proclaimed him someone who preferred to keep the reins of his business firmly in his own hands.

Relief coursed through Sarah, who had feared being sent away by an assistant before she could get near Mr Trenery.

The other man, wearing work clothes, had his back to her, yet he looked vaguely familiar. As he glanced round, Sarah's stomach clenched. Nathan Keast's shock quickly became a smirk.

'All right, Sarah?'

Ignoring him, Sarah kept her gaze on the man she had come to see. 'Good morning, Mr Trenery. I apologize for calling without an appointment. Could you spare me a few moments?'

He studied her. 'You're George Govier's girl. I knew your father. A good man, he was.' He shook his head. 'A sad business.'

Not sure if he was referring to her father's death or her own situation, Sarah stood perfectly still.

'Come in, come in.' He shifted his gaze to Nathan Keast. 'Get back to work. And you mind what I said.'

Raising a finger to his forehead in a salute that bordered on insolence, Nathan Keast turned to the door. With his back to his employer, he made a soft sucking sound as he passed Sarah. Her loathing masked by composure, she ignored him.

As the door closed, Thomas Trenery came from behind the table, lifted a pile of papers from a chair and drew it forward.

'Please,' he gestured before returning to his own seat. 'What can I do for you?'

Sarah sat, removing her gloves and holding them in her lap. 'Mr Trenery, you may have heard rumours that Talvan quarry is in trouble and I am about to sell to Kinser Landry.'

'You know what this town's like for rumours.'

'Indeed I do.' She saw realization cross his face at her quiet reply. Anxious that he should not feel uncomfortable, which might make him less receptive, she continued smoothly. 'This is why I came in person to tell you that I am not selling.'

'You're not? Well, I've got to say I'm glad to hear it. I know your father hoped your boy would take it over one day. But you didn't come all the way down here just to tell me that.'

'No.' She paused, marshalling her thoughts. It would be all too easy through nerves, or eagerness, to say more than was necessary. 'Mr Trenery, Jeb Mundy informs me that within a very few weeks Talvan quarry will be able to supply dimension stone of the highest quality. Would you be interested? Obviously you will want to visit the quarry to see the granite for yourself to be assured of its standard and suitability.'

'If it's as good as Jeb claims, then certainly I'm interested. You talked to anyone else about it?'

'You are the first merchant I have approached,' she replied adroitly. 'My father always spoke well of you.'

He nodded, as if it were no more than his due. 'Well, you've come to the right man. Subject to inspection, I'll take all your granite. I'm one of the suppliers to Grissell & Peto, the contractors for the new Houses of Parliament up in London.' His smile deepened the creases at the corners of his eyes. 'Landry bid, but they turned him down.'

'Mr Trenery, that is indeed excellent news.' In their brief shared glance she read understanding. He knew that she was not referring solely to his offer, or to his successful bid. 'My congratulations. You must be delighted. Now, concerning the matter of transport. I assume you will wish to use your own wagons to collect the granite from Talvan?'

He sucked his teeth and puckered his forehead. But Sarah knew that was simply part of the negotiating process. Telling her about winning the contract had revealed how much it meant to him. Landry's failed bid was simply the icing on Mr Trenery's cake. If she could supply the granite he needed, he would not risk losing her to another merchant.

After a further quarter of an hour of hard bargaining they agreed that he would supply two wagons and teams while she would pay for hiring however many more were needed. After arranging a day and time for him to visit the quarry, Sarah rose.

'My apologies for calling without an appointment, Mr Trenery.'

He came round the desk and took the hand she offered. 'No apologies necessary. I'll have my clerk draw up a contract—'

'Would you be kind enough to allow me two copies?'

'Two?' He tipped his head sideways, clearly curious.

'Yes, if you please.' Smiling, she drew on her gloves, seeing no need to tell him that one copy was for James Crago. 'You'll let me know when they are ready for signature?'

'It'll be within the week,' he promised and opened the door. 'You just hang on a minute, Miss Govier.' Looking past her, he raised a hand to summon a workman. Sarah froze. But it was a tall, skinny tow-headed lad who hurried forward, snatching off his cap.

'Yessir?'

'Where's Sully?'

'Over in the warehouse, Sir,' the lad pointed.

'Fetch him, will you? That boat's going nowhere till the tide comes in. He's to drive Miss Govier home.'

'Mr Trenery, there's really no need—'

'It's no trouble. Don't you fret about your dress. I wouldn't ask you to ride on one of the wagons. I drove down in my gig. That'll take you home in comfort.'

'And in great style.' She smiled and saw his pleasure at the compliment. 'You're very kind.'

'If your granite is as good as you say, 'tis the least I can do.'

Nine

During the week that followed Crago completed the orders for Carwhidden quarry and Porkellis mine. Then, on a fresh, sunny morning, after taking Sam Venner aside and telling him that the new stonemasons would be dividing their time between the farm and Talvan quarry, he saddled his huge thoroughbred and rode across the moor to introduce himself to Jeb Mundy.

'I know who you are, Mr Crago,' Jeb said, looking first at his feet, then off to one side and finally over Crago's right shoulder. His arms were folded and his boots planted firmly on the gritty boulder-strewn quarry floor. 'But I don't know what you're doing here. Miss isn't selling, and I got nothing to say—'

'I know she isn't,' Crago interrupted. 'She told me so herself, when she stormed on to my property last week to scold me for stealing two of her masons.'

Startled, Jeb met Crago's gaze for the first time. '*Scold?* She scolded *you?*' he repeated.

As Crago nodded, the foreman's astonishment dissolved into a grin. Shoving his cap back, he shook his head. 'Well, I never.' He glanced over his shoulder at the two men who had stopped work to watch. 'What're 'ee waiting for?' he shouted. 'They holes won't bore theirselves.'

'She also told me about Landry's attempt to trick her into selling this quarry,' Crago said.

'She did? Skiddery as an eel, he is,' Jeb growled. 'He like to think he got the world by the ass. But he won't best her, not if I can stop'n.'

'I'd like to help. In fact,' Crago added drily, 'Miss Govier has insisted on it. She says I owe her compensation.'

Jeb gaped. 'Dear life! She don't want for nerve, I'll say that.'

'My sentiments exactly,' Crago muttered.

Once more Jeb stared at his boots and Crago sensed the foreman's inner battle. 'Look, maybe it isn't for me to say, but don't you go giving her no trouble. She've already had too much of it.'

Crago bit back his anger. Damn it, *she* had come to *him*. 'Miss Govier is fortunate indeed to inspire such loyalty.'

'I've knowed her all her life. She was only five year old when her mother passed away, dear of her. If it hadn't been for Becky Hitchens – then all that other – and losing her father. Well, like I say, we wouldn't take kindly to anyone giving her grief.'

'Mr Mundy,' Crago hissed softly, his impatience tinged with envy. 'I may look like a fiend, but that does not make me one.'

The foreman started and his cheeks flushed crimson.

Knowing his point made, Crago continued. 'If you are referring to the ganger, she told me what Flynn did, and that she has dismissed him.'

'Good riddance, too. Look, I didn't mean . . . no offence intended.'

'None taken.' Crago said wearily. *What would be the point? It would not stop sidelong glances and horrified shudders.* 'She mentioned a new bed of granite?'

Visibly relieved, Jeb nodded quickly. 'I knew there was better than that poor stuff we been pulling out since Christmas. I could smell it.'

'Will you show me?' Crago said.

'Over yonder.' Jeb tipped his head sideways. 'Know what you're looking at, do you?'

'No. You're the granite expert. My expertise is in blasting powder.'

Jeb sniffed. 'Flynn got ours. I dunno where. But 'tis awful lumpy stuff.'

Unease slithered like ice down Crago's spine. 'Don't use any more. Get rid of it. It sounds like cheap mill cake.'

'That bad, is it?'

'Very. It's extremely dangerous.'

'I s'pose yours is safer?'

Appreciating the droll note in the foreman's question, Crago nodded. 'Yes, it is. And it's more reliable. But you judge for yourself. I've developed a new mix. The captain at Carnkie mine is delighted with it. He's placed a regular order, and I've just sent five barrels over to Porkellis mine. I told Miss Govier I'd welcome the chance to try it here at Talvan.'

'How's yours different, then?' Jeb demanded. 'If you don't mind me asking.'

'Not at all.' Crago guessed the foreman was still bitter at being taken in by the ganger. 'Gunpowder only contains three ingredients:

sulphur, saltpetre and charcoal. But it's the proportions of each ingredient in the mix that determines what the powder will be used for. It could be cartridges or safety fuse or blasting. I sieve my mill cake to break down the lumps and remove the dust. Then, after air-drying, the grains are rolled in a barrel with graphite to give them a hard, shiny surface.'

'I never seen powder like that. What do you do that for?'

'Two reasons. First, it makes weighing out a charge easier and more accurate. Second, the powder will store longer because it doesn't absorb moisture.'

'Sounds a damn sight better than the stuff we been using,' Jeb said.

'It is,' Crago's tone was dry. 'Miss Govier and I have reached an agreement over the two masons. You let me know when the granite is ready for dressing and I'll send them over, though I doubt two will be enough. She said you would also need a blacksmith to work on site, and men to operate the crane.'

'We'll need to set up a spider as well,' Jeb said.

'*Spider?*'

'Movable crab winch,' Jeb explained. 'To haul the stone to the crane, and to shift the waste.'

'I assume you'll hire men you know, hard workers you can trust?'

'She don't need to worry. Nor do you. I'll find they easy enough. Only thing is, it'll cost . . .'

'That is all in hand. You just find the men.'

'Here,' Jeb clambered over scattered blocks to the huge stepped face. 'Here it is.'

About to follow him, Crago paused, studying the rock. 'Why are some holes round and others triangular?'

'Don't miss much, do you? Depends who's boring. See Timmy there?' Jeb pointed to the man standing on top of a large uneven block. 'He's holding the jumper, the hand borer. Now, every time Ben hit it with the sledgehammer, Timmy do turn the jumper in the hole. Timmy like a round hole when we're going deep for blasting. So he fit a steel collar just behind the cutting edge of the borer. They're only making three-inch holes now, for plugs and feathers.'

'What?'

'Plugs and feathers,' Jeb repeated. 'To split the stone down smaller. A plug is a tapered iron wedge put in between two half-round iron pieces – that's the feathers – in the hole. Hit them with the sledge and the rock will split. You got to hit them just right, mind, nice and level. Anyhow, for blasting I just twist the borer half a turn as he go down. See, most times I can tell from the face of the hole where the blast will crack the rock.'

'You know that just by the way the borer feels in the hole?'

Jeb nodded as if surprised. 'Most times. But when we was doing that one, the bore was eight foot deep and I couldn't be sure. So we put in a small charge, just enough to spring'n.'

'Open up a fracture?'

Jeb nodded. 'You got it.' Enthusiasm, and relief at knowing he'd have the men and equipment he needed, demolished the last of his reserve. 'Anyhow, next charge we put in was twenty-five pound of powder. Shifted that great block a yard from the face. Damn thing was flawed and broke in pieces. But there, behind it, see? Beautiful that is.'

Pleasure glowed on Jeb's seamed face. 'Lovely even colour, close texture and small grain. Be lovely to work, it will.' He turned to Crago. 'It'll take some shifting, mind. We got a couple of carts for carrying setts, kerbs and light stuff down to the quay. But for dimension stone, we'll need heavy wagons.'

'You'll have them. Anything else?'

Jeb shook his head. 'I reck'n that's it for now.' He touched his cap, briefly meeting Crago's gaze. 'Much obliged.'

Returning the salute, Crago re-crossed the quarry floor. As he walked up the ramp to where his horse grazed on new spring grass amid gorse, heather and tumbled stone, the rhythmic ringing tone of the hammer stopped once more. The men would want to know the reason for his visit and Jeb would be delighted to tell them.

A smile lifted one corner of his mouth as he swung himself into the saddle. Behind the foreman's gesture – one expert acknowledging another – Crago recognized acceptance and was surprised at the pleasure this gave him.

Cantering along the track, he slowed as he came to the crossroads, patting his mount's glossy shoulder. 'Which way?' He told himself he would leave the decision to Balal. And he knew he lied. The horse tossed its head. 'It's only polite,' Crago murmured. 'A courtesy. Keeping her informed.'

A light touch on the rein and gentle pressure with his knee

turned Balal towards a scattered group of cottages. As he approached the first and largest, he saw the front door was wide open. A wooden fence surrounded the garden, presumably an attempt to keep rabbits out. On one side of the path leading from latched gate to front door were neat rows of potatoes, cabbages, onions, turnips and leeks. On the other were beds of sage and thyme, cushions of lavender, rosemary and myrtle bushes and, tumbling along and over the fence, dog roses and honeysuckle. A gnarled elder tree stood by the fence. Amid fresh green leaves, flower heads as big as tea plates were just beginning to open.

Dismounting, he looped the reins over Balal's head and tied them to the fence. The horse lowered his head and began to graze. Aware of his quickening heartbeat, and mocking himself for a fool, Crago opened the gate.

He walked up the path, his mouth watering as he inhaled the fragrance of fresh baking. Approaching the open door, he heard the clatter of metal on stone. Taking off his hat, he raked a hand through his hair and tapped his knuckles on the painted wood.

'Come in, Ivy,' he heard Sarah call. 'They're just off the baking iron.'

Tilting his head to avoid the low lintel, he stepped inside just as she turned from the hearth, holding a cooling tray with a dozen golden-topped scones.

'Oh!' The tray tipped and she dived forward. The scones nearest the edge of the tray fell on to the table. 'Mr Crago. You startled me.'

Her face was rosy. Was it from the heat of the embers, or at seeing him?

Setting the tray down, she replaced the three scones and quickly removed the coarse apron covering her gown.

'I've just come from the quarry.' He was disconcerted by his desire to reassure her and explain himself. Damn it, it was *his* money. 'It occurred to me that your foreman would welcome reassurance that he will have the men and equipment he needs.'

'How thoughtful. I did mean to go and tell him myself,' she added quickly. 'Only—'

'It was no trouble. In fact, I found it most interesting.'

She tucked a stray curl behind her ear. 'I'm glad you're here. I–I mean – glad you stopped by. Because I have some news as well. I went into town this morning, to see Mr Trenery. Thomas Trenery, the granite merchant?'

'Is his the yard on Glasney Creek?' Watching her clasp her hands and then release them to smooth down the front of her skirt, he found it reassuring that she seemed as unsettled as he was.

She nodded.

'Was it a successful interview?' He deliberately shifted from one foot to the other.

Her colour deepened and she immediately indicated the chair closest to him. 'I beg your pardon. I–I'm – Will you sit down, Mr Crago?'

'Thank you.' Setting his hat and gloves at the far end of the table, he pulled out the chair and then remained on his feet, waiting. 'Miss Govier, I cannot sit unless you do.'

'Oh.' Retreating to the armchair by the fire, she perched on the edge, stiff-backed, folding her hands as he sat.

'What did Mr Trenery say?'

'He put in a bid to supply granite to the contractors building the Houses of Parliament, and he has been successful. I'm sure you can imagine his delight as he shared this news. It means that, subject to a satisfactory inspection, he will take all we can produce.'

'Well done indeed, Miss Govier.' Watching pleasure bloom in her cheeks, he was aware of an odd sensation in his chest, like the first stirring of spring after a long, cold winter. 'Your foreman showed me the granite. I confess I had no idea what I was looking at. But he described its exceptional qualities with such enthusiasm that Mr Trenery cannot fail to be impressed. When does he wish to make his inspection?'

'I suggested the end of next week. Jeb will want to blast out a sizeable block.'

'I will take a barrel of powder over to Talvan tomorrow.' He studied her. 'I think, perhaps, you have more to tell me?'

She nodded, her eyes shining. 'Mr Trenery has also agreed to provide two heavy wagons needed to move the granite from the quarry to his yard. He was reluctant, but in the end I was able to persuade him.' Her smile faltered. 'Of course, we will have to provide at least one more, maybe two. But—'

'Bravo, Miss Govier,' he said softly. Not for a king's ransom would he tell her that, had he been in charge of the negotiations, Trenery would be supplying all the wagons. Like him, she was practised at concealing her emotions. But while relating her achievement, she had radiated pride. These past few years could have afforded her few such opportunities. 'Congratulations on a most successful morning.'

Behind her, hanging from its hook over the fire, the kettle began to boil. She glanced at it and then back to him, clearly uncertain. Reluctant to go, but with no reason to stay, he started to get up.

'W—would you like a cup of tea, Mr Crago?'

'That is most kind. I would indeed.' He saw from her surprise that she had anticipated refusal, braced herself for it. What was it like for her? Branded a tart and a sinner by people smug in their self-righteousness: people without a fraction of her courage.

Watching her take cups and saucers from the dresser, then lift the beaded muslin from the milk jug, he thought of his own rare and reluctant visits to town, of steeling himself to ignore the inevitable stares and mutters.

As she poured the milk, the jug clattered against the rim of a cup, and he realized that his silence was responsible. He was making her nervous. He searched for something to say. Business had brought them together. Surely he could think of something relevant?

He cleared his throat. 'Did Mr Trenery mention any other merchants or quarry owners bidding for the London contract?'

She nodded. 'Kinser Landry also put in a bid.'

'That would explain his desire to buy your quarry, especially if he had learned from Flynn about Jeb's discovery of high-quality stone.'

'Yes, but he wasn't successful.' Taking the tea caddy from the mantelshelf, she glanced at him as she spooned tea into the warmed pot. 'Mr Trenery's manner as he shared that information makes me think he has no more liking for Mr Landry than I do.'

'What was his manner?'

A smile trembled on her lips. 'Gleeful.'

'If his bid was rejected, Landry will be angry and disappointed.'

'I don't think that troubles Mr Trenery in the least.'

It wasn't the granite merchant he was concerned about. Landry was wealthy and powerful; a man used to getting what he wanted. Losing a major contract was a blow. But being outmaneuvered by a young woman, especially one stigmatized and considered beneath his notice, that would infuriate him.

Putting the lid on the pot, she returned the kettle to the hearth. 'Mr Trenery is having a contract drawn up. I asked him to allow two copies.'

'Two? Did he ask why?'

'No, though it was obvious he wanted to.'

'But you didn't tell him.' What a surprising and complex young woman she was.

She shook her head, keeping it tipped as she poured the tea, so he could not see her face. 'No. I wasn't sure . . .' Setting the pot down, she moistened her lips and deliberately met his gaze. 'It occurred to me that you might not wish our association to become public knowledge, which it almost certainly would if I had told him that the other copy was for you. People love to gossip, as we both have reason to know.' Her tentative smile wrenched his heart. 'Anyway, I didn't think explanations were necessary. Most likely he thinks I asked for two copies in case I mislay one.'

Before he could respond, booted feet scampered up the path. Watching her, Crago saw her shyness eclipsed by pleasure as her mouth curved in to the first completely natural smile he had seen.

Ten

'Ma, I'm home! There's a handsome great horse . . .' Jory burst through the doorway, his boots skidding on the flagstones. 'Mr Crago! Is he yours?'

'Jory!' Sarah chided quietly. 'Where are your manners?'

'Good afternoon, Mr Crago,' Jory gabbled. 'Is he yours?'

'Yes.' Reaching into his coat pocket, Crago looked at Sarah. 'I always carry sugar lumps. Would you have any objection to Jory giving one to my horse?'

'Can I, Ma? Can I? Please?' Jory jumped up and down in an agony of impatience.

'All right. But make sure you hold your hand flat, and—'

'Keep my thumb out of the way,' he finished, then turned to Crago. 'Jenny bit me. But she didn't mean to. And it was only the once.'

'And Jenny is?'

'Our donkey. What's he called, your horse?'

Crago dropped the sugar into a small, grubby hand. 'Balal.'

'I never heard that name before.'

'It's an Arabic name. It means hero.' Crago started to get up.

'I can do it by myself,' Jory said quickly. 'Anyhow, you haven't drunk your tea. Ma never lets me get down from the table till I've finished.'

Sarah gave a small helpless shrug and Crago managed not to laugh. As their eyes met, he heard Jory's piping voice, then more footsteps hurrying up the path.

Clearly flustered, Sarah started towards the door. Crago rose to his feet as a short plump woman hurried over the threshold and stopped, breathless, one hand pressed to her bosom as she looked up at him.

'Ah. Mr Crago, is it?' Suspicion battled with curiosity.

'That's right, Mrs . . .?'

'Hitchens. Becky Hitchens. I live next door. I seen you in town once or twice.' Her bright, sharp gaze switched to Sarah. 'You all right, bird?'

'I'm fine.' Laying a reassuring hand on Becky's arm, Sarah turned to Crago. 'As well as being my neighbour, Becky is my very dear friend.'

'No one could doubt it.' He watched her blush deepen.

'That'll be your horse, then,' Becky said. 'So what brings you here?'

'Quarry business, Mrs Hitchens.' With a smile and nod, he turned to Sarah. 'I'll leave you now. Forgive me for calling unannounced. But I wanted you to know I've spoken to your foreman. I'm delighted to hear of your achievements this morning.'

'Thank you. Your tea,' she blurted. 'I . . .'

It warmed him to see dismay rather than relief at his departure. 'Another time, perhaps?' He picked up his hat and gloves. 'Good afternoon, Mrs Hitchens.'

As he stepped outside, Sarah followed him on to the path, with Becky close behind.

'Mr Crago, Jory loves going with Noah. But I would not want him to be in anyone's way.'

'Noah tells me he's very useful. So as long as he does as he's told and does not stray off the property, I have no objection. Good day, Miss Govier.' He replaced his hat, adding drily, 'You have yet another visitor.'

Shading her eyes, she looked past him. 'It's Ivy. Mrs Triggs. Noah's wife,' she added in explanation.

Becky had followed them out. 'Sarah do make scones for Ivy to take to the Women's Bright Hour at chapel,' she told him. 'Got a lovely light hand with baking, she has. I wouldn't give they gossips the time of day meself. But Noah's good with Jory, and Sarah don't believe in debts.'

'Becky!' Sarah whispered, clearly startled.

'She's fortunate indeed to have such a loyal friend,' Crago said, then turned and touched his hat to Noah's wife.

'Mr Crago,' Ivy nodded, curiosity avid on her face.

'Mrs Triggs.' He walked down the path to the open gate and took the reins from Jory, who had unfastened them from the fence.

Sarah heard him ask, 'Still got all your fingers?' Grinning, Jory held up both hands.

'Good man.' Gathering the reins, Crago placed one booted foot in the stirrup and swung himself on to the horse's back. He nodded at Sarah, his eyes gleaming beneath the brim of his hat. 'Miss Govier.' Then he turned towards the crossroads.

'Ma!' Jory called. 'I'm going up the field to groom Jenny.'

Waving acknowledgement, Sarah went back inside.

'Well! That was a surprise!' Becky said as Ivy followed her in and Sarah took another cup and saucer from the dresser. 'I told you he was some great, lanky chap, didn't I?'

'Mind if I sit down a minute, Sarah?' Ivy pressed a hand to the stiffly boned bodice of a dark blue gown trimmed with white lawn frills at the collar and cuffs. Beneath her bonnet she wore a frilled cap that revealed greying hair parted in the centre and drawn over her ears.

Catching Sarah's eye, Becky raised her own to the ceiling and shook her head. Sarah had to agree. Ivy's new hairstyle did not flatter a round and ageing face.

'I haven't stopped all day.' Ivy sank on to the chair that Crago had just occupied.

Sarah reached for the teapot. *Another time, perhaps.* Had he meant it? Or was he merely being polite without committing himself. She did not blame him for leaving. Becky had behaved very strangely; on one hand protective, on the other singing her praises. And Ivy had made no effort whatsoever to hide her curiosity.

Sarah would have liked some time alone to relive the past half hour and everything he had said. But that would have to wait. This was the first time Becky or Ivy had spoken to him. They would be anxious to compare what they had heard with their own impressions. *Would he be doing the same?* Because, despite the rarity of his visits to town, he was sure to have heard about her.

'Well, there isn't no way around it,' Becky announced, 'that's some wreck of a face. But you can't fault his manners. Here, give us that pot, bird,' she ordered. 'Shaking like a leaf in a gale, you are.'

Putting the teapot on the table, Sarah retreated to the chair by the hearth. 'I wasn't expecting . . . He just arrived. I thought he was you, Ivy.'

'I meant to come earlier. But, like I said, I'm all behind today.' Ivy drew the filled cup and saucer towards her. 'Noah says Mister is the best he've ever worked for. Be sorry when they've finished up there, Noah will. They still got a bit to do yet, though. Living in the kitchen, Mister is, bed and all, along by that new range. And he leave tea for the men each morning.'

'He's no fool,' Becky said. 'You catch more flies with honey than with vinegar.'

About to chide Becky for her cynicism, Sarah bit her lip and said nothing.

'True,' Ivy agreed. 'But he don't have to do it. It must be some lonely for him. 'Tis a huge great place for a man on his own.' Resting her wrists on the table, she leaned forward. 'Now, you know I aren't one to gossip . . .'

Briefly catching Sarah's eye, Becky leaned forward as well. 'No one could ever say that about you, Ivy. But seeing as he was just here, if there's something we ought to know . . .' she waited.

'Well, Noah don't know the whole of it, but Mister was a soldier out in India. And from what Noah can make out, there was a girl. There was more to it, some kind of trouble. Look like whatever it was, Mister come off worst.' She shuddered. ''Tis all right going to these here foreign parts. But they aren't like us, are they? Get the wrong side of them and they cut 'ee to ribbons.'

Sarah's breath caught in her throat as her imagination combined Crago's face and Ivy's words, producing horrific images.

'Well, he look lively enough to me,' Becky said. 'Anyhow, our army been fighting out there for years. He could have got that scar in a battle.'

'True,' Ivy admitted. 'But you got to think. His face is bad enough, poor soul.' Her voice dropped. 'What about the rest of him?'

'What about this girl?' Becky demanded. 'What happened to her?'

'Noah don't know.' Ivy shrugged. 'Maybe she up and married someone else, one of her own kind. Maybe that's why Mister came back.' As Becky glared at her, Ivy clapped a hand to her cheek. 'Oh my Lord. Sarah, I never thought. You know I didn't mean no harm. My tongue do run wild sometimes. Be the death of me, it will.'

'It's all right, Ivy,' Sarah reassured. 'Really.' Though she had told no one but Becky and her father, somehow word that Philip Ansell had seduced and then abandoned her in order to marry Margaret Tregenza had spread quietly among those close to her. They had closed ranks against the rest of the town, deflecting curiosity and pretending ignorance, for which she was infinitely grateful.

Some might have seen Jory as a painful reminder. But Sarah did not. He was the light of her life, a constant joy. As for the rest, it was all a long time ago and no longer had the power to hurt.

Draining her cup, Ivy set it on the saucer. 'Oh, I needed that. Right, I'd best get on.' She beamed up at Sarah, who had risen from her chair. 'They scones look handsome.'

'They're still warm.' Fetching a clean linen towel from the dresser drawer, Sarah wrapped them carefully.

Ivy picked up the bundle. 'Thanks, my bird.'

Becky closed the door behind her, and then returned to help Sarah clear the table. 'You know she do pass them off as her own.'

Sarah nodded. Setting the big kettle in the sink, she worked the pump handle. 'I guessed as much. I don't mind. In fact, it's better that way. I certainly wouldn't want Mrs Trembath and her ladies worried that I might wish to join them and wondering how to turn me down.' She replaced the lid, hefted the kettle out and hung it on the hook over the fire.

Becky covered the milk jug with bead-edged muslin and put it on the slate slab in the larder. 'Put the fox in the hen house, that would!' she grinned. 'But it isn't for you, bird. Be bored to sobs, you would.'

'I know. Making scones for Ivy every few weeks is my way of thanking Noah for taking Jory along with him.'

Becky joined her at the sink. 'Like I said, you got a heart as big as that there quarry.'

Sarah nudged her. 'Get on with you.'

Riding into the yard, his thoughts still with Sarah, Crago glanced towards his house. Through the windows and back door, all wide open, he could hear hammering, sawing and shouted banter. The sounds of men happy in their work.

Standing in her kitchen, he had deliberately manipulated her into inviting him to sit. Her kitchen was large, old-fashioned, warm and fragrant. The oval baking iron reminded him of his childhood. Sitting there with her he had felt . . . comfortable.

Watching her face as she told him about her visit to the granite merchant, he had become aware of an unfamiliar sensation. For a moment he had wondered, and then recognized *enjoyment*.

Gazing at her, fascinated by the blush of rose-pink along her cheekbones, he had remembered a morning in India. Standing on a mountainside above a cloud-filled valley, waiting for the order to proceed, he'd had no idea how deep it was or what might be waiting when he reached the bottom.

He knew the memory was a warning. He was advancing blind. All kinds of danger might be waiting. *But she had looked into his face without flinching.*

A small figure tottered out of the back door, his arms laden with off-cuts of wood. 'Afternoon, Mr Crago,' Jory panted, grinning. 'I got to put this in the barn for Uncle Noah.'

Crago looked down at the boy. 'Well done.'

'When I've dropped it, shall I help you put your horse away? I know what to do.'

About to decline, Crago hesitated. The little boy was so willing. *And apparently oblivious to his disfigurement.* He had not realized – no, that wasn't true. He knew all too well how much he hated the horrified stares or swiftly averted eyes that invariably greeted his appearance. Occasionally he was tempted to shout that *inside* he was still the same person he had always been. But that wasn't true, either. He had changed. How could he not? He had become solitary, wary, *lonely*. 'All right. If you like.'

Beaming, Jory quickened his pace and disappeared inside the barn.

Dismounting, he led Balal into the stone-built stable, aware of a pulling in his puckered cheeks. *He was smiling.*

Putting the horse in a large, airy stall, he fastened a chain across to prevent Balal from backing out. He had just unfastened the girth and was removing the saddle when Jory reappeared.

'Take it to the tack room, shall I?'

'It's heavy.'

'I won't drop it. I'm very strong, honest.'

Crago flipped the girth over the saddle, put it gently in to Jory's arms and watched the boy stagger along the wide passage between the stalls and the outer wall to the harness room at the far end. He half-expected to hear it drop. Instead, he heard a grunt of effort as Jory heaved the saddle on to one of the wooden trees. He stepped swiftly back into the stall so the boy wouldn't know that he had been watching.

'Stay that side of the chain,' he warned as he unfastened the chinstrap buckle. 'Balal doesn't like people in his stall.' He handed over the bridle.

'Does he try to squish you against the wall?' Jory clutched the looped reins and straps, his eyes bright with interest. 'Jenny tried that with me once. I kneed her in the belly and she moved over. I didn't tell Ma. She'd only worry. I hate it when she cry. She wait till I'm in bed 'cause she don't want me to know. But sometimes I hear.'

Crago felt a wrench in his chest and saw sudden anxiety on Jory's small face. 'You won't say nothing, will you?'

'Not a word.'

'Promise?' Jory persisted.

'I promise,' Crago said gravely, then indicated the bridle. 'Hang it on the peg.'

'Shall I rinse the bit? Ma always does when she takes Jenny's off.'

Crago nodded. 'There's a pail in the tack room, and plenty of rags in the cupboard. Use the pump outside and don't fill the pail above a quarter.' He doubted the boy would be able to lift it, let alone carry it any distance. But to spare Jory's pride, he found a reason. 'I'd rather not have the leather soaked.'

As he followed, Jory glanced back. 'You don't need to come. I can do it.'

'So I should hope, a young man of your experience. But I have to change.' He pointed to the old breeches and work shirt he had left hanging on a peg, then took off his coat.

Jory grinned. 'Ma would be some pleased with you. She always make me put on my old stuff before I brush Jenny and clean out her shed.' He staggered away, leaning sideways for balance, the pail clanking against his boot.

Changing quickly, Crago opened the cupboard and took out brushes, a currycomb and a cloth, and dropped them into a leather bucket. Lifting a halter from the peg, he returned to the stall. *Ma would be some pleased with you.*

Slipping the halter over Balal's head, he tied the rope through an iron ring and began to groom the big horse.

He could not deny that he was drawn to her, and not solely because she had not fled from him, screaming. Even her son had offered him sympathy and reassurance. Her son: living proof that she had been with a man.

He had seen others in her position, watched them fall further. Because once virtue was lost, there was no way back. The increasing number of young women whose bodies were fished out of the Thames was proof of that.

Abandoned by lover and thrown out by family, some struggled on for a while. With no home and no money, desperate for food and shelter, they ended up in the workhouse, their child taken from them. Or, with nothing to sell but their bodies, they joined the swelling ranks of streetwalkers and prostitutes. Until abuse, disease or sheer hopelessness drew them to the river.

Those with harder hearts or stronger spirits quickly sought a protector. Provided they were shrewd, accommodating and, above all, discreet, they could acquire considerable wealth in money and jewels: a nest egg for when they were no longer young, fresh and desirable.

Crago shook his head. Swapping the currycomb for a round bristle brush, he worked along the horse's body with smooth sweeps, pausing frequently to remove the dust and hair from the bristles.

He had never questioned society's rules granting men the freedom and opportunity to indulge every sexual appetite, while condemning the women they used. It was simply the way things were.

But Sarah – a fallen woman loved and protected by her friends – baffled him. Her arrival in the valley to demand his help had struck him as bold and foolhardy. Yet in her own home, clearly startled by his unexpected arrival, she had seemed genuinely shy.

Tossing brush and currycomb in to the bucket, he picked up a cotton cloth and wiped it hard along the horse's coat. Then he rubbed Balal's legs and picked up each hoof in turn, attending to the bends of the joints.

She was the first girl – no, not a girl, for she would be twenty-five or twenty-six now – the first young woman – to have captured and held his attention. Isolated by choice on the farm or in the woods, for a long time he had relied on Sam, Noah or Zack to fetch necessary supplies. His reclusive way of life was less painful than the reaction to his face on his rare visits to town.

But Sarah, shy Sarah, had held his gaze. Sarah, whose illegitimate son made her as much an outcast as his scar made him. She knew – who better –what it felt like to be rejected, reviled. He knew his face was shocking. But she had refused to turn away: refused to reject him the way that she had been rejected. Why? Why would she care?

Balal snorted and skittered sideways. Absently, Crago stroked the horse, his mind elsewhere.

What if her response to him was simple kindness? What if he

allowed his interest to grow and deepen, then she backed off
claiming he had misunderstood? Better to remain aloof. It was
lonely, but he was used to that. He could live with that.

He could – if she wanted, and he prayed that she did – still be
a friend to her. But, damn it; what he felt for her already went
beyond mere friendship. That was *his* problem, he must not make
it hers. Recalling Jory's anxiety over her crying at night, he knew
that he would do anything to spare her further worry.

After brushing Balal's mane and pulling his ears, which the big
horse loved, Crago picked up both leather bucket and water pail,
ducked under the chain and headed for the harness room and feed
store.

Maintaining an emotional distance was best. It would spare him
rejection, and spare her the embarrassment of having to tell him
that, though she thought him a kind benefactor, she could never
consider a closer, more personal relationship.

Jory came back, carrying the bridle over his outstretched arms.

'Here, Mr Crago. I done it.'

Crago bent to examine the bridle, finding it cleaner that he
expected. 'That's a good job, Jory.' Outside, Noah was calling the
boy's name.

'Hang it on the peg there, then off you go.'

There was yearning on Jory's face. 'Uncle Noah won't mind if
you got another job for me.'

'Maybe another time. But thank you.'

'All right. Bye.' Flashing a grin, the boy scampered away and, as
Crago followed him to the doorway, he heard Jory telling Noah
what he'd been doing, saw Noah pat the boy's head, their voices
fading as they went back in to the house.

Rinsing the water pail, he refilled it at the pump and carried it
back to the stall. Yes, he had it all worked out. The trouble was
that his presumed understanding of Sarah Govier's thoughts and
feelings sprang entirely from fear.

The longer he knew her, the more he wanted to know her
better. Which deepened his worry that she did not, could not, feel
the same about him. So he would not even ask?

During his youth and his years in India he had often been
afraid. But he had never let it hold him back. The roar of
cannon and crack of musket fire, the desperate fight to gain
ground and avoid injury amid the acrid stench of gunpowder

and smoke, had sharpened his senses and quickened his reactions. But fear had been the spur.

He had survived attempted murder and the death of a girl he had loved. Time had worked its magic, healing his face, his body and, almost without him noticing, the deeper wounds to his heart.

Now, when he least expected it, destiny was offering him another chance at happiness. Because of his past, and hers, the stakes were far higher. So were the risks. She had ignited a spark of hope. Rejection would be devastating. But not even to try? A single tremor shook his hand as he patted Balal's neck. Then he went to fetch oats and fresh hay.

Eleven

Noah and Jory were last to leave. Jory had stood quietly to one side while Noah showed Crago the completed bed and then discussed the size and design of the wardrobe. When they had gone, closing the front door behind them, the house was very quiet.

Crago looked in to each of the bedrooms, inhaling in the smells of fresh plaster and paint. As he descended the stairs, the banister rail felt satin-smooth against his palm. Sam, Noah and the others were doing a superb job.

Still clad in his working clothes, he washed his hands in the kitchen sink, then picked up his coat, waistcoat and trousers from the back of the chair. He had just placed them on hangers when he heard loud knocking on the front door.

Opening it, Crago saw a portly man turn from surveying the garden and fields beyond. His gaze met Crago's and instantly slid away to focus on the doorjamb. Crago stiffened, his face an expressionless mask.

The man's attire indicated wealth: a knee-length cutaway coat of fine black cloth, glossy top hat, pristine starched linen, a silver brocade waistcoat with a gold watch chain looped across it and immaculate dove-grey trousers held taut by straps beneath his highly polished shoes. A supercilious expression and air of barely controlled impatience suggested displeasure at the circumstances necessitating this visit.

Behind him on the drive stood a smart gig drawn by a pair of horses whose coats gleamed like polished chestnuts. The driver wore dark green livery that matched the gig's paintwork.

Guessing the identity of his visitor, Crago felt curiosity stir. 'Good afternoon.' He was coolly polite.

'Mr Crago, I am a busy man with little time to waste so—'

'One moment, if you please.' Crago raised his hand.

Shock crossed the fleshy face. 'I am not used to being interrupted.'

'No? You surprise me,' Crago remarked. 'You appear to know my name. However, there you have the advantage. We have not, to the best of my knowledge, been introduced.' Watching anger darken the man's florid complexion to the colour of brick, Crago lifted one eyebrow and waited.

'Landry. My name is Kinser Landry. I'm a force to be reckoned with in these parts. A fact it would serve you to remember.'

'Really?' Crago said. 'Why?'

Landry gaped at him. 'Because . . . Because I have an interest in many of the commercial ventures in and around Penryn.'

'How very satisfying for you.'

'Yes. Well, one of these is the Cosawes gunpowder mill. I hold a considerable number of shares. It is my understanding that you have a little venture of your own and turn out quite reasonable powder. Though with a workforce comprising yourself and a deaf-mute woman, it can hardly be described as a viable business.'

Crago's brows rose. 'Good heavens, Mr Landry. Surely you cannot consider my *little venture* a threat?'

'Certainly not! The idea is ridiculous. However, as I say, word has got around concerning the quality and reliability of your powder. You may or may not be aware that I own several quarries in the area. I anticipate acquiring another very shortly.'

'Indeed?' Crago's interest sharpened, but he was careful not to show it. 'I was not aware any of the local quarries were for sale.'

'No reason you should be,' Landry snapped. 'You're not a quarryman.'

'True,' Crago allowed. 'But as I supply powder to two – no, three – local quarries as well as a number of mines, naturally I'm interested. To which quarry do you refer?'

'Talvan. I hope to take possession soon. When I do, my requirements for blasting powder will increase. So it occurred to me that you and I—'

'Talvan? But surely – didn't I hear the stone there is poor stuff?'

'That is so. However, there is a possibility that with sufficient investment, which I am in a position to provide, stone of high quality might yet be uncovered.'

'You are willing to commit substantial funds to mere possibility? That is either very shrewd or remarkably foolhardy.'

'When the risk is great, the eventual prize is all the more rewarding,' Landry smirked.

But you're not risking anything because you already know there's high-

quality granite in Talvan. Flynn saw it and told you. Concealing his disgust, Crago eyed his visitor. 'So what are you proposing?'

'A partnership.'

'On what terms?'

'You must know how people talk.' Landry's smile never reached his small eyes. 'Especially about a man with an air of mystery about him such as yourself. I'm given to understand that you have practically rebuilt this house. And setting up your mill will have involved considerable cost. In other words, Mr Crago, it is clear to me that that you are a man of significant means. What I propose is an alliance that will be a benefit to both of us. As well as supplying the blasting powder, were you to match my investment in the expansion and development of the quarry—'

'But you do not own it yet.'

Landry dismissed the objection with a careless gesture. 'A mere formality. Miss Govier knows she cannot possibly continue. She has lost customers. Orders have been cancelled.'

'You're certain of that?'

'Oh yes,' Landry nodded. 'Such information is easily obtained when one knows who to ask.'

Or has had a hand in bringing it about, Crago guessed.

'Indeed,' Landry continued. 'I am doing her a kindness. Relieving her of a burden. My offer is more than fair. I fully expect her acceptance within a day or so.' He sighed, brushing a speck of lint from his lapel with gloved fingertips. 'Indeed, I should have received it a week ago. This delay is most discourteous. But I suppose one can expect no better. My nephew had a fortunate escape.'

Crago thought quickly. Sam Venner had mentioned a connection between Landry and – who was it? – *George Ansell.* He was a cargo broker with offices in Bohill. He had a son, Philip, married to Horace Tregenza's daughter Margaret. *Sarah and Philip Ansell?*

'Your offer is interesting, Landry. If only for its breathtaking duplicity. But I must decline. Enter in to partnership with a man whose dealings are based on lies? I think not.'

Shock blanked Landry's face for an instant. '*Lies?*' He blustered. 'How dare you! I'll—'

'Show me the survey of Talvan quarry?' Crago suggested.

As startled realization give way to fury, Landry's colour deepened to crimson and saliva gathered at the corners of his mouth.

'It seems I was mistaken in you. But be warned, Crago. You would be unwise to interfere. This is none of your concern.'

'Oh, but it is.' Crago spoke softly, his voice razor-edged and lethal. 'You see, I already have a business arrangement with Miss Govier regarding her quarry. Which makes it very much my concern. She is not selling Talvan. No doubt you will shortly receive a letter from her to that effect. Meanwhile take heed, Landry. Anyone attempting to cause trouble for her will have me to deal with.'

'How dare you threaten me!' Landry spluttered.

'You make it so easy,' Crago said. 'We have nothing further to say to each other. Good afternoon.' He shut the door.

'Come in, Philip. Cognac?' Horace Tregenza poured the spirit in to two balloon glasses. Handing one to his son-in-law, he indicated a chair. 'Sit down.'

Reminded of a summons to the headmaster, Philip sat. Determined to show how relaxed he was, he leaned back, crossing one leg over the other.

'It was most encouraging,' Tregenza said, 'to see Margaret eat a proper dinner.'

'Yes.' Philip waited.

In his button-back armchair of rich brown leather Horace Tregenza gently swirled his glass. After inhaling the bouquet, he raised the glass and drank. Philip did the same. He could not understand why, despite being similarly furnished, his own small study lacked both the comfort and the *gravitas* of this room.

'As our only child, Margaret is very dear to her mother and me.'

'As she is to me,' Philip said quickly.

'Quite.' Something in Tregenza's tone made Philip sit a little straighter in his chair. 'Dr Prout is an old family friend. As such, he was kind enough to inform me of the true state of affairs concerning Margaret's health.' He paused to swallow cognac.

Philip raised his own glass and gulped a large mouthful as dread clenched icy fingers beneath his breastbone.

'Another?' Tregenza enquired, indicating Philip's glass.

Sorely tempted, Philip shook his head. 'Thank you, no.' He needed to remain sharp and focused.

Rising, Tregenza added a little more cognac to his own glass, then returned to his chair. 'It seems her condition is delicate and likely to remain so for some time. Under such circumstances a man might consider making arrangements to relieve his wife of demands, the results of which, given her current state of health, could endanger her life. Provided they were conducted with absolute discretion, such arrangements would have my blessing.'

'No!' Philip blurted in horror. He didn't want a mistress. He wanted freedom.

'Your reaction does you credit.' Tregenza cleared his throat. 'No doubt hearing your wife's father speak of such matters is unexpected. But you need feel no embarrassment. Your situation is one with which I am familiar. I too hoped for a son. But the good Lord saw fit to bless us with only one child, our daughter. My wife was not strong enough to risk further childbearing. I, however, was not yet forty and in robust health.'

As Philip stared at him, dumbstruck, Tregenza drained his glass. 'So you see, I have considerable understanding of your position.'

His perception of his father-in-law irrevocably changed, Philip blurted his first coherent thought. 'Does your wife know?'

'My wife is a woman of uncommon good sense,'Tregenza replied, studying his empty glass. 'Situations that pose no threat to her are simply ignored.' He turned to Philip. Though his mouth curved in a smile, his eyes were hard. 'She has been a loving mother to our daughter. She is an excellent hostess and manages our home exactly as I like it. Anyone foolish enough to upset her would find me . . . unforgiving. But that is by the way.'

Philip started to rise. 'I really ought to—'

'Sit down. I haven't finished.'

Bemused and deeply uneasy, Philip subsided again.

'Where was I? Ah yes, Margaret. Mary and I have doted on her, perhaps more than was wise. When she chose you as a husband, we were pleased to welcome you in to the family. However, the tragic losses she has suffered during the past two years and her current state of health have forced me to consider the future. God forbid that anything should happen to my daughter—'

'Indeed,' Philip said quickly, then tried not to squirm as Tregenza shot him a glance so shrewd, so *knowing*, that for an instant Philip feared his father-in-law could read every thought in his head.

'But should such an unhappy event occur, it is reasonable to assume that after a period of mourning you might wish to remarry. Indeed, though *our* loss would be irreplaceable, how could we begrudge you another chance of happiness? However, with regard to my two granddaughters, I thought it wise to consult my attorney.'

'Oh?' was all Philip could manage as his throat grew dry.

'I know you will applaud my decision to secure the girls' future comfort and security by making them my heirs.'

Philip had to clear his throat before he could speak. 'That is most generous of you.' He waited for the rest, guessing it would not be to his advantage.

'They will be the sole beneficiaries of my estate. To keep everything simple, and spare you an unnecessary burden, their inheritance will be administered by a trust until each of them reaches the age of twenty-one.'

He could not have made it plainer. While the girls would be wealthy, their father would not have access to a single penny. But Philip had his pride. He'd be damned before he'd give his father-in-law the satisfaction of seeing his furious disappointment.

Baring his teeth in a smile, he stood and offered his hand. 'Let us hope such arrangements prove unnecessary.'

Tregenza's handshake was brief. 'Indeed. However, I'm a great believer in foresight. My ability to look ahead and recognize potential problems has proved invaluable in protecting and expanding my interests while others have watched theirs dwindle.'

As heat climbed his face, Philip's head came up. 'You are fortunate indeed, Sir, that your interests do not depend upon conditions outside your control.'

Tregenza patted Philip's shoulder. 'My dear boy, I intended no slight on your father. Indeed, the loss of so many cargoes to Falmouth would have finished a lesser man. But I understand he has weathered that particular storm and is prospering once more with the upsurge of traffic in granite and tin.'

'You will excuse me, Sir,' Philip said stiffly. 'I must return to Margaret. She frets if I am away from her too long.'

'Of course, of course. I'm so glad we had this little chat. I feel we understand each other far better now, don't you?'

Seething, Philip bowed briefly and then strode from the room. There was no escape now. He was trapped.

Twelve

Waking from a restless sleep, Sarah slid out of bed and crossed to the window. Drawing back the curtains, she looked out. In the east the sky was turquoise and pale primrose. The wind had not started moving, and trees were black silhouettes against the pastel shades of sunrise.

Changing her nightgown for a clean shift, stays, calico bodice and her old serge skirt, she left her hair in its thick plait and pushed her feet into worn kid slippers. On the landing she paused outside Jory's room and peeped around the half-open door. He lay on his back, deeply asleep, arms flung wide. His lashes lay like small fans against his rosy cheeks.

Watching him for a moment, love swelling her heart, she crept downstairs, coaxed the embers to life with furze, and then filled the kettle and pulled it over the flames. While it heated, she pumped water into an enamel basin and washed her face and hands.

Moving quietly about the kitchen, she prepared breakfast and the food Jory would take with him, all the while thinking about James Crago.

Since the afternoon in the woods when she had seen him for the first time, he had rarely left her mind.

There had been no man in her life since Philip. Her father had made it clear to her that while he was prepared to accept her child in to his house, he expected her to devote herself to domestic duties and her son's care. The town would be watching and judging her.

She had shamed him once. He would not accept a second embarrassment. By choosing to keep her son, she had forfeited any right to the dances, parties and social gatherings enjoyed by other girls her age.

How right he had been about the scrutiny and criticism. But why had he not warned her about predatory men? Perhaps being a man himself he shied away from acknowledging the self-serving callousness of his own sex. Or maybe it had simply not occurred to him because his presence protected her.

In his youth he had been a wrestler of renown. His father had owned several acres of rough land covered with huge moorstones. A skilled stonemason, he had supplied granite blocks for harbour works at Charlestown and St Ives. When the surface stone was no longer sufficient to supply expanding markets, he and her father had blasted open the ground to reach the granite underneath, thus creating Talvan quarry. Both achievements had earned Henry Govier the reputation of a man it was wise not to cross.

But within a few months of his death, men had come sniffing round like dogs. At first, still naïve, it had not occurred to her that offers of help would have a price attached. Then one day, demanding more than the beer and pasty she had offered him as thanks for a load of logs, Will Laity had tried to kiss her. He received a stinging slap for his impertinence. From that day on she refused gifts and paid cash for her wood.

She continued to live by her father's rules, determined to protect her son for as long as possible. Prompted by Ivy and Becky, Noah stepped in as a substitute grandfather and invited Jory to help him mend his garden fence. The pair got on so well that once the fence was fixed, they made a new chicken fold for the orchard.

Meanwhile a local widower had let it be known through Ivy that he was looking for a housekeeper and would be willing to accept the boy. Sarah declined, wary of what additional duties might be expected of her. Besides, she and Jory both deserved better than grudging acceptance. Nor was she interested in looking after someone else's house. She already had her own to take care of and the quarry to run.

Because she could not bear to think of Jory being hurt, or of having to face even more criticism, it was simpler to live a blameless existence. In any case, none of the men she encountered had inspired the slightest interest. Until now.

Meeting James Crago had forced her to face the fact that, after years of steadfastly refusing to mourn all those things her circumstances had put beyond reach, there was a yawning emptiness at the heart of a life she had persuaded herself was full and satisfying.

In reality she was living like a widow without ever having known the warmth and companionship of marriage. And it wasn't enough. She yearned for a man's protection. For someone she could talk to and laugh with. And love. She longed to love. She ached to be loved.

Nor was what she felt the nebulous fantasy of a naïve young girl. It was the yearning of a woman who had experienced passion, who had been held in a man's arms, felt the weight of his body and matched the urgency of his desire. Memories long buried resurfaced. But it was not Philip whose face she saw. Not Philip's arms she imagined around her.

She pressed her palms to her burning face. In his initial shock and anger her father had called her wanton, his expression reflecting discomfort and dismay. Was she? Was there something wrong with her that she should be gripped by such powerful emotions? Was this why Philip had abandoned her and married Margaret instead?

Becky had sworn it was not so. That she was guilty only of loving a man who didn't deserve her. She wanted so much to believe that. To be reassured that she was worthy of being loved.

James Crago knew her circumstances and her shame. Yet he had called on her to tell her of his visit to Talvan and his discussion with Jeb. When Becky and Ivy arrived, he had withdrawn into politeness and quickly taken his leave. She could not blame him for that. In fact, she was glad he had gone. She knew Becky had sensed her confusion and, ever protective, was making her own assessment of him, which she would not hesitate to impart when she felt the moment was right.

As the kettle began to boil, she emptied the teapot into the bucket under the sink. The spent leaves would go on her garden. She warmed the pot, spooned in fresh leaves, added boiling water and set the pot on the hearth to brew.

Though she could not regret Jory's existence, she bitterly regretted giving herself to a man who, despite swearing he loved her, clearly had not. Fetching milk from the larder, she took out a cup and saucer.

James Crago's face seemed not to bother Jory at all. Arriving home yesterday afternoon, he had talked as much about helping Mr Crago with Balal as he had about the jobs he'd done for Noah. But for either of them to become fond of a man whose work was so dangerous, was that wise?

Crago knew what was coming. But he could not stop it, couldn't escape. Images crossed his mind like flashes of sunlight in a forest: the sloping stone ramparts of the fort; the massive gateway of white arches leading into an open square. Anjuli's maid whispering that he should go to the garden known as Raja's Seat, not once meeting his eyes as she dropped the bracelet in to his hand so he would know the message came from Anjuli.

He could hear the voice of Ralph Sawyer, his brother officer and friend, warning him it might be a trap. Walking in to the garden, he saw Anjuli sprawled on the grass, the front of her pink-and-gold sari crimson with blood.

With a roar of grief and rage that tore his throat, he began running towards her. Catching movement from the corner of his eye, he saw a turbaned man, a cloth covering the lower half of his face, spring from behind dense shrubbery, sword swinging, dazzling, blinding in the sunlight.

He swerved but could not escape the arcing blade. It sliced through his clothes, scoring his side from spine to ribs. He turned his head, but he was too slow to avoid the serrated metal wrist guard. It smashed in to his face, breaking his nose and splitting the flesh on both cheeks.

A white-hot flash of agony, the hot, salty taste of blood, shouts. He felt himself dragged, heard Sawyer's voice, running feet, more voices.

Then everything else faded as he saw Anjuli where he had first seen her, standing in the garden by the low wall, looking out at the panorama of forested hills and valley clearings. He knew he was calling to her, felt his throat strain with effort. But no sound emerged. Nor did she turn. She walked slowly away, her image dissolving like mist. He knew she was gone forever. And he could not remember her face.

Bolting upright with a gasp, he wiped a hand across his forehead. It came away slick with sweat. Swinging his legs out of the cot, he stumbled across to the sink and worked the pump, cupping cold water over his face and the back of his neck.

If the dream meant that it was time to let go of the past, time to move on, why then had he relived the wound to his face? He could not leave that behind. He was scarred, disfigured and always would be.

He dried his face, tossed the towel on to the table, then raked the embers and added kindling. Within minutes the fire blazed bright and comforting. He pulled the kettle on to the hotplate, fetched milk and took down a cup.

He could vaguely remember fighting people as they held him

down, and strange dreams filled with terrifying images. Then long periods of nothing. The drugs, he supposed. The Commanding Officer's own doctor had done his best to repair the terrible damage.

Anjuli's death had been one murder too many. After fourteen years of sadistic rule over a kingdom rife with rebellion, Chikka Vira Raja had been deposed. Kodagu had come under British protection and he had been sent home.

His face had healed. So, eventually, had his heart. Now he was facing a choice. He could remain solitary, a fugitive from society trapped in the past. Or he could move forward. Risk loving again, losing again.

After seeing Jory off and completing her household chores, Sarah washed and changed, putting on a gown of maroon glazed cotton with a double-layered muslin pelerine that crossed over the bodice. Then she loosened her plait and brushed her hair until it crackled before coiling it neatly, high up on her crown. Her simple bonnet was trimmed with ribbons that matched her gown. She wanted to look her best for the quarry inspection with Mr Trenery. After a critical look at her reflection in the long glass, she allowed herself a brief nod of satisfaction.

Downstairs in the kitchen she slipped her feet into brown boots and fastened the laces. They were neither dainty nor fashionable. But she was walking to Talvan and had no wish to turn an ankle.

Reaching the quarry, she waved to Jeb and waited for him to join her up on the grass. On the opposite side of the gaping twenty-foot-deep hole, three men had just finished re-siting a timber mast with a fixed jib and iron-tipped base that sat in a foundation stone. Four of the long-linked chains that radiated outwards from the top of the mast had been anchored in a semi-circle at the quarry edge. While she watched, they fixed the remaining two.

As Jeb started up the slope, she heard her name called and looked over her shoulder.

'Good morning to you, Miss Govier.' Mr Trenery rode up on a smart bay gelding. Reining to a halt, he raised his top hat.

'Good morning, Mr Trenery.'

'Lovely day for it,' he beamed, then dismounted. A green spotted cravat knotted over his upright collar added a jaunty note to an otherwise conservative ensemble of brown long-tailed coat, cream waistcoat and fawn trousers tucked into polished black top boots.

'It is indeed,' Sarah smiled. 'Ah, Jeb.'

'Morning, Miss.' Jeb nodded, raising a finger to the brim of his cap.

'Mr Trenery, may I introduce my foreman, Jeb Mundy, who will be able to tell you everything you wish to know.'

Thomas Trenery didn't offer his hand, but his smile was warm. 'Your reputation goes before you, Mr Mundy.'

Jeb touched his cap once more. 'Best if your horse stays up here, Sir. Don't want him upset by the noise.'

'Oh, yes. Of course.' Trenery glanced round, as if looking for something to tie his mount to.

'All right if I . . .?' As Trenery gestured acceptance, Jeb reached for the rein, flipped it over the horse's head and tied it to an iron ring that had once held a guy chain.

'Lead on, Mr Mundy. I understand you have uncovered a new bed?'

Sarah followed as Jeb led the granite merchant down the slope and across the quarry floor to examine an area of the fresh rock face.

'See, we left this line of plugs overnight,' Jeb explained. 'Then they was hammered again this morning and cleaved down fifteen foot to the bedrock.'

'I thought it was common practice to use jumpers for making blasting holes, and to keep plugs and feathers for breaking the blocks once they were out,' Mr Trenery said.

'That's right,' Jeb nodded. 'But when I was looking for the next cleaving line, I seen a hairline crack from the last blasting. Can't waste a gift like that.'

'Too true.' Sarah saw Mr Trenery smile as he nodded. Then he stepped closer and ran his hand over the granite while looking carefully at it.

As Jeb glanced back, she gave him an encouraging nod, indicating two more stonemasons thirty feet away, boring holes ready for the next blast.

'I see you got a crab winch,' Mr Trenery observed.

'Heavy old thing, he is,' Jeb said. 'But he's some useful. We can move'n wherever he's needed and he'll haul the cut blocks across to the other side so the crane can load them on to the wagon. Should be blasting again tomorrow.'

'How much hand dressing will you do here?'

'We'll scapple the blocks to an inch or two of the size you want,' Jeb answered.

Trenery nodded. 'I expect each block to be checked to ensure it's free of defects.'

Seeing Jeb about to take offence at the implication that he would allow a flawed stone to leave the quarry, Sarah spoke up.

'Mr Trenery, I give you my word that you may safely rely on my foreman. Jeb Mundy's name and integrity are known throughout Cornwall.' She saw a faint wash of colour stain Trenery's cheeks.

'So I've heard. And I wouldn't be here now if I thought different. But I like things plain and clear. Then we all know where we stand and what's expected.' He turned to Jeb. 'No offence meant.'

'None taken.'

Taking a folded piece of paper from his waistcoat pocket, the merchant handed it to Jeb. 'I'd be obliged if you would make sure these numbers are painted on each block after it's inspected and before it leaves the quarry. They'll tell me the block size, the code for this quarry and the reference number of the contract.'

'Right.' As Jeb tucked the folded paper away, Trenery turned and started back towards the slope.

'I got a mind to put up a dressing shed in my yard and take on some skilled masons to hand dress the blocks before they ship to London.' He looked at Sarah. 'Miss Govier, your granite is every bit as good as you promised.' Removing a thicker wad of folded papers from inside his frock coat, he offered them to her. 'Your two copies of our contract as agreed.'

'Thank you.' Sarah inclined her head, thrilled and relieved and trying to hide both.

He looked around at the tumbled blocks. 'What do you do with the waste slabs or blocks that are too small?'

Catching her eye, Jeb's brows climbed.

'Would you have a use for them, Mr Trenery?' Sarah enquired.

'I would, yes. I've been thinking for a while about expanding in to monumental masonry work. There'll always be a market for a nice polished granite headstone.' Trenery's eyes gleamed. 'I've just bought an old "waggon" polishing machine.'

'I've heard of they,' Jeb said. 'But I never seen one.'

'Some brave great thing, it is,' Trenery's tone reflected his enthusiasm. 'Got these flat cast-iron rings that spin round.'

'What do it use for an abrasive?' Jeb asked.

'Sharp sand and water. The whole thing moves back and forth on rails.'

'How good a finish would you need on the granite before you started polishing?' Jeb enquired.

Trenery shrugged. 'I wouldn't like to say. What do you think?'

Jeb pursed his lips. 'I s'pose a fine axed-finish would be all right. Do that, shall we?'

'Could you?'

Jeb glanced at Sarah, who gave a tiny nod. 'We could, no trouble. ''Course, it would add a bit to the price. But then it would save your masons time they better spend on carving and polishing.'

Trenery's forehead puckered. He thought for a moment and then gave a decisive nod. 'You're right. Time is money.' He turned to Sarah. 'I'll work out some figures. Perhaps if you're in town during the coming week, you'll call in? But I can always post—'

'I wouldn't hear of it, Mr Trenery,' Sarah said, amazed that she could sound so calm when inside she was jumping up and down with delight. 'It would be no trouble at all for me to call.'

'Don't mind me asking, Mr Trenery,' Jeb said, 'about this here polisher. How do it work?'

'Normally by two men turning a wheel,' Trenery explained. 'But I reckon it might be possible to connect it with a belt to a small steam engine.'

'Dear life,' Jeb's brows disappeared beneath the brim of his cap. 'I wouldn't mind seeing that.'

As they reached the top of the slope, Trenery pointed to the mast and jib. 'That's some spider, Mr Mundy. I see you've got a hand winch attached to the lower part of the mast.'

Jeb nodded. 'We'll use the crab winch to haul the blocks away from the face to where the masons want them. Then the spider will lift them on to the wagons.'

While Jeb released the rein and held the horse, Trenery offered Sarah his hand. 'Thank you, Miss Govier. A most interesting and instructive visit.' Then he turned to Jeb and touched the brim of his hat. 'We'll meet again, Mr Mundy.'

Jeb nodded. 'Well, Miss,' he grinned as they watched the merchant ride away, 'look like things is on the up.'

'I'm so grateful to you, Jeb.'

The foreman glanced away. 'Get on. 'Tis no more than you

deserve. I just wish . . .' He shook his head and looked at the ground.

Sarah's pleasure ebbed. 'Wish what? What is it, Jeb?'

'Well, 'tis only what I heard, and I wouldn't like to swear to it, but word is that Mr Landry been putting pressure on other quarrymen and mine owners not to use Mr Crago's blasting powder.'

Sarah's temper flared and she forced herself to remain calm. 'Is he having any success?'

Jeb grinned briefly. 'Not as much as he'd like. There's quite a few owners like you with just the one quarry. And they're pi—' he hastily corrected himself. 'They're fed up with him. He got big ideas about buying up everything between here and Longdowns. Word is that some are weakening. Others don't want to sell. They just want to go on quiet like they always have. So he's trying to put pressure on them in other ways. Like with the blasting powder. He want them all to buy from Cosawes because he got shares in the company. But Mr Crago's powder is better quality and more reliable.'

'Well, if that's the case, I don't see what Mr Landry can do,' Sarah said. 'He can't force them. It's their choice to buy what they want.'

'See, that's what I'm saying, Miss. Mr Landry can't stand anyone getting the better of him. Carry a grudge for years, he will. I wouldn't put it past him to try and get rid of Mr Crago.'

Sarah stared at him. 'Jeb! You can't mean. You really think . . .? I can't believe he would dare . . .'

''Tis only what I heard, Miss,' Jeb shrugged. 'And you know how people talk. But I got a bad feeling. Been a day or two since Mr Crago came by so I haven't had a chance to say nothing. You tell him, Miss. Tell him to be wary and watch his back.'

Thirteen

Sarah straightened up, pressing one hand to the small of her back. It was late afternoon and the breeze had dropped. The air was fresh, warm and fragrant with the melted-butter scent of brilliant yellow gorse blossom. A short distance away a skylark trilled as it fluttered above new green fronds of bracken and cushions of purple heather. Puffs of white cloud floated across a clear blue sky.

Glancing round, she saw her son hauling a branch of dead furze twice his height. Becky stood watching him, hands on her hips, a smile curving her mouth.

'You're doing some brave job there, boy. But how are we going to fit'n on the shay?' She nodded towards the donkey standing patiently between the shafts of the small flatbed cart.

Jory looked from her to the branch. Then his grin reappeared like the sun from behind a cloud. Sarah was swamped by a wave of love for him.

'Don't worry, Auntie Beck.' Propping the branch against a large weathered chunk of granite and steadying himself with one hand, he stepped up on to the branch and began jumping up and down. With a sharp crack, the branch snapped and Jory lurched forward on to the grass. 'See?' He waved his arms to celebrate his success.

'Some bright spark, you are,' Becky praised. 'Right, put'n with the rest. Strong enough, are you?'

''Course.' Grunting from the effort, he heaved the first piece of branch on to the pile near the shay, then went back for the other half.

Throughout the past two hours, Sarah had heard the crump and rumble of explosions at various quarries. Blasting was usually timed for late afternoon so that the dust would settle overnight. The sound was so much a part of her daily life that she often didn't notice it unless it came from the nearest quarry, her own.

Jory had straightened up and was watching a group of boys dragging dead branches, rotting tree trunks and furze to the top of the hill for the midsummer's eve bonfire.

'Ma, can I go and help?' He looked longingly at the boys as they shouted to each other.

Sarah opened her mouth to refuse.

Becky caught her arm. 'No.' She turned her head so Jory would not hear. 'Let him go.'

'Becky, they'll turn on him.'

'They might, they might not. But either way he's got to learn to deal with it.'

'He's only six.'

'He'll manage. And if he's hurt, you'll give him a cuddle. But he's got to stand on his own feet, bird.'

'I know you're right, but . . .'

''Tis hard to let'n go. I know. But he's got to learn.' She waved him away. 'Go on then, boy.'

'All right, Ma?' Jory fidgeted, poised to run.

'Off you go, my love.'

'Come on.' Becky dragged Sarah's attention back to the pile of wood they had gathered. 'We'll get this lot loaded up then it'll be time to go home. Hear that, can you?'

'Hear what?'

'The teapot calling to me.'

Rolling her eyes, Sarah smiled.

They had stacked half the furze branches on to the shay when Jory returned. Sarah felt a clutch at her heart as she saw that his little face was flushed red and his eyes were bright with tears. But none had fallen.

'All right, boy?' Becky asked carelessly as she bent to pick up another branch.

'They called me names.' Jory wiped his nose with the back of his hand.

Sarah couldn't speak for the lump in her throat. She wanted to march up the hill and bang all their silly, mean, spite-filled heads together. Even as she raged inside, she tried to remember that they were only children. They aped their parents, repeating what they had heard.

'You know what?' Becky said. 'I'm some glad you're back. I was just wondering how me and your ma was going get all the rest up on the shay.'

Jory managed a wobbly grin. 'Don't worry, Auntie Beck. I'll do it.' As he trotted away, Becky turned to Sarah and simply raised her brows.

'Yes, all right,' Sarah muttered.

'What you say?' Becky demanded. 'I can't hear you.'

Sarah dissolved into laughter, shaking her head. 'You were right,' she said loudly.

'What, Ma?' Jory puffed up to them, dragging another dead branch. 'What was Auntie Beck right about?'

'You.' Sarah ruffled her son's curly hair. 'She was telling me what a big boy you are now.'

'Look!' Jory pointed. 'There's Mr Bottrell. He's got rabbits.'

Wearing a shapeless coat over a wool shirt, a red-and-white spotted kerchief loosely knotted at his throat and brown serge trousers with leather gaiters buckled over his sturdy boots, Zack touched his battered brown hat as he reached them. 'Afternoon.'

'Good afternoon, Mr Bottrell,' Sarah smiled. 'I don't believe you've met my dear friend and neighbour, Mrs Hitchens. Becky, this is Mr Bottrell, he makes charcoal for Mr Crago.'

'Mizz Hitchens,' Zack nodded.

'I believe I've seen you around,' Becky said.

'Daresay you have. We're here April to October.'

'That's right, you got your daughter with you.' She nodded at the dead rabbits dangling from his fist. 'You done well.'

'Like a couple, would you? More here than we need.'

'Kind of you, I'm sure. But—'

'I don't want paying.'

'And I don't like owing.'

Sarah watched and listened, intrigued. She saw Jory tugging at Becky's apron.

'Auntie Beck,' he whispered loudly. 'You could make Mr Bottrell one of your heavy cakes to say thank you.' He turned to Zack, beaming. 'Auntie Beck makes the bestest heavy cake.'

A slow smile spread over Zack's face. 'I'm very partial to a nice bit of *hevva* cake. You put peel in along with the figs?'

'Of course!' Becky bristled.

'All right, Auntie Beck?' Jory grinned. 'Will you have the rabbits now?'

Becky clicked her tongue and sighed. 'Can't say no, can I?' As she turned to Zack, Sarah noticed a definite rosy tint to her cheeks. 'Much obliged, I'm sure.'

Handing them over, Zack touched his hat and walked on.

Becky tucked the rabbits in to a corner of the shay. Wiping her hands down her apron, she turned towards Sarah. 'What?'

'Nothing,' Sarah said, compressing the smile on her lips.

'That's all right, then.' Becky was brisk. 'Come on, time we got this lot home, seeing I got rabbits to skin now.'

Philip Ansell glanced up from the newspaper as the landlord set down a pewter tray containing a pot of coffee, milk, sugar and two cups and saucers, then he continued to scan the pages.

Her Majesty's birthday had been celebrated in Falmouth by a royal salute from HMS *Astrea*. A day of thanksgiving for the providential escape of the Queen and Prince Albert from an assassin had been observed at the New Street chapel, and an address signed by the minister and congregation forwarded for presentation to Her Majesty. Smallpox in Redruth was attacking vaccinated persons as well as those who had not obtained such protection. Samuel Bailey had been convicted of the most grievous offence of wounding with intent to murder, and sentence of death had been passed. And at a local inn a man had swallowed two live eels for a wager.

'Morning, Philip.'

Quickly refolding the paper, Philip half-rose as his uncle settled in to the seat opposite.

Kinser Landry was frowning, his mouth a thin line of irritation. 'Something wrong, Uncle?'

'There most certainly is. I have this morning received a letter from Miss Govier declining my offer for her quarry. As it happens, I was already prepared for her refusal—'

'You were? But when we last spoke, I thought—'

'Yes, well, things have happened since then. So it was not quite the shock it would otherwise have been.'

'But annoying just the same,' Philip commiserated. He knew how much his uncle had wanted Talvan, so a show of sympathy would not go amiss.

'*Annoying? Annoying?* It is a great deal worse than that. During a thoroughly infuriating encounter with that – that – upstart Crago, I learned that he and Miss Govier have entered into a business arrangement regarding her quarry.'

Shock jolted Philip. 'Sarah? With that scar-faced brute?' His first thought was to dismiss the idea as ridiculous. But his uncle would not have made a mistake over anything that adversely affected his plans.

'He even had the effrontery to threaten me. *Me!* Well, I am not so easily dismissed. So he will discover.' He leaned forward and picked up the cup that his nephew had just filled. Taking a mouthful, he replaced the cup on its saucer and sat back. 'Judging by your expression, you are no more contented than I this morning.'

Sarah and Crago? This was news he could have done without. Did he not already have enough to contend with? He had plans for Sarah Govier and no intention of permitting some scar-faced incomer to disrupt them. But he needed time to decide what to do. In the meantime resentment over Tregenza's announcement still seethed within him.

He glanced round to be certain that no one could overhear. 'My esteemed father-in-law has only seen fit to cut me out of his will.'

Landry's brows lifted. 'What?'

Philip nodded. 'He made a point of informing me that he has settled his estate on my two daughters.' In other circumstances Philip would have relished his uncle's startled expression. Though he was easily angered, Kinser Landry was hard to shock.

'But what about Margaret?'

Philip shrugged in fury and frustration. 'He claimed it was *because* of Margaret's fragile health that he had taken action. Apparently Doctor Prout is a personal friend of long standing, a lever Tregenza had no hesitation in employing. Prout told him details of Margaret's condition that are no one's business but mine. I am her husband.'

'Yes,' Landry broke in impatiently. 'But *what* did Prout tell him?'

'That it was unlikely Margaret would survive the strain of another pregnancy.' He gestured in disgust.

'Ah,' Landry nodded, his eyes narrowing as he gazed at his nephew. 'And you had been thinking that in a few months you would return to her bed. But now that Tregenza is aware of the risks, your route to freedom is cut off.'

Briefly astonished at his uncle's swift and accurate grasp of the situation, Philip raised his upturned hands. 'Can you blame me? What have I to look forward to? I have endured years of her ill health, yet am to receive nothing. If I could've had a son with her,

Tregenza would never have been able to cut me out. As it is . . .' he hissed in disgust.

'On his death the girls' inheritance will be administered by a trust until each of them attains the age of twenty-one.' His hand shook with barely suppressed rage as he picked up his coffee. 'Then, after making it plain that should Margaret die I am to be cast out of the family, he throws me a bone, a toy to play with in my cage.' He nodded in response to Landry's raised brows. 'Oh, yes. To demonstrate his understanding of my *situation*,' he mocked savagely, 'he announced that should I wish to take a mistress, thus sparing Margaret any further risk to her health, he would not object. Provided, of course, that I am discreet.'

Landry drained his cup and set it down. 'Tregenza is hardly in a position to object, considering he has kept a mistress these twenty years.'

Philip blinked, convinced he had misheard. 'Tregenza? A mistress?' As Landry frowned, Philip lowered his voice. 'But when he said – I thought he meant—'

'Someone like Sally Jenkins?'

'Well, yes.'

'Oh, dear me, no. Cheerful and obliging Sal may be, but she's just a common whore. She would not do at all for a man who stands so much on his dignity.'

'Then who?'

'Her name is Ellen Foster. He set her up in a little cottage off West Street. She's a widow, no children. Her husband was lost at sea. I daresay you'll have seen her about the town. Neat little woman, very presentable, keeps to herself.'

'Twenty years? Good God,' Philip finished his coffee, replacing the cup. 'I had no idea.'

Landry shrugged. 'No reason you should. Though to some of us, it's been an open secret for years.' He lowered his voice. 'If you wish, I could arrange an introduction to someone I know. She is most discreet. The success of her establishment depends as much upon the secrecy it affords clients as the range of services offered. I'm sure she would find someone to suit you.'

'I appreciate the offer, Uncle, but I prefer to make my own arrangements. I already have someone in mind. Bearing in mind your own news, I think you'll approve.'

*   *   *

Sarah broke off flat, saucer-sized sprays of tiny white elderflowers and dropped them in to a shallow trug.

'You going to put some of they in the jam?' Becky enquired from beside a row of gooseberry bushes where she was picking off ripe fruit.

Sarah nodded. 'Yes. I'll keep two or three for Jory. He loves them dipped in batter and fried, then sprinkled with sugar.'

Becky carried her brimming basket to the path and stood watching Sarah. 'What's wrong, bird? You haven't been yourself for days.'

Sarah shook her head. 'I don't know what to do.' She didn't have to explain; Becky would understand what she meant.

'Follow your heart.'

'Becky, it's not that simple.'

''Tis only as difficult as you want to make it.'

'But it's not just about me. There's Jory. He used to come home full of what he'd been doing with Noah. Now all he talks about is Mr Crago. How he's helped with his horse, or fetched feed or brushes. You know as well as I do how dangerous gunpowder is. What would it do to Jory if – God forbid – the man was injured or killed?'

'He'd get over it. Dear life, girl, you can't spend your life fearing the worst. That won't stop it happening. All it does is cast dark shadows. Happiness is a rare creature; it don't turn up that often. So when it do, you'd better have your wits about you. 'Cause if you leave it pass by, it might not come back. You listen to me, bird. When you get old, it won't be the things you done that you regret. It's what you could have done but didn't, because you was hiding in a corner waiting for the sky to fall.'

Later that afternoon Sarah peeled and chopped onions, sweet young turnips and spring cabbage, watching Becky scoop a lump of butter from the dish and drop it in to a shallow pan resting on an iron trivet over the glowing embers. As the butter melted and frothed, Becky lifted the joints of rabbit, now coated in seasoned flour, and bent to lay them in the pan. Immediately the kitchen filled with the savoury aroma of frying meat.

Becky looked over her shoulder. 'When are you making the jam?'

'Tomorrow. Why?'

Crouching, Becky turned the joints, her back to Sarah. 'I s'pose I'll have to get on and make that *hevva* cake for Mr Bottrell.'

Sarah caught her lower lip between her teeth to hold back a smile. 'It does seem only fair,' she agreed, 'as we're having the rabbit tonight.'

'That boy,' Becky sighed. 'The things he get me into.' She looked up at the sound of running feet on the path. 'And here he is.'

''Lo, Ma, 'lo Auntie Beck,' Jory panted, dropping his canvas bag on to the floor. 'You'd never guess what I been doing.'

'What's that, my bird?' Becky said over her shoulder, as she spooned juices over the browned meat.

'Only helping Mr Crago. He let me clean out the stable.'

'He did?' Sarah feigned amazement, putting the chopped onion and turnip into an iron pot.

'And he sent me to fetch oats and hay for Balal all by myself. I'm sure Balal knows me now. When I come in the stable, he looks round and blows down his nose.'

'I reckon that's a sure sign.' Becky lifted the rabbit joints out of the frying pan and laid them on top of the vegetables, then poured stock in to the frying pan, stirring until it bubbled and thickened.

Sarah watched her son clamber on to the chair, resting his elbows on the table and propping his chin on his fists. 'What is it, love? Is something wrong?'

Jory sighed. 'I wish I had a pa like other boys. I like Uncle Noah a lot, but he's a bit old. Ma? Do you think Mr Crago might like to be my pa?'

As Sarah caught her eye, Becky shrugged and tipped the thick-ened gravy over the rabbit and vegetables, then carried the empty pan to the sink.

Taken aback by a question she realized she should have seen coming, Sarah hung the pot on the hook in the chimney, fitted the lid and added more furze to the fire. The thought of James Crago with her son, the three of them together, made her heart ache with yearning. But it was the stuff of dreams. Reality meant trying to find her way through a situation laden with the poten-tial for hurt, embarrassment and misunderstanding.

Crossing to his side, she stroked Jory's curly head. 'To be your pa would be a proud honour for any man, Jory.'

He looked up, his eyes round and serious. 'But I don't want anyone else, Ma. I really, really want Mr Crago.'

'Why, sweetheart?' She played for time, desperately hoping for inspiration. How was she supposed to tell this trusting little boy that the man he so admired might not want the responsibility? But in that case, what was Crago doing? Why was he allowing – encouraging – Jory to spend time with him? Could it be . . .? Did he *want* to know Jory better? She tried to stop her thoughts from racing off in to the realms of wishful thinking. 'What do you like about him?'

'Lots of things.' He shrugged. 'He looks at me.'

'Looks at you?'

He nodded. 'When he's telling me something, he stops what he's doing and looks at me. Uncle Noah never looks up.'

'Perhaps that's because Uncle Noah is working?' Sarah suggested. 'So he has to concentrate?'

'I s'pose.' He swung his legs to and fro. 'Mr Crago tells me stuff.'

'What kind of . . . stuff?'

'Like he didn't have a pa when he was small. So that makes him the same as me, don't it? But he didn't have a ma, neither 'cause she died, too. So he lived with his grampy at Jericho Farm. But then he went away to school and after that he went on a ship and sailed all the way to India.'

'Goodness. That must have been interesting,' Sarah said. But Jory wasn't willing to be diverted.

'And he lets me help him in the stable. He doesn't let anyone else in there because Balal doesn't like it. So that means I'm special, doesn't it?'

Sarah knelt and hugged him, nuzzling her face into the soft, sweet-smelling skin on his neck. 'You certainly are. You are the most special boy in the whole world.' He wriggled and she released him, remaining on her knees so that her face was level with his. Though the prospect made her quake, there was only one way to deal with this.

'I think I'd better ask what he thinks of the idea.' Perhaps, unused to children, James Crago was simply being kind and had no idea of the impression he had made. But if that was all he intended, then he had to be told. For between them they would need to find a way to let Jory down lightly.

'Yes!' Jory's grin split his face and his eyes shone as he nodded. 'I'm sure he'll want to, Ma.'

'Maybe. But until I've had a chance to talk with him, it's best that you don't say anything. We'll keep this just between us, all right?'

Jory sighed. 'All right. Will you ask him soon? Please?'

'As soon as I can. But he's a busy man. I've promised,' she said as he opened his mouth. 'Now off you go and feed the chickens. Give them some crushed eggshells with their corn.'

As he scampered out, Sarah turned. 'Oh Lord, Becky. What am I going to say?' She could hear the panic in her own voice.

'It'll come to you, bird.'

Fourteen

The following afternoon Sarah fetched all the empty jars from the bottom of the larder in preparation for making gooseberry jam. It wasn't only her promise to Jory that made her yearn and fear seeing James Crago.

She was attracted to him. It was not possible to be unaware of his disfigurement. Yet the longer she spent in his company, the less she noticed it. He had beautiful eyes. Fringed with thick, dark lashes, they were the same vivid blue as speedwells. But even as her gaze sought his, she was afraid to hold it too long. Afraid of what he might see.

What did he think of her? He had surprised her with his swift decision to invest in Talvan. But as he had made clear, it was a business decision based on the prospect of an excellent return.

She knew that she was delaying because she could think of no way to broach the subject of her son's wish without risk of it appearing that she, rather than Jory, was behind it. That she was seeking a man to marry in order to reclaim a measure of respectability.

In fact, she had long since stopped worrying about respectability. If there was any truth in the rumours and gossip that Ivy could not resist sharing, then there were married women in Penryn living far less respectable lives than hers.

Being an outcast still hurt, but less than it used to, for she had grown accustomed to it. Nor was she without friends. Not with Becky, Ivy, Noah and Jeb so much a part of her life. In town Miss Nicholls, Mrs Tallack and Mr Trenery had continued being pleasant to her.

Though *she* no longer cared what people thought or said, it was wrong that her son should suffer for something that was not his fault. Yet nor could she insult James Crago by allowing him to think that her only interest in him was on Jory's behalf.

All day she had moved from one task to another, finding reasons – *excuses* – for not walking over to Jericho Farm. Because once the words were spoken, they could not be called back. It was too late now, anyway; Jory would be home soon.

Early that morning Becky had gone into town with Ivy. For the first half hour Sarah enjoyed the solitude. But then, too late, she realized that being alone was a mistake. Her thoughts pulled her one way and then the other.

Crago was kind to Jory. But that did not mean he wanted a closer relationship. They had only met because Noah had taken Jory to work with him. In the eyes of the town she was a fallen woman and her son a bastard. Why would any decent man wish to associate himself with them?

As her thoughts went round and round, she finished washing out the last of the jars. Drying each one carefully, she set it down on the table.

The door stood wide open, letting in light and fresh air. At the sound of a brisk knock, she looked up.

'I'm coming.' Dropping the cloth on the table, she tucked a loose curl behind her ear. But as she started towards the door, a man's shadow fell across the threshold. *Crago?* Her heart leaped into her throat, kicking hard against her ribs.

A head appeared. Shock tingled unpleasantly across her skin as her breath caught. Before she could speak or stop him, Philip Ansell stepped in to the kitchen.

He smiled, clearly expecting her to be pleased to see him. 'You did say come in.'

'No, I didn't. I . . .' She stopped, her heart thudding. She didn't want him in her house. 'What do you want?'

His smile faded to hurt. 'I had hoped for a warmer welcome.'

Smart in a dark blue coat and matching cravat, biscuit-coloured trousers and glossy top boots, he had brushed his fair hair forward from a side parting so that it curled over his ears. Since the last time she had glimpsed him in town, he had grown a moustache. It did not flatter.

'Why have you come here?'

Holding his top hat and riding crop in one hand, he splayed the fingers of the other against his chest.

'After all this time I am desolate to find you still angry.'

She would not make excuses for her reaction. He deserved none. 'Why are you here, Philip? We have nothing to say to one another.'

'Sarah, my dear Sarah, that is where you are wrong. There is so much I want – need – to tell you. The first is that I never loved Margaret.'

Sarah stared at him. 'But you abandoned me for her.' The words were out before she could stop them. With all her heart, she wished she could call them back. 'Though that is long past and no longer of any account,' she added quickly. She would not allow him the satisfaction of thinking that it still mattered.

'I was under pressure from my father, who was anxious for an alliance with Horace Tregenza.'

But you never thought to tell me. After persuading me to believe that I mattered, that I was important to you. Growing steadier as shock receded, Sarah moved around the table so that it was between them. 'Then you will have made him very happy. You made your choice, Philip. There is nothing more to—'

'Sarah, I still love you,' he interrupted, his voice vibrant with emotion. 'I never stopped.'

She studied his once-handsome face, noting the incipient fleshiness beneath his jaw, the clipped bar of bristles between his nose and upper lip, the lines of dissatisfaction dragging at the corners of his mouth, and wondered why she had ever thought him attractive. An image of Crago's ravaged features flashed across her mind.

She regarded Philip calmly. 'You never loved me.'

'I *did*. I still do.'

'No, you simply said the words.' Yet it was not fair to hold him solely responsible. She had believed because she wanted to believe. But she had been young and naïve. While he, more experienced and determined, had taken advantage of that.

He grasped the back of the nearest chair. 'Can't we sit down and talk?'

'Philip, you have your life. I have mine. It's far too late for talking.'

'What do you mean?' He took a watch from his waistcoat pocket and shot her a teasing smile. 'It's barely four o'clock.'

'That's not what I meant, as you well know.' Beneath her impatience, anxiety began to stir. She didn't want Jory to come home and find Philip here. She didn't want Philip anywhere near her son.

'I hear you are expanding your quarry. I have money to invest. I would be delighted to—'

'No, thank you. Now you must excuse me. I have things to do.'

'How can you be so cold, so heartless?'

'I am neither, but I am busy. And you are married with a family. You should not be here.'

'Why not? Surely two old friends may discuss business . . .?'

'We are not friends.'

'No,' he said softly. 'We were far more to each other than that.'

'Philip, stop it!'

'How can I stop when I think of little else? You are on my mind day and night.'

Anger burst through her increasing unease. 'That's enough. You have said far too much. You have no right to talk that way. You have a wife, children—'

'Whose every need is provided for, have no fear. The world will still see me as a devoted husband and father. But Sarah, what you and I once were to each other, we could be again.'

What we once were? He had used me, abandoned me and refused to acknowledge the result. 'No.'

'You would want for nothing.'

Appalled, Sarah strode to the door and stood beside it, trembling with anger. 'Get out. I told you we had nothing to say to one another. I was right. How little you know me if you imagined the promise of money would win me back. Nothing you offer will ever change my mind. Now you will oblige me by leaving.' Her back straight and face flaming with indignation, she grasped the latch.

He stepped outside, then turned to face her. 'You don't understand.' His expression beseeched, but in his eyes she glimpsed something darker.

'No, I don't. Nor do I wish to. Just go.' At the sound of hoofs, she glanced over his shoulder and saw Crago approaching. He had Jory in front of him on the horse. Relief at seeing the tall, dark man who was rarely out of her thoughts was swept aside by panic. Had Jory been hurt?

Her son's wide grin and cheerful wave reassured her. But her relief was short-lived. Philip turned to see what had caught her attention.

Crago remained astride the horse, bending over to swing Jory down.

Sarah bit her lip. She wanted to scream with frustration. Would Crago assume that she had invited Philip? Had seeing them together cost her his good opinion? But considering her situation, could she ever really have had it? What mattered now was to get Jory inside as quickly as possible.

Thanking Crago, Jory ran up the path. A happy grin lit his face and his croust bag bounced against his hip. Sarah hurried past Philip to greet her son. She kissed him, then put a protective arm around his shoulders. For an instant her gaze met Crago's. She wanted to explain. But with Philip watching, listening, she couldn't. She felt helpless, hopeless. Her throat was dry. 'Thank you.'

Touching his hat, Crago turned the big horse away. She closed her eyes against the stab of pain. Then, still with her arm around Jory, she walked him down the path.

'Good afternoon, young man.' Philip reached out a hand as if to pat Jory's head, but Sarah moved between them.

'In you go,' she said softly, ushering her son over the threshold. 'I'll be there in a moment.' She turned around in the doorway, ready to defend her home and her child. 'Go away, Philip.'

'I'll come back at a more convenient time.'

'Don't. There is no point. We have nothing to talk about.'

Philip smirked. 'Don't be silly, Sarah. Of course we do. There's our son's future, for a start.' Replacing his hat, he raised his crop to the brim in mocking salute. Then he sauntered down the path to where his horse waited, tied to her fence.

Fear knifed through her as Sarah shut the door. *Why now, after all these years? What possible interest could he have in Jory's future?*

Jory had taken off his cap and put his croust bag on the table. 'Who was that man, Ma?'

She swallowed and forced a smile. 'Just someone I knew a long time ago.'

'What did he want?'

'He was just passing and stopped to say hello.' She hated lying, but could not bring herself to tell him the truth. Kneeling, she opened her arms. 'May I have a hug?'

As he flung his arms around her, she closed her eyes and held him close.

'Ma?' he whispered in her ear.

'Yes?'

'Will you ask him tomorrow?'

After this afternoon it would be far more difficult. 'Jory, important questions have to wait for the right moment. I will ask him. But . . .'

'All right.' He sighed. 'Can I have some milk and a piece of cake?'

Coughing to clear her throat of clogging fear, she forced a smile. 'I'm sure you've got hollow legs.' Releasing him, she went to the larder.

'Did you see me on Balal, Ma? Isn't he handsome?'

'He certainly is. It was very kind of Mr Crago to give you a ride home.'

'Uncle Noah was busy and didn't want to leave till he finished.' Jory scrambled up on to the chair as Sarah set the milk in front of him. Then she saw his hands.

'Oh no, you don't. Over to the sink with you.'

'Aw, Ma!' He rolled his eyes, then grinned up at her. 'I had a lovely day.'

Guessing Sarah would be reluctant to talk while Jory was in the house, Crago knew that he would have to wait until the following day. Sensitive to his master's moods, Balal tossed his head and skittered sideways, suddenly twitchy.

Crago turned the horse towards the moor. When Balal tired after a pounding gallop, Crago turned back and called at the quarry. On the slope he met Jeb, who raised a finger to his cap in greeting.

'You look weary,' Crago observed.

''Tis hard graft,' Jeb admitted. 'But we're coming on. Should blast again tomorrow.'

'Have you got everything you need?'

Jeb nodded. 'Much obliged.'

'Then I'll leave you to it.'

Jeb returned to the quarry and Crago headed for the farm, exchanging salutes with his homeward-bound workmen on the way.

After grooming Balal and giving him hay and fresh water, Crago entered the kitchen. Nessa had left a freshly baked pasty on the table.

Sweating, tired and deeply unsettled, he sat and pulled off his boots. Then, knowing himself alone, he stripped off the rest of his clothes.

Taking a cake of soap from the sink and a clean towel from the wooden drying rack above the range, he walked barefoot in to the yard.

He rested the soap on the stone rim of the well, hauling up the bucket and tipping it over his head, before gasping at the shock of the cold water. After another bucketful, he lathered his body with soap, his fingers sliding over the ridged flesh along his ribs, then rinsed off with several more buckets.

Refreshed, he wrapped the towel around his waist, picked up the soap and returned to the kitchen. After rubbing dry his hair, he reached for a fresh towel. Once dry he pulled on a clean shirt, cotton drawers and trousers, pushed his feet into slippers and hung both towels over the drying rack.

Tidying his hair by raking both hands through it, he poured himself a glass of beer from the keg in the larder. As he sat down to eat his pasty, he thought about the tableau he had witnessed: Ansell defiant and smirking, Sarah anxious and unhappy. What did it mean?

Using a dipper to pour boiling jam in to the warmed jars, Sarah filled each almost to the brim. Philip's visit the previous day had left her shaken. He had never acknowledged Jory as his, so why was he now talking of *our son*?

Was that supposed to persuade her to take him back? If so, he was wasting his time. The past was long dead. As for his claim that he still loved her, she didn't believe it for an instant. Far from feeling beguiled by his declarations, she found them distressing and distasteful.

She hated that he had walked in to her house, as if he were entitled. This was her home, hers and Jory's. He had no right of entry. If he did return as he had promised – *threatened* – she would not allow him to put one toe across the doorstep. Even so, she dreaded him coming back. And hated even more that she was afraid.

Right now Jory was safe with Noah at Jericho Farm. Becky had taken the shay and gone in to town for shopping, but she would not be away long.

Filling the last jar, she scraped the remaining half cupful of jam out of the pan and in to a dish, then carried the pan to the sink and pumped cold water in to it.

Circles of oiled paper waited to top the jam when it was cold. The table was lined with squares of tissue paper, a paintbrush, a bowl containing the white of an egg and labels on which she had already written GOOSEBERRY and the date, June 1840.

As she wiped her hands on a cloth, a knock on the closed door sent her heart in to her throat. She froze. No, it couldn't be. Not so soon. But what if it was? If she kept quiet, would he go away?

Her mouth dried and her heart thumped painfully as she heard a rattle and saw the latch lift.

Fifteen

Her hand flew to her mouth and she gasped in relief as Crago's head appeared.

'I did knock . . .'

'Oh, it's you. I . . .' *was terrified*. She shook her head.

'Is this an inconvenient time?'

'No, not at all. I am just making jam.' Embarrassment flushed her cheeks. 'As you see,' she said, indicating the jars.

He remained on the doorstep, his dark brows drawn together. 'Might I speak to you for a moment?'

'Jory?' She blurted, instantly fearful.

'To the best of my knowledge, he's fine.'

Relief coursed through her. 'I thought . . .' She tried to smile but her face felt stiff. 'Forgive me, I must sound very foolish. An overanxious mother.' She tipped her head and tidied the already neat oiled circles.

'Not at all. He's very young. He's been ill. Of course you will worry.'

His kindness nearly undid her. Swallowing hard, she looked up. 'Would you like to come in?'

'Thank you. Shall I leave the door open?'

About to ask why, she managed to stop in time. His consideration swelled the lump in her throat. He must know that she had no reputation left to lose. But his question made her aware of the heat in the kitchen and the heavy sweet-sharp scent of boiled fruit and sugar.

'I appreciate the thought, yet I would prefer it shut.'

Stepping inside, he closed the door behind him. When he turned to her, his frown was deeper. 'On such a lovely day? Then I must assume that you do not desire visitors.'

'One particular visitor.' She straightened the tissue paper squares. How could she explain? What would be the point? Philip's presence on her doorstep must invite the worst speculation. How could she tell this man, the man her son wanted to be his pa, the shaming, degrading fact that Philip had come hoping to *buy* her?

'You are upset.'

She would not insult him by denying the obvious. 'Yes, but it's of no consequence.'

'Indeed it is. You know it and so do I. Yesterday – did Ansell come here to try and resurrect the past?'

Her head flew up. She was horrified that he had guessed, yet relieved for the same reason. 'How . . .?'

A muscle jumped in his jaw. 'All he can offer you is secrecy and shame.' His voice was harsh.

She looked away, her eyes stinging. 'Do you imagine I don't know that?' Coming here, offering her money, only proved how little true regard Philip had for, her despite his protestations.

'You are worth more.'

That Crago should think it, let alone say it, brought hot tears to her eyes. Blinking them away, she raised her head. 'Yes, I am. Though I fear few would agree with you. In town people cross the street rather than speak to me.' She wiped her eyes with the corner of her apron.

He gestured impatiently. 'That is their loss, not yours.' Startled, she stared at him as he continued. 'Mr Trenery holds you in high regard. I am sure he is not alone. As for those pillars of respectability who gaze down on you from their moral high ground, I imagine all are devoted church-goers?'

Her faint smile held irony. 'Oh, yes.'

'No doubt they find it easier and more comfortable to deplore the sins of others than to examine their own actions. Such people clearly have great need of the Church. Though I would not hold my breath waiting for them to absorb its teaching of tolerance and compassion.'

She gave a weary shrug. 'Perhaps I am unfair. They were prepared to forgive me.'

'Indeed?' He indicated the chair tucked under the kitchen table. 'May I?'

'I beg your pardon. My manners have gone begging. What happened yesterday – it was . . .'

'A shock?' Pulling the chair out, he waited.

She nodded. 'Please, sit down. I'll make—'

'Later, perhaps.' He indicated the chair on her side of the table. 'I think we have been here before.' He waited for her to sit and then followed. 'They were willing to forgive you?'

She nodded, clasping her hands on the table. 'Like every woman who bears a child – and despite the fact that – that I was unmarried, I could have been churched after Jory's birth.'

His gaze searched hers. 'But?'

Vivid memories of the vicar's austere expression and thinly veiled disdain brought heat to her cheeks. 'But I was informed that it would be necessary for me to make a public penance during the service.' She swallowed. 'As punishment for my fornication.' What was she doing, telling him what she had shared with no one but her father and Becky? Yet it was better that he knew the worst, and that he heard it from her rather than as gossip from anyone else.

'You refused.' His tone made it a statement.

'Yes, I refused. I was already whispered about, pointed at in the street, treated with scorn and contempt. Being churched would not have stopped that. If anything, it would have made matters worse, because more people would have been aware of my wrongdoing. But the main reason I refused was anger, anger at the injustice. Philip faced no punishment, no public shame. His morals were not questioned. His reputation remained intact. I bitterly regret what I did. But I never have, and never will, regret my son.' Facing him, half-expecting condemnation for her defiance, she gave a helpless shrug. 'My refusal earned me even greater criticism.'

'It must have been very difficult for you.'

Sarah plucked at her apron. 'I could not have coped without Becky. My father . . .' She shook her head, then met his intent gaze. 'He insisted on a meeting with Philip's father. I begged him not to, I knew it was pointless.'

'Why?'

'Because by the time I realized I was . . .' She straightened the tissue squares once more. 'Philip had married Margaret Tregenza.'

His brows rose. 'What was Mr Ansell's response?'

'That he had no idea what my father was talking about.'

'How very convenient.'

'He might have been speaking the truth. Philip had never introduced me to his family. Mr Ansell told my father that Philip was recently married and away on his honeymoon. And while he sympathized with what was obviously a distressing situation, I had no proof that his son was responsible.'

Her cheeks burned at an implication that still had the power to hurt as Crago's breath hissed between his teeth. 'He warned that if my claim was repeated either in public or private, he would go to law.' She drew a shaky breath. 'It was my word against theirs. My condition meant that my morals were already in doubt and my reputation ruined. Pursuing the matter would have cost Father money he couldn't afford, made an even greater fool of me and changed nothing.'

She rose from her chair, bent to add chopped furze to the embers, then turned to him. 'Mr Crago, you cannot know how grateful I am that you brought Jory home yesterday. Your timely arrival helped me out of a deeply uncomfortable situation.'

He stood, his head almost touching the beams. 'It should not have been necessary.'

She flinched. 'You cannot believe I *invited*—' She turned away.

'No! God, no.' Taking a quick stride forward, he touched her shoulder, drew her round to face him, then quickly dropped his hand. 'I never meant – I wasn't blaming *you*.' His voice was husky. 'I meant that he had no business here and should not have come.'

'Oh.' Her heart fluttered like a trapped bird.

His blue gaze was intent. 'Miss Govier—'

The gate slammed, small feet raced up the path and Jory burst through the door. 'Mr Crago!' He beamed. 'I saw Balal, so I knew you was here. Stopping for tea, are you? Ma said you wouldn't stay last time because Auntie Beck and Auntie Ivy came.'

'Thank you, Jory.' As a blush flooded her face, Sarah darted a wry look at Crago and lifted the kettle from the hearth.

Dropping his croust bag on the table, Jory grinned at her. 'I been ever so busy.' With a quick glance at Crago, he beckoned her down to his level, and when she bent, whispered, 'Did you ask . . .?'

She shook her head. 'Remember what I said?'

He turned to Crago. 'Have you got sugar lumps? Can I give some to Balal? Please?' he added quickly after a glance at his mother.

Clutching three, he raced out, leaving the door open.

'I'm curious,' Crago smiled. 'What does he want you to ask me?'

With her back to him, Sarah pumped water into the kettle, refitted the lid and hung it above the flames, struggling to find the words.

'Though I think I can guess.'

She whirled round. 'You can? You don't mind?' she added anxiously.

A smile warmed his eyes. 'Why would I mind? It was the reason – one of the reasons – I came over. On our way here yesterday afternoon Jory talked of nothing else.'

Sarah's hands flew to her cheeks. 'Oh no. He promised me he would wait.'

'Small boys can't wait. So,' he dipped his head for a moment, then raised it again. His blue gaze held hers. 'Miss Govier, will you do me the honour of allowing me to escort you and your son to the Midsummer Eve bonfire?'

'B–bonfire?' she stammered blankly, realizing they had been speaking of different things.

He nodded. 'Jory informed me he is desperate to go.'

'*That* was what he . . .?' She stopped. 'Oh, Mr Crago—'

'James. Please.'

'James,' she whispered, joy battling anguish. 'I can't.'

Naked hurt was stark on his face for an instant. Then his expression blanked. 'I see.' He stepped back. 'Forgive me. I–I– forgive me.' He bowed and this retreat in to formality was more than she could bear.

She gripped his arm. 'No, you misunderstand me. Mr – James, you never venture in to town because of the stares, the remarks. For you to appear at a public event—'

'Will doubtless provoke as much attention as one of the sideshows,' he said drily. His gaze dropped to her hand on his forearm and she snatched it away, twining her fingers. 'But that—'

'That alone,' she broke in, determined he should be aware of what he risked. 'Would be unpleasant for you. But attending a public event with *me*? Do you not realize what being seen in my company will do to your good name and reputation?'

Reaching for her hand, he held it between both of his. Gently, as if he were holding something precious. The calluses on his palm were rough against her knuckles. 'And do *you* imagine I have not already considered that, then dismissed it with the contempt it deserves?'

'Oh.' He would brave all that for *her*? As her throat ached and her eyes swam, she looked away.

'I am still waiting for your answer,' he reminded.

'James—'

'Wait. Listen to me. Individually, you and I are already subjects of gossip and rumour. You have suffered this for a lot longer than I have. If we go, people will see us together. No doubt they will talk. So what? We owe no explanations. Sarah, look at me.' His gaze held hers and his voice softened. 'You would like to go, wouldn't you?'

After an instant's hesitation she nodded. 'Oh, yes.' She had missed so many feast days, carnivals, fairs and bonfires, preferring to stay away rather than risk exposing Jory to the unkindness of people who would scorn him, scorn them both. She had told herself that it hadn't mattered. But it had.

'Then it is agreed. While you are with me, you need fear no insult. And while I am with you, if people should stare and whisper about my face, I will have no time to notice. Jory will make sure of that. Yesterday as we were riding here from the farm, he asked a remarkable number of questions.'

Sarah bit back a smile. 'Oh dear.'

'His belief in my ability to supply answers is a compliment. But one I'm not entirely sure I deserve.'

'He was telling me what he liked about you.'

'May I ask?'

'He said you look at him. You stop what you're doing and look at him.'

She saw a flicker cross his face as he nodded. 'I just wanted you to know that he noticed.'

A painful smile lifted one corner of Crago's mouth. 'If I didn't *know* he has the eyes of a hawk, I would assume . . .' He shook his head, running his fingers down his scarred and broken nose. 'It's as if he doesn't even *see* this.'

'Perhaps he doesn't. Not any more. He sees you.'

He raised her hand. As his lips touched her knuckles she felt her breath catch. 'Miss Govier—'

'Sarah,' she whispered, and laid her hand lightly, tentatively, on his.

The kettle boiled just as Jory scampered in, and they stepped apart.

'You can't go yet!' Jory cried. 'Ma, Aunty Beck's coming up the road.' He turned to Crago. 'She always asks me to put Jenny away. You'll stay and have your tea? Ma?' He turned, pleading.

'If Mr Crago has time and would like to stay,' she caught Crago's eye. 'He is very welcome.'

'Mr Crago?' Jory hopped up and down, anxious.

'I should like it very much.'

As Jory raced out, grinning, Sarah took cups and saucers from the dresser. 'You do realize that as soon as Becky knows you're here, and Jory is probably telling her even as I speak—'

'You will have additional company.' He nodded. 'She is very fond of you.'

They shared a smile. As Sarah turned to fetch the milk, the door opened.

Crago rose to his feet. 'Good afternoon, Mrs Hitchens.'

'Mr Crago.'

'Come in, Becky,' Sarah knew Becky must see her happiness. She felt as if it were radiating from her like sunshine. 'The kettle's just boiled.'

'I won't say no. Dry as a bootjack, I am.' She waved Crago to his chair. 'Sit down, my 'andsome. You'll be in the way, else.'

Seeing Crago bite back a smile, Sarah turned to Becky. 'Mr Crago has kindly offered to escort Jory and me to the Midsummer Eve bonfire.'

'He has?' As her eyebrows climbed, Becky dipped her chin and looked hard at him.

'I have. Would you care to join us?'

'Me?' Becky said, startled. 'You don't want me along.'

'Mrs Hitchens,' Crago said gently. 'It would be a pleasure to have you with us.'

Becky's eyes sparkled as she pressed one hand to a rosy cheek. 'Well! I take that very kindly. Very kindly indeed.'

Sixteen

Sarah clicked her tongue. Jenny's ears twitched, signalling that she'd heard. But though this stretch of road was level, her pace remained a steady plod.

Smiling, Sarah tilted her face to the sun. It was another warm, dry day. Water-filled ruts had dried and the frequent passage of carts and wagons over the hardened mud had broken it down. The air was fresh and fragrant with the scent of new grass and clover blossom. The birds had stopped singing while they renewed their plumage after nesting.

Above her in the clear blue sky two buzzards soared in slow circles with mewing cries as they taught their fledgling to ride currents of warm air reflected off the outcrops of granite.

She was on her way to Talvan with two barrels of ale and two big slabs of *hevva* cake cut in to squares. Though long hours and hard work were earning the men good money, she wanted to show her personal appreciation for their efforts.

Every time she visited, the quarry was bigger as each blast lifted out yet another huge block of granite. Thanks to Crago's investment and his excellent blasting powder, Talvan was on its way to success. After the difficulties of the past few years, this improvement deserved celebration.

As she followed the quarry edge, she saw a huge block, rough-dressed by stonemasons to the approximate size and painted with Mr Trenery's code numbers. Chains had been fastened around it and looped on to the crane's hook. As two men turned the winch handles to lift the block, two more swung it round to load it on to a heavy wooden wagon with an iron-reinforced bed, while the team of four powerful horses waited patiently.

Then she noticed Jeb gesturing angrily as he argued with the wagon-driver. Pulling on the reins to stop the donkey, she slid off the shay. Jenny immediately put her head down and started to crop the lush, sweet grass. Sarah hurried towards her foreman.

'Jeb?'

He spun round. "Af'noon, Miss.'

She nodded to the driver, then turned back. 'Is something wrong?'

Disgust curled Jeb's mouth. 'Says he won't carry no more loads for us.'

"T'isn't my fault!' The driver shot back.

Sarah looked from one to the other. 'Will one of you please tell me what the problem is?'

'Sorry, Miss. This is the last load I can do for you.' The driver would not look at her.

She felt a heaviness in her chest. Everything had been going so well. She forced herself to remain calm. 'I don't understand. We have an agreement.'

'Look,' the driver said miserably, 'I don't like it no more'n you do. But I got no choice.'

'What do you mean? No choice?'

'Bloody Landry,' Jeb spat. 'Begging your pardon, Miss.'

'All right, Jeb.' Touching her foreman's brawny arm, Sarah addressed the driver. 'What does Mr Landry have to do with this?'

'See, what it is,' the driver said, 'you only have one or maybe two loads a week for me. But Mr Landry give me at least one load every day.'

Sarah shook her head. 'I still don't see the difficulty. You have time to carry two loads a day from the quarries to Penryn quay. So surely—'

"T'isn't the number of loads, Miss. Look, to put it plain, if I carry any more stone for you, Mr Landry won't use my wagons no more.' He shrugged, embarrassed but adamant. 'I can't afford that. I got a family.'

Moistening her lips, Sarah nodded. 'Of course.' She should have expected something like this. Should have prepared for it. She ought to have known that Kinser Landry would interpret her refusal to sell him Talvan as a personal affront. This was his revenge. It was annoying and inconvenient, but if he imagined it would change her mind, he was going to be disappointed.

'I'm sorry, Miss.'

'I do understand.'

After Jeb had lifted the beer and cake from the shay, Sarah turned the donkey towards home. Thank heaven she still had Mr Trenery's wagons. But given Talvan's expansion, those two alone would not be enough. Approaching any one of the other transport firms would be a waste of time. No doubt Landry had already warned them off as well. What was she to do? James Crago would know.

No doubt he would. But he had his own business to take care of. Talvan and its problems were her responsibility. She found her immediate reaction to ask his advice unsettling. It showed how quickly she had come to rely on him. But what if he didn't want that?

Wearing a dark green coat, a matching cravat knotted over a shirt Nessa had bleached in the sun, fawn trousers and polished boots, Crago set his top hat low over his eyes. As he crossed the yard to the stable, Noah emerged from the barn, carrying a saw. Jory was quick at his heels.

'Cor, Mr Crago!' Jory's eyes widened. 'You look handsome!'

As Noah turned, rolling his eyes, Crago's mouth quirked.

'Thank you, Jory. That's not something I hear very often.' He mounted up, and as he headed out of the yard, he heard Noah's mutter.

'Dear life, boy. Be the death of me, you will.'

'Well, he does,' Jory said, totally uncrushed.

Riding through Penryn, he ignored startled glances and open stares. Not so long ago he would have found them intolerable. With nerves stretched taut by anger and bitterness, he would have been fighting the urge to snarl and lash out. Echoes of that temptation still lingered. But now he found it easy to ignore. Nothing had altered, yet everything was different. A change he owed to Sarah, an outcast like himself, and her son.

Every time he saw her, he learned a little more. And it was never enough. Sometimes shy, sometimes spirited, she was fiercely loyal to her friends and had been kind to him.

Were gratitude and sympathy all she felt? He hoped not. He wanted more, much more. Sometimes he sensed deeper emotions, then feared he was simply reflecting his own hopes and wishes.

Long before he met her, he had heard the gossip about her past. In a small community it was impossible to avoid. Then she had marched in to the valley, her indignation a wafer-thin veneer covering anxiety that verged on panic.

Far from trying to elicit his sympathy she had told him things he would never otherwise have learned. It was as if she wanted him to know the worst of her, and to hear it from her own lips. Why had she done that?

His investment in Talvan was a sound business proposition, completely independent of liking, let alone the friendship that had sprung up between them.

But was friendship all she wanted? Were her revelations intended to keep him at a distance? If so, was it to protect herself? Or to spare him the embarrassment of being seen in her company? There was only one way he would find out.

He had set up his mill knowing the risks and the dangers. They hadn't mattered then. Now they did. So did she. More than he could ever have imagined.

He turned down the hill and in to the stable yard behind Simmons' Hotel. Leaving Balal in the care of a bandy-legged ostler with a seamed face the colour of teak, he crossed the main road and walked down Bohill.

As he entered the general office of Ansell's Cargo Brokerage, he saw a door on the far side close. Ignoring the young clerk perched behind a sloping desk and peering at him as if mesmerized, Crago approached the counter.

A thin, middle-aged man dressed in black looked up from an open ledger. 'May I help you, Sir?'

Crago removed his hat. 'I wish to speak to Mr Philip Ansell.'

'I'm sorry, Sir. Mr Ansell is not available at the moment.'

'Then perhaps you will conduct me to Mr George Ansell. No doubt he will pass a private message to his son.'

'If you will wait one moment, Sir,' the clerk said smoothly, 'I will ascertain whether Mr Philip has completed his business.' He knocked on the door Crago had seen close and entered without waiting for a response.

Crago heard quiet murmurs followed by a short silence. Then the clerk reappeared, came to the counter and pointed to his left. 'Through the first door, Sir.'

'Thank you.' The clerk had not asked his name. It was not necessary; his face identified him.

Crago did not knock. Opening the door, he saw Philip Ansell seated behind a large oak desk. Several piles of papers, a penstand and an inkwell were lined up in front of him. Apparently engaged in writing a letter, he did not look up.

Briefly amused at this childish attempt to demonstrate power,

Crago did not wait. Nor did he raise his voice. 'I will be brief. You are not welcome on Miss Govier's property. That includes her quarry, her house and the land in between.'

Philip's head jerked up. 'You take a lot upon yourself,' he snapped. Then his mouth twisted in to a sneer. 'You might fancy yourself her champion. But you cannot seriously believe any woman in her right mind would choose to be seen in public with you.'

Crago merely raised one brow. 'I hope I have made myself clear?'

Pushing his chair away from the desk, Philip stood. 'Better you should mind your own affairs instead of—'

'That is precisely what I am doing. Miss Govier is a business associate as well as a friend. Should she be subjected to any more of your unwanted attentions, the magistrate will be informed.'

Blood rushed in to Philip's face. 'How dare you come in here and threaten me! My relationship with Miss Govier is a private matter and no concern of yours.'

'According to Miss Govier, there is no relationship. Nor does she desire one.' He reached for the door handle. 'Keep away, Ansell.'

'You're making a big mistake, Crago,' Philip hissed. 'You'll regret this. Just wait and see.'

Closing the door, Crago replaced his hat, left the building and walked back up the hill. Checking the time on the new clock tower, he entered the hotel.

'There's a gentleman waiting to see you, Sir,' the landlord said. 'I directed him to the coffee room.'

'Do you have a small parlour?' Crago asked. 'I have some business to transact and would prefer to conduct it in private.'

'Just down the passage, Sir. First door on your right. I'll bring the gentleman to you, shall I?'

'Thank you.' Crago passed him a coin.

'Coffee and brandy for two, Sir?'

'I should be much obliged.' A few weeks ago he could not have envisaged what he was about to do. It was a leap of faith. If it failed, he would lose everything. That was a chance he had to take.

A few moments later he heard footsteps. The door opened and he rose to greet his guest.

'You coming, then?' Becky demanded, poking her head round the back door. 'You didn't ought to be sitting in here on a lovely afternoon like this.'

Sarah looked up from the newspaper spread over the kitchen table. 'I was hoping to find a carter's advertisement. But . . .' She stopped as Becky's question registered. 'Coming? Where?'

Becky clutched the handle of her basket with both hands, her knuckles as white as the cloth-wrapped parcel. 'I can't go down there on my own. I don't want him getting ideas.'

'Who? Becky, I'm sorry, but I don't know what—'

'Zack Bottrell. I promised – well, Jory promised – for the rabbits.' She lifted her basket. '*Hevva* cake. I made it this morning. I thought I'd take it down there now. 'Tis lovely out. Do you good to have a walk. Only if you aren't too busy, mind.'

Sarah knew better than to take those last words seriously. Becky wanted company, wanted her. How could she refuse? Besides, she was intrigued.

'Of course I'm not too busy. A walk would be lovely.' She folded the paper and stood up. She had dressed that morning in an old summer gown of apple green with elbow-length sleeves and a round collar. Just for an instant she wondered if she should change and quickly dismissed the notion.

She was not going on her own account, but for Becky's sake, and only as far as the clearing. It was most unlikely that she would see James Crago. He would be busy at his gunpowder mill. Quickly, she fetched a light shawl and tied the ribbons of her bonnet.

'Have you been to the clearing before?' Sarah asked as they set off.

Becky shook her head. 'No. Never had no call to. I wouldn't be going now if that dear boy of yours hadn't put me up for it.'

'Mr Bottrell and his daughter have got the prettiest little . . . Becky, that's it! That's the answer!' Sliding her arm through Becky's, she squeezed. She'd have kissed Becky's flushed cheek had their bonnet brims not prevented it.

'Prettiest little *what*? Dear life, girl. What are you on about?'

'Wagons, Becky. Mr Bottrell is used to driving a wagon. Perhaps he might be willing to drive for me. If he's not too busy and Mr Crago can spare him.'

'I don't think you need to worry about Mr Crago being willing,' Becky said drily. 'Do anything for you, he would. No, don't you laugh,' she said as Sarah shook her head. 'I see the way he look at you. Like he can't believe what's in front of his eyes. Anyhow, if you got a driver, all you need is a strong enough wagon.'

'Perhaps Mr Trenery might—'

'No doubt he will. But if I was you – and 'tis only a suggestion – I'd ask Mr Crago to ask'n.'

'Becky, I'm perfectly capable—'

''Course you are. Did I say you weren't? But truth is, bird, Mister
will get a better price. That's just the way of it. And seeing how
'tis his money . . .' she shrugged.

Sarah sighed. 'You're right.' It was a legitimate reason to see
James again, soon. As they walked on, that thought kindled excitement, anxiety and a powerful yearning.

Seventeen

'Again!' Jory begged.

'This is the last time,' Sarah warned.

'High. Please, Ma, Mr Crago. Swing me high.'

Holding his hands, Sarah and Crago counted to three, then lifted and swung so that Jory's booted feet flew up level with their heads. Joining in her son's squeal of pleasure, Sarah glanced across at Crago, and saw him watching her. His smile made her quake inside.

Wanting to look her best for this outing – it was her first since Jory's birth with a man who was not her father or Noah – she had put on her green checked gown and a bonnet of pale straw. When Crago had arrived to escort them and she saw that he was wearing his dark green coat, her heart had floated even higher.

Passing him on the step, Becky had remarked how well they looked together. Now as she met his gaze, the apprehension that had haunted her all day began to dissolve. Despite her efforts, she had been unable to pin her unease to a specific cause. *Would he come?* As it had been his suggestion, his invitation, why would he not? *What if Philip turned up?* What if he did? James had promised to shield her. With him beside her, she had nothing to fear.

'That's enough for now, Jory,' Crago said. 'We must allow your mother's arm time to return to its normal length.'

'All right. But if I'm very good, can we do it again d'reckly?' He looked from one to the other with a winning smile.

'We'll see.' Sarah shook her head at him but couldn't hide her amusement.

'The art of persuasion.' Crago laughed.

Sarah rolled her eyes. 'He's an expert.'

'Ma? Tell Mr Crago what you was telling me last night. About the bonfire.' Jory skipped along between them, still holding their hands.

'I'm sure he knows already.'

'Tell me anyway,' Crago said, his eyes gleaming in the golden light of the setting sun.

'All right.' She was intensely aware of him and her body responded to his gaze with a wave of heat that made every nerve tingle. She cleared her throat. 'On Midsummer Eve, that's today, the sun reaches its highest point in the sky. And what does the sun do?' she asked her son.

'Gives us light and warmth and makes the crops grow,' he recited.

'That's right. And because the sun is so important, long long ago on this special day people would light bonfires in its honour. The heat and light of the fire reminded them of the sun.'

'Those people also believed that the sun had the power to destroy evil,' Crago said. 'So they thought their bonfires would do the same. That's why everyone dances in a circle around the fire. Then when it dies down to embers, they jump through the flames.'

Jory looked up, his eyes wide. 'Will it stop bad things happening to us?'

Sarah's eyes met Crago's. She stopped and bent to look in to Jory's eyes. 'Nothing bad is going to happen us. But just to be extra sure, shall we jump through the flames?'

As he nodded, they started walking again.

'You know those explosions we heard this morning?' Sarah said. 'They were set off by miners up on the carns to let everybody know that today is Midsummer Eve.'

'Did the miners use your powder, Mr Crago?' Jory demanded.

'Some would have done.'

'I 'spec' they made the biggest bangs.'

A large crowd had already gathered as they approached the hilltop.

Jory jumped up and down. 'I can't see.'

Before Sarah had a chance to say anything, Crago handed her his hat. Then he bent and hoisted Jory up on to his shoulders.

'Is that better?'

'Handsome!' Jory patted Crago's dark head. 'I can see everything now.'

Crago led the way up a shallow incline to the top of a grass-covered ridge. Sarah followed. 'Can you see?' he asked her, holding Jory's ankles. 'Or would you like to—?'

'This is perfect.' They were at the back and away from the crush. Looking to her left, she saw more people arriving. All wanted to be as close as possible to the enormous conical pile of logs, branches and furze.

The sun had set in a glorious blaze of orange and gold. Sarah watched the dazzling brilliance soften to apricot, rose and lilac.

Then as the sky overhead turned from turquoise to aquamarine and dove-grey dusk crept in, excitement rippled through the crowd.

A girl dressed in white and wearing a wreath of blossoms around her head approached the fire carrying a bunch of herbs tied with a rainbow of long ribbons.

'Who's she, Ma?' Jory asked, holding on to Crago's head.

'The Lady of the Flowers,' Sarah told him. 'Listen now.'

A man held up a flaming torch and the crowd joined in as he shouted the familiar words in Cornish.

'I set the pyre at once on fire. Let the flame aspire over many a parish.' Then he plunged the torch in to the massive heap. The long spell of dry weather ensured that it caught at once. The flames swiftly gathered strength, leaping into the darkening sky and sending up showers of sparks.

As the Lady of the Flowers flung her bouquet into the flames, the crowd gave a roar of approval.

'Look, Jory,' Sarah pointed to distant hilltop where a similar bonfire had been lit. 'There will be fires like this on hilltops all over Cornwall.'

Down nearer the fire the number wanting to take part was sabotaging attempts to form a circle. As scuffles erupted Sarah, was glad they were not closer. Yet part of her yearned to circle the fire and jump the flames. Logic and common sense told her that belief in the protecting power of the flames was simply superstition. But another deeper part of her could not so easily dismiss it. This ceremony had been performed for thousands of years. Why, unless they believed, would people continue to honour it?

The squabble was defused as a group organized a second ring outside the first. Now there was room for everyone who wished to join in. Someone started to sing. Everyone joined hands, and the circles began to move. The chant was picked up, voices rising and falling with the flames.

She saw faces she recognized: Mr Trenery and his wife; Miss Nicholls from the haberdashery; Philip's parents. Mr Tregenza and his wife had their two granddaughters between them. Mrs Tallack tripped daintily around, followed by Ivy, Noah, Becky, Zack and Nessa. Even Sally Jenkins was part of the outer ring; her head thrown back, her bare shoulders gilded by the flames.

Sarah watched, longing to be part of the community, if only for this one night. But she had suffered too many rebuffs to willingly invite another. James had shrugged off the likelihood of nudges and stares in order to come. She was aware of them and they were discomfort enough. For herself, she didn't care. But she was angry on his behalf. If people knew him as she did . . . But they didn't. Because – like her – he was intensely private.

What if the circle refused to let the three of them in? She gasped as two groups of young men and boys raced past, whirling blazing torches above their heads. Crago bent, lifting Jory down.

'Come on!' he cried. 'We're going to join the circle.' As Jory squealed with delight, Sarah hung back for an instant and felt Crago squeeze her hand. As he looked into her eyes, she knew he saw her fear. 'It will be all right. Trust me.'

She nodded. Then they were running forward.

With Jory between them, they broke in to the circle between Noah and Becky.

''Bout time!' Becky beamed, flushed and breathless. 'I was wondering where you was to. Some crowd tonight. I never seen so many.' She rolled her eyes. 'Dear life, I haven't moved so fast in years!'

Singing and skipping, the two rings circled the fire.

'All right?' Crago grinned down at her, shouting above the noise.

'Never better!' Sarah yelled back, laughing. It felt wonderful to be part of the circle and the celebration. His little face bathed in the glow from the flames, Jory was grinning from ear to ear, singing only one word in every ten, but clearly having the time of his life.

As the fire began to settle, men with long staves poked and spread burning logs and embers over a wider area. Then, with a wild cry, one of them leaped over the flames. Others followed. Fathers jumped with children, husbands with wives and young men with their chosen sweetheart. As each couple prepared to jump, the circle closed up so they remained within its protection. Cheers and clapping greeted each leap.

Sarah saw Jory turn an excited face up to Crago and felt a pang as she heard her son's excited plea. 'I want to do it. Please, Mr Crago? Jump with me? I'm too heavy for Ma.'

Crago looked at her, waiting for her permission. She nodded. She could not disappoint Jory and knew he was in safe hands. Crago released her and Zack clasped her fingers, closing the circle.

As Crago swung Jory over the flames, Sarah saw people nudge each other. But the song continued, the mood and the circle unbroken, and Sarah released a shuddering breath. Holding Jory under his arm, Crago leaped over the embers and back again.

Back on his feet, waving his arms in excitement, Jory raced towards her. 'Now you, Ma! You've got to jump.'

'Oh!' Sarah gasped as Crago's strong hands grasped her waist. She just had time to put her own hands on his shoulders before he whirled her in to the air and over the flames. Her heart beat wildly and she was laughing as he set her down.

'Now we jump,' he said, clasping her hand. 'Ready? Now!' They leaped, over and then back.

'Now you're safe,' he said, looking in to her eyes. As she and Jory rejoined the circle, Crago grabbed a startled Becky, whirled her over the flames and made a courtly bow as he released her.

'Well, I never!' she gasped, blushing like a girl as all around people whirled and leaped, claiming protection for the year ahead.

'Time you did, then,' he grinned.

'Get on with you!' She gave him a playful slap. Then darting Sarah a smile, he reached for Nessa, whose face lit up as she held his hand and leaped with him.

In that instant Sarah realized. *He's protecting everyone he cares about.* Back in the circle once more, he smiled at her over Jory's head and she felt her heart crack wide open. When Zack seized Becky's hand, *and she didn't send him packing*, Sarah cheered and laughed with the others.

Twenty minutes later, finally succumbing to excitement and exhaustion, Jory turned his face up to Sarah. 'I'm tired, Ma.'

'So am I,' she smiled. 'Shall we go home now?'

'Would you like to ride on my back?' Crago offered.

'Oooh. Yes, please.'

Saying goodnight to Becky and the others, they left the circle. Crago hoisted Jory on to his back and they turned towards home.

'Did you enjoy yourself?' he asked.

'It was a wonderful evening.' She smiled up at him. 'Truly magical. Thank you so much.'

'I would not have missed it.' The warmth in his voice enfolded her like a blanket.

'We'll have good luck now,' Jory said sleepily, his head on Crago's shoulder.

Please let it be so, Sarah thought. Five young men ran past, flaming torches made from tar-wrapped rags bound to thick sticks held high as they headed towards the town.

The crack and pop of squibs shattered the night quiet. Rockets fizzed into the indigo sky, trailing showers of golden sparks. Soon people would leave the hilltop and make their way to the bars and inns in the town centre where revelry would continue long in to the night.

'Mr Crago,' Jory said, settling his head more comfortably. 'Will you be my pa?'

'Jory . . .' she began, thankful that the darkness hid the rush of heat sweeping up her throat to burn her face.

'Ma said she'd ask you, but—'

'I know I did, sweetheart. But—'

'See, all the other boys got one,' Jory continued, his voice so thick with sleep that Sarah wondered if he'd even heard her. 'They go on to me and call me names. Will you, Mr Crago? If I promise to be good?'

Sarah pressed her fingers to her mouth, her throat painfully stiff.

Crago turned his head so that the boy would hear but kept his voice low. 'Jory, you have paid me a wonderful compliment. I am flattered to be asked, but . . .'

But. Though she had braced herself for it, Sarah felt a weight on her chest, as cold and hard as stone.

'What's flattered?' Jory mumbled.

'It means to be proud and pleased. What you feel when Noah tells you you've done something well.'

'Or you, like when I washed Balal's bit.' He yawned hugely.

Taut as one of the stays on the crane, Sarah hardly dared breathe as she waited for what her son might say next. But as the silence stretched, she realized that he had fallen asleep.

She moistened her lips. 'I'm sorry—'

'Don't be. It's not necessary.'

Opening the gate, she led the way up the path and unlocked the front door. 'Shall I take him?'

'No. Just tell me where—'

'First on the right at the top of the stairs.' She followed him up and pulled back the covers as he lay Jory down and removed his boots.

Then he stepped back. 'I'll wait downstairs.'

She had expected him to make some excuse and leave. Afraid to hope, she tried not to think at all as she quickly stripped her son and tucked the bedclothes around him.

In the kitchen Crago had stirred the embers in to life and was sitting in the armchair by the fire, forearms on his thighs, his fingers loosely linked between them. As she reached the bottom of the stairs, he stood up.

She moistened lips that were suddenly dry. 'Would you like a glass of beer? You must be thirsty. Jory is no lightweight and—'

'Thank you,' he broke in gently. 'That would be most welcome.'

Carrying two glasses to the larder so he should not see how her hands shook, she poured beer for him and elderflower cordial for herself.

Taking the glass, he indicated the door. 'Shall we sit outside? It's a beautiful night. And there is something I wish to say to you without the risk of Jory overhearing.'

Torn between hope and dread, she led the way out to the old bench seat against the front wall.

As he sat down beside her, she lifted her glass. It rattled against her teeth as she took a nervous gulp. The cordial slid cool and soothing down her parched throat.

He raised his own glass and she heard him swallow. He was sitting half-turned towards her but with his head tipped so that she could not see his face.

'I would be happy to give Jory the support he is seeking. The only reason I did not say so immediately was because the decision is not mine.'

Sarah gripped her glass with both hands. He must mean Philip. She cleared a slight hoarseness from her throat. 'When you brought Jory home and found Philip Ansell here, it was the first time I had spoken to him in almost seven years. I wish it might also be the last. I have no idea what had prompted him to come. But I left him in no doubt that he is not welcome.'

Crago touched her arm gently. 'I have not expressed myself well. What I meant was that I would enjoy spending more time with Jory. But that decision must be yours. Do you have any objections? Obviously, I will not allow the boy anywhere near the mill.'

Her heart quickened. But she was afraid to assume too much, to hope for too much.

'No, I have no objection.'

'Good.'

'I think I should warn you, he does ask a lot of questions.'

Crago laughed softly. 'You're too late, I know. The first time I met him he was clutching one of Noah's wood planes. He stared at me, then asked if my face hurt. No.' He touched her hand, and when she didn't pull away, grasped it. His palm was warm and her heart skipped a beat. 'Don't apologize for him. There is no need. He was simply being a child. His openness is one of the many things I like about him.'

'And does it?' Sarah asked softly. 'Hurt, I mean.'

Taking her hand, he lifted it to his face and used her fingers to trace the jagged ridge of white skin. 'The scar has no sensation. But above or below it,' he released her fingers, sliding his own gently over her knuckles and then dropping his hand, 'that I can feel.'

As she explored his damaged face with her fingertips, she knew that what she felt for this man wasn't pity or gratitude, or even admiration. It was all that and more, so much more. She had imagined that she loved Philip. But what she had felt then was a pale shadow of the emotions that James Crago ignited in her.

'How . . .?' Her voice cracked and she cleared her throat. 'How did it happen?' Taking her hand, he kissed her fingers. Sarah caught her breath. Should she have asked? Was the memory still painful?

The corners of his mouth tilted and one dark brow arched. 'Ivy hasn't told you yet?'

Eighteen

The lingering tension inside her evaporated. She felt light and happy and, for the very first time, *safe*.

'Ivy is a dear. There's no harm in her. She's just very interested in people. Someone like you . . .' she stopped, hesitated.

'Someone like me?' he prompted quietly.

'A man on his own, keeping himself apart, involved in dangerous work—'

'And ugly as the devil. No, Sarah,' he warned before she could speak. 'I want no pretence, not between us.'

Us. No longer two isolated people, separated from others by their pasts, denied what others took for granted. Though she was reluctant to assume and risk disappointment, to hear him speak of *us* kindled a warm glow of excitement and hope. 'She said – she heard there was a girl.'

He nodded. 'There was.' He released her hand and linked his fingers around his glass, separate once again.

She spoke quickly. 'If it's too painful . . .'

He glanced up. 'Not any more. Her name was Anjuli. She was descended from the ruling family of an ancient kingdom in the south-west of India called Kodagu. Her great-uncle was a good man. When he died, his son succeeded him as ruler. But though he was only twenty years old, Chikka Vira Raja was already notorious for his cruelty and self-indulgence. To protect himself from any challenge for the throne, he ordered the slaying of every member of his predecessors' families. Anjuli's father was spared only because he was too useful a member of the government.'

'Why were you there?'

'In India? I was an officer in one of the East India Company's artillery regiments. I was in Kodagu because I could speak Hindustani and had a working knowledge of several dialects. I was attached as interpreter to the party of British officers sent in to try and bring about an end to the fighting between the people who had been driven to rebellion and the soldiers loyal to the Raja. It took weeks of negotiation before we were even admitted in to the Raja's presence. He would agree a meeting, or summon the delegation, then leave us waiting, often for hours.'

'How very rude.' Sarah was indignant.

'It was. But as absolute ruler, he was answerable to no one and could do as he pleased. He was also making a political point. He knew the British powers in India would prefer a negotiated settlement.'

'Why?'

'Because using force against a sovereign state might cost the British government votes.'

'Oh.' Her ignorance made her feel foolish.

'There is no reason for you to have known that.' The light reassuring pressure of his hand sent pleasure fizzing along her limbs. 'Sometimes an official or minister would be sent to speak to us. Anjuli's father was one of the chief ministers. Balaji Singh could see that my superiors were losing patience. In fact the delegation had begun to talk about removing the Raja regardless of the political repercussions. Balaji Singh invited us to his house in an attempt to defuse the tension.'

'That was where you met her?'

He nodded. 'She was seventeen years old, very beautiful and utterly terrified. The young man she had been about to marry had been killed in the fighting, and the Raja wanted her as a concubine.'

Sarah caught her breath. 'Oh, dear Lord.' She remembered her own devastating sense of loss after Philip's brutal abandonment. But then to be chosen not as a bride but a mistress by a young man already infamous for his cruelty. She could not begin to imagine how that must have felt.

'Could her father not have refused?'

He shook his head. 'Defying the Raja meant certain death. But so, too, did failure to please him. Anjuli told me of one girl who simply disappeared. According to rumour, she had disappointed the Raja. He sent her back to her family, and her father killed her for bringing dishonour upon the family.'

Sarah gasped.

'I'm sorry. I did not intend to—'

'No, no. I'm all right. It's just . . . the *poor* girl. Please go on.'

'Anjuli said she would kill herself sooner than submit to him. But she knew her father's position and that of the rest of her family would be in jeopardy if she disobeyed. I worked out a plan to help her escape. I told only one person, a brother officer I knew I could trust.' He looked down at his glass. 'He warned me against interfering. He said it was dangerous, foolhardy and might well see us both killed. Even if somehow we managed to get Anjuli away, there could be no future for her and I.'

'Why?' Sarah asked. 'Did the law forbid . . .?'

'No. In fact the officers, both married and single, often took Indian women as mistresses. They were mostly beautiful, well educated, trained in singing and dancing and skilled in the arts of love.'

Sarah was glad that the darkness hid her blush, though she was more curious than embarrassed. Having borne a child herself, she knew how one was created. But to learn there were skills in such matters, *that* she had not known.

She sipped her cordial to wet a throat dried by shyness at the images that his words provoked: images of her and James. She pushed them back, her skin burning. 'Weren't such relationships frowned upon?'

'Not at all. In addition to their other talents, Indian women were sound domestic managers, ensuring servants did not steal or waste money. They were also excellent nurses. Which, bearing in mind all the illnesses Englishmen fell prey to, was very useful. Having an Indian mistress made practical sense. But marriage to an Indian girl was unacceptable.'

'Why?' For Sarah, branded immoral, her reputation forever tarnished because she had yielded to persuasion *without* the sanction of a legal ceremony and a wedding ring, this was hard to understand.

'Because it suggested that you had gone native. Such an accusation was likely to bar a man from further promotion. Also the new bride would find herself isolated. The English wives would refuse to receive her and her own people would scorn her. I knew all that. But I could not turn my back. I thought if I could just get her out of Kodagu, then . . .' His shrug conveyed helplessness. 'I had no idea what to do next. But at least she would be safe.'

'What happened?' Sarah whispered.

'The night before we were due to leave, I received a message to meet her in a garden outside the palace fort. We had walked there several times. It was a beautiful spot with glorious views over miles of forested hills and valleys. The servant who brought the message gave me a bracelet Anjuli always wore, to prove it had come from her.'

Sarah felt an unpleasant tightening in her stomach. She guessed that what came next would be difficult to hear. But how much harder for him: facing it then, reliving it now.

'It hadn't?'

He shook his head. 'Somehow our plan had been discovered. There were always servants around. When I arrived at the garden, she was already there, dead. She had been stabbed. Then I was attacked. That was when—' he indicated his face, 'Sawyer got me away. Were it not for him . . .' He inhaled deeply. 'While I was recovering, the Raja was deposed and Kodagu became a province of British India. But because of my actions – not to mention my appearance – I was an embarrassment. My resignation was accepted and I came home.'

'Did you ever learn who was responsible?'

'For the attack on me? Or for Anjuli's death?'

'Both, either.' Tentatively she touched his hand, wanting to convey – What? Empathy? Understanding? 'Answers would have changed nothing, I know that. I just thought if the person concerned had been brought to justice—'

He gave a bitter laugh. In the moonlight his eyes glittered. 'My dear, sweet Sarah.' His gentleness was at odds with his fierce expression. 'Concepts of honour and justice have a different meaning in India. Anjuli's reluctance to submit to the Raja insulted him and undermined her father's position as a trusted minister. Neither man would have permitted such defiance to go unpunished. As for which of them actually wielded the dagger . . .'

She gasped. 'You mean her own *father* . . .?'

He shrugged. 'It's not unusual. She was doomed long before I became involved. Sawyer warned me. And I knew there was little chance my plan would succeed. Yet . . .'

She heard him swallow. 'You had to try. And paid dearly.' She made no attempt to comfort. She knew from her own experience that, no matter how well meant, words never helped. Only time could smooth grief's raw edges. As weeks and then months passed, blade-sharp stabs of pain gradually dulled to an ache. Eventually, even that faded.

'The company was generous. I received all the prize money due to me. My length of service meant I had also accumulated a substantial pension. I returned to Cornwall a wealthy man. But one whose face terrified children and caused women to faint.'

'You do not terrify Jory and I have not fainted,' she reminded softly.

Setting down his glass, he took hers, put it on the ground and drew her to her feet, holding her hands against his chest. 'Once I believed I would never forget. Now there is much I cannot remember. I am content with that and would not wish it otherwise. But you and I will never entirely escape the past. I have my scars. You have your son. Yet without them, we would not be who we are. Nor would we be here now, together. Sarah—'

A loud cough made them both look round. He stepped back, releasing her, as Ivy and Noah, Becky and Zack passed the garden gate. Fond though she was of them all, Sarah wished fervently that they might have chosen another moment to return.

'Night, my bird!' Becky called. 'Night, Mr Crago.'

'Goodnight!' they called back in unison.

'I should go,' he said.

'Thank you for a wonderful evening. And I truly appreciate – it cannot have been easy for you to talk about what happened.'

'Easier than I anticipated and now laid to rest. It was another life.' Raising one of her hands, he kissed it. 'For you, revisiting the past must have been far more difficult. Yet you did not spare yourself. You have more courage . . .'

Her fingers tightened on his. 'Oh, James. I do not deserve such praise. It was not courage but fear that drove me. Had I not told you, sooner or later someone else would have. So if you were going to turn away, I wanted you to do so before . . .'

'Before?' he prompted softly.

She hesitated, then plunged on, the darkness making it easier. 'Before I could begin to care.'

'And do you?'

'Care?' Was she wise to tell him? Was she sensible to lay bare her heart and risk another rejection? But if she were not honest with him, how could she expect honesty in return? 'Yes.' More than she would have believed possible. More than she was ready for.

He laid one rough-palmed hand along her cheek. 'I will not turn away, Sarah.'

'W—would you like to come for supper next week?'

'I should like it very much. '

'Wednesday?'

'Wednesday.' Lifting her hands, he kissed the knuckles of each in turn, then released them to cup her face. 'Sarah,' he whispered, then lowered his head to brush his lips over hers. It was a kiss as soft and light as feathers, a kiss that cherished. A kiss that held a world of promise.

Her eyes closed and she stopped breathing. Then his mouth moved on hers with increasing pressure and her heart quaked. A tremor shook him. She sensed restraint, and the hunger beneath it, and her own yearning flared. Her lips parted beneath his, moved on his. She inhaled him, tasted him, pouring in to the kiss all the longing in her heart.

He made a sound deep in his throat as his mouth plundered hers, giving back everything he took. Still holding her face, he eased his lips from hers and both drew a shaking breath as he pressed kisses on to her closed eyelids, cheeks and the corners of her mouth. Then he stepped back.

As he dropped his hands, so did she. Where his palms had been warm on her face, the night air was cool. They stood a foot apart and Sarah felt pulled towards him by a powerful force. She ran her tongue over her lips to moisten them, tasted him and felt a melting inside her.

Taking her arm, he led her to the door and opened it. 'For pity's sake, go inside,' he rasped.

'Goodnight, James.' Her voice was husky and shook slightly.

'Sarah?' He kept his voice low. 'I haven't the words to tell you how much I enjoyed this evening.'

'Really?' She whispered, making no attempt to disguise her delight and eagerness.

'It was magical.' He touched her cheek lightly with his finger-tips. 'Sleep well.'

As she closed the door, she saw him turn towards the gate. She pushed the bolt across, put the glasses in the sink and climbed the stairs. While she undressed, she thought about the evening: of jumping the flames together, of the honour this reclusive intensely private man had paid her in sharing his past. He had even touched upon his financial status. On Wednesday he was coming to supper. And his kiss, his kiss . . . She was still smiling when she blew out the candle.

★　★　★

The following morning Becky popped in after breakfast.

'Just wanted to make sure you was all right, bird.'

'I'm fine, Becky. Apart from having my ears talked off.' Smiling, Sarah rolled her eyes. 'If Jory has told me once, he's told me ten times that last night he had the best time in his whole life *ever*.'

'Dear little soul.' Becky sighed. 'I didn't think he'd be up to go with Noah this morning.'

Sarah shook her head. 'Not a bit of it. He woke at the same time he always does. He only stopped talking long enough to swallow his breakfast, then raced off as usual. I feel sympathy for anyone working at Jericho Farm today. I expect all of them went to the bonfire. But that won't stop Jory telling them about it.'

'Don't you fret about that. If Noah want a bit of peace, he'll send the boy off to fetch a hammer or a bit of wood.' She tucked a stray wisp of hair in to her bun. 'I got to say, Mr Crago gave me some start, swinging me over the fire like that. But I seen what he was about.'

'You did?' Sarah stopped wiping the table and looked up, wanting to hear what Becky had made of James's actions.

'Protecting us, he was. I knew he'd look out for you and Jory. And Nessa Bottrell, 'cause she do work for him. But I never expected . . . Gave me some shock it did when he picked me up.' Her face grew pink at the memory. 'He's a dear soul and that's God's truth.'

She sighed. ''Tis funny. First going off, that face of his was some awful shock. I didn't b'lieve I'd ever get used to it. But now, I still *see* – well, you can't miss it, can you? But it don't bother me no more. I tell you what, bird. He got a lovely smile.' Clicking her tongue, she tossed her head. 'Not that you'd have seen it, standing out there in the dark.'

Carrying the cloth to the sink, Sarah rinsed and then wrung it out. 'Mr Bottrell looked very happy last night. He certainly seemed to be enjoying the dancing. Did he like the cake?'

'Said it was the best he ever tasted. Which it prob'ly was.' Suddenly looking around for something to do, Becky carried the milk jug to the larder. Returning to the table, she picked up dishes and put them on the dresser, then pushed the chair in under the table.

Sarah recognized the signs. 'Becky, why don't you tell me what's bothering you?'

'There isn't nothing *bothering* me. 'Tis just . . . see, Zack – Mr Bottrell – said his girl want to know how to make it like I do. What d'you think? Should I ask her round my place?'

'I think you'd both enjoy it. Being deaf, Nessa won't find it easy to make friends. It must be lonely for her. I'm sure her father does his best, but it's not the same as having another woman around. I don't know what I'd have done if you hadn't been there for me.'

'Well, I was. Nor wouldn't have missed a day of it.'

Sarah smiled. 'Can I make one suggestion?'

'You will anyway. What?'

'Invite Zack as well. No, listen,' she said before Becky could argue. 'He'll help you understand what Nessa is saying. Once the two of you are comfortable together, he wouldn't need to come every time. But you might find that you enjoy his company.'

'You sure you wouldn't mind?'

Crossing the kitchen, Sarah threw her arms around Becky and hugged her. 'Why would I mind? It's about time you had a gentleman caller.'

'Get on!' Becky pushed her. 'No such thing. Just making a cake is all.'

Sarah returned to the sink and washed the breakfast dishes. 'When will you have them over?'

'Well, they're both working, so it depends what day they're free. I'll go down to town this afternoon then walk over to Jericho tomorrow and see what's what.'

'You won't lose by it, Becky.'

'How do you mean?'

'Zack knows you don't like being beholden. He might feel the same way. Especially where Nessa is concerned. So if you invite the two of them over, it's more than likely he'll bring something for the pot.'

'Well, now,' Becky nodded. 'You can't say fairer than that.'

Sitting on the wooden bench in the afternoon sun, Sarah topped and tailed the plump, glossy blackcurrants she had picked an hour earlier. A white apron covered her blue calico gown and she had perched a wide-brimmed straw hat on her head to shade her eyes.

While her fingers were busy, her thoughts drifted through the previous evening: Jory's squeal of delight as he was lifted on to James's shoulders; the way her heart had leaped when James gripped her round the waist, then whirled her over the flames as if she were weightless. Last night in the moonlight he had held her hands and talked to her as no man ever had. Then he had kissed her.

Remembering the warm pressure of his lips on hers and the rough skin of his palms cupping her face so tenderly, her heart did a little flip.

Seeing Becky dancing with Zack Bottrell had surprised her, considering their initial prickliness. But maybe that prickliness had simply been protective, hiding an interest that had caught them both unawares. Would anything come of it? She hoped so. Both were loyal and generous. But it was up to them. Becky baking with Nessa was surely an excellent start.

Lifting the basin of blackcurrants from her lap, Sarah placed it beside her on the bench and then gathered up the corners of the cloth containing the tufts and stalks.

Philip Ansell had dismounted some distance from the lime-washed cottage and left his horse in the leafy shade of an oak tree. He had told both his father and senior clerk Ernest Scoble that he was visiting a client.

As he drew closer to the cottage, he saw the front door was standing wide open, which meant that Sarah was at home. Though compelled to come, he would have resented making the journey for nothing. Relief gave way to a pleasant buzz of anticipation.

Then he saw her. She was sitting on a bench seat in front of a window to the right of the doorway, her head tipped. Today she wore blue. Last night she had worn green. Her layers of petticoats had flashed white as that ugly brute Crago had whirled her over the flames and then jumped through them with her. Crago had carried the boy under his arm, then on his shoulders. Playing father to *his* son, and making eyes at *his* woman.

He refused to believe she could prefer that mutilated wreck to himself, who, since his youth, had been noted for his handsome face and elegant physique. It wasn't rational.

Images of Sarah with Crago had seared his brain and now burned like acid in his gut. He tried to push them away. But they clung, colouring his voice with echoes of bitter fury as he approached.

'What a pretty sight on a summer afternoon. Good afternoon, Sarah.' He reached for the latch.

Bolting to her feet, she dropped the cloth. It fell to the ground, scattering bits of leaf and stalk. She took a few steps forward, stopping abruptly in the middle of the path. 'Stay where you are!'

He straightened. 'I beg your pardon?'

'I know you are not deaf, Philip, so you will have heard me. Step away from the gate.'

No woman had ever used that tone to him. He didn't like it. Nor would he allow it, as she would soon learn. But for now he was determined to be patient. He tipped his head to one side and offered what he knew to be a winning smile. 'Come now. We cannot possibly have a conversation from opposite sides—'

'I told you the last time you came here, and I'm telling you again now. We have nothing to say to each other. Please leave.' She regarded him steadily, her expression closed and cold.

Anger stirred. He wanted to hit her. The urge was so strong, it made his palm itch. He curled his fingers into fists. What right had she to speak to him like that, or to look at him with such contempt? Who did she think she was? 'Be warned, Sarah. My patience is wearing thin.'

'As is mine,' she retorted. 'You have left me alone for almost seven years . . .'

Relief washed over him. 'So *that's* what has upset you. I thought I explained: my father insisted. It was my filial duty.' He pulled a face, implying *you know what fathers are.* 'But everything will be different now, I promise. You will want for nothing. Pretty trinkets, nice clothes, you shall have everything you desire.' There would be plenty of time to show her who was in charge once he got her in to bed. 'There was such passion between us, Sarah. I will rekindle that fire in you, a fire that has lain dormant for too long—'

'Stop it! Stop it at once!'

He stared at her. She should be smiling, blushing prettily, perhaps pretending shyness, but all the while knowing that they would soon be lovers again. It was inevitable. They were meant to be together. Why could she not see it?

But she wasn't smiling. Her face was pale as milk and rigid with disgust.

'You could offer me no greater insult. Perhaps among your acquaintance there are people willing to be bought with such promises, but I am not one of them. If you open that gate and set one foot on my property, I will report you to the magistrate.'

'On what grounds?' he sneered. She was bluffing. She would not dare take such action. Then he saw her shoulder lift.

'Trespass, harassment. It hardly matters. Within an hour the fact that I have laid a complaint against you will become public knowledge. Is that what you want?'

How *dare* she defy him? He had been patient, but such rebellion and hostility were not to be borne. She must be brought to heel.

'An empty threat, Sarah.' He waved it away. 'But mine is not. You have had my son for six years. Long enough, I think. It is time he was sent away to school instead of being allowed to run wild.' The boy was her only weakness. If he had to use the child to bend her to his will, she had only herself to blame.

But as she faced him, her eyes those of a hunted animal, he felt a twist of fear. He suppressed it, ignored it. She would break now. She must.

Instead, her chin rose. 'You have no proof that Jory is yours.'

He snorted impatiently. 'Don't be silly. My father knows he is. Your father told him so.'

'And *your* father refused to believe it,' she retaliated. 'He claimed I had no proof, then threatened legal action.'

Philip brushed her words aside as he would a fly. 'My uncle knows, too. Kinser Landry?' He had powerful allies, as she would do well to remember. Her flinch on hearing Landry's name gave him considerable satisfaction. 'I'm the boy's father. I have rights.'

'You also have responsibilities,' Sarah shot back. 'You have two daughters.'

'I want a son.'

'That is a matter for you and your wife. Jory is mine.' Turning on her heel, she picked up the basin of fruit and went in to the house.

'Sarah!' he shouted. 'Are you absolutely certain James Crago wants *you*? Did it never occur to you that his real interest is Jory?' He saw her stumble, felt a thrill of savage glee. That shot had found its target. 'With a face like his,' he fired the words at her, 'what chance has he of finding a wife and having a family? But you, all alone for seven years and desperate for a husband to win you some respectability, you were ripe for plucking. Fool yourself if you wish, but he's not having my son. And without the boy, will he still want you? I doubt it.' He'd made his point. It was time to be conciliatory. 'Sarah, please. This is no way for us to—'

The door slammed shut and he heard the bolt shoot across. He slammed his fist down on the gate. Why wouldn't she listen? She could bluff as much as she liked, but they both knew that the boy was his.

He turned and walked back towards his horse. Damn it, all his life he had done everything expected of him. In a few years' time he would take over his father's company. He wanted – needed – a son to follow after him, continue the tradition. If Margaret couldn't give him one, why shouldn't he have Jory?

He had come with the intention of persuading Sarah to rekindle their relationship. That was still his objective. The boy was simply a means to an end. Yet the more he thought about it, the more the notion of acknowledging his son appealed. After all, what would he be risking?

His job was secure. So was his marriage, for Horace Tregenza would never countenance the stigma of divorce. Once he had the boy, Sarah was as good as his, for she would never abandon her son. That would put paid to James Crago. A most satisfactory outcome all-round. He smiled, his good humour restored.

Nineteen

Sarah laid a circle of oiled paper on top of each pot of cooled jam with hands that still trembled. She knew Philip's parting words had been a deliberate and spiteful attempt at revenge because she had rejected him. He had deliberately set out to upset and unsettle. She knew that, and hated that he had succeeded.

Why *would* James Crago be interested in her? He was charming, intelligent and kind, as well as a shrewd businessman. If she was able to see past his scars to the real man beneath, then surely others must, too? He had so much to recommend him, so much to offer. Whereas she – in the eyes of many in the town she was soiled goods, an affront to moral womanhood.

At least she had been able to maintain her financial independence, avoiding the additional stigma of having to apply to the parish overseers for Poor Relief. But it had been a close-run thing. For without James's investment and his blasting powder, sooner or later she would have been forced to sell her quarry.

Her hands still unsteady, she dipped a pastry brush in to the bowl of beaten eggwhite and dampened both sides of each tissue paper square. Then one at a time, she laid them over the top of the jars and gently pressed each moistened paper against the rim. As the tissue paper dried, it would harden, excluding air and preserving the jam.

A tear gathered in the inner corner of her eye and slid down her nose. She wiped it away with the back of her hand. In just a few short weeks her life had changed completely. James Crago was responsible for that. She had quickly come to admire and respect him. Now she loved him. She loved him for his courage, his kindness, his dry humour, for the way he had supported and helped her without attempting to take over, as most other men would have done.

Philip had mocked her loneliness, claimed her friendship with James had sprung out of desperation. It was true that she had sometimes – often – felt lonely. But being alone was infinitely preferable to the risk of making another disastrous mistake.

James Crago made her feel special, worthy of his time and interest. He had kissed her with tenderness and with passion, and her heart had opened up like a flower. Once, a long time ago, she had believed herself to be in love. Now she saw so clearly the difference between mirage and reality.

Philip was arrogant and selfish, used to having his own way. Faced with rejection, he had retaliated by undermining her peace of mind and attempting to destroy her happiness. He might try, but she would not allow him to succeed.

Yet the seeds of doubt he had so skilfully planted had already taken root. Was it *her* that James cared about? Or was her son the true object of his interest? *Trust me*, he had said. Could she? Should she? Another tear fell.

As she carried the empty bowl and brush to the sink, she heard the gate slam. Quickly wiping her eyes with the corner of her apron, she returned to the fire and pulled the kettle over the flames as the door opened. Becky's bare head indicated that before coming round she had first gone home to remove her bonnet and leave her shopping.

'Got the kettle on, have you? Dry as a boot, I am. I unhitched Jenny and turned her out in the field. Here, you'd never guess—'

The two cups Sarah had taken from hooks on the dresser slid from her unsteady hands. She flinched as they smashed on the stone floor.

With a quick frown, Becky hurried towards her. 'What's on, my bird? White as a sheet, you are. Here, sit down.'

'The shards—'

'Leave 'em. I'll brush up in a minute. Tell me what's wrong.'

'I'm fine. Really.'

''Course you are,' Becky pursed her lips. 'I aren't in my dotage yet. I can see you been crying. What's happened?'

Sinking on to the chair that Becky pulled from beneath the table, Sarah covered her face with her hands, her shoulders shaking.

'Camomile and honey is what you need,' Becky announced. Taking a tin of dried herbs from the dresser, she moved about the kitchen. 'Come on, my bird. I can't abear to see you like this.'

Sarah wiped her eyes. 'I'm all right now.' She took a deep breath. 'Philip came. He . . .' She swallowed hard. 'He wanted . . . he promised trinkets and clothes.' Disgust thickened her voice. 'He tried to buy me. And when I rejected him, he . . . Becky, he says he's going to send Jory away to school.'

'He never!'

Scalding tears slid down Sarah's face once more. 'He said James only wants me because of Jory. Because he'll never be able to have a son of his own.'

'That's a pack of lies! Rubbish, the lot of it!' Becky exclaimed. 'For a start there id'n no way he can take your boy. As for what he said about Mr Crago, 'tis plain ridic'lous. Ivy and Noah and me all seen the way he was looking at you last night. 'Tis you got his heart. He's fond of the boy. 'T would take a hard heart not to be. He's a dear little soul. If Mr Crago take time with him, it's because he knows he'd have no chance with you if the boy didn't like him. I tell you, bird, if you b'lieve a word that Philip Ansell says, you need a good shaking. Dear life! Like a spoilt child he is. Can't get his own way, so he'll kick the cat.'

Sarah cleared the hoarseness from her throat. 'I was so frightened, though I didn't let him see it.'

'I should hope not. If I'd been here, I'd have given him what-for. Bloody nerve of him! Coming round here, upsetting you like that. Well, I aren't having it. Drink your tea.' Startled by Becky's rare fury and her unheard-of use of a swear word, Sarah sipped the herbal brew and felt soothed and reassured.

'I know what's behind all this,' Becky said. 'When I was in Rogers' shop, buying currants and peel, Mrs Tregenza was talking to Mrs Eddyvean and I couldn't help but hear. Margaret Ansell lost another baby a few weeks ago. This is the third. They was all boys as well.'

Setting the cup on the table, Sarah kept her hands round it, drawing comfort from the warmth. 'Oh, poor Margaret. She must be devastated. How *could* Philip come here making overtures to me while his wife is grieving?'

'Because he don't care about no one but himself,' Becky snorted. 'He should be home where he belong. Not that he'd be much comfort. Some husband he is. Neither use nor ornament. 'Tis a sad business for Margaret, but she'll get the care she need. Her mother and father will make sure of that. Come on, now. Time's getting on and Jory will be home soon. You don't want him seeing you like this.'

'I'm better now.' Sarah forced a smile. 'Really.' She did indeed feel calmer, soothed by the camomile and honey and by Becky's spirited reassurance.

Perhaps Philip had been driven here by grief at losing another baby boy. It would be a terrible blow, especially to someone like him who considered a son his entitlement. But that did not justify him taking Jory. Nor would she allow it. As for what he'd said about James . . .

'Come on, bird,' Becky urged. 'Wash your face and tidy your hair. Look like you been pulled through a hedge backwards, you do. I see you done the jam.' She picked up a jar and examined it. 'Set nice and firm, too. Remember last year? That blackcurrant jelly? Boiled it up twice and he still wouldn't set. We done it in the end, though. Handsome it was.' She prattled on, standing to one side with the towel while Sarah pumped the handle and splashed cold water over her face.

'Stay for tea, Becky,' Sarah blurted, clutching the towel to her chest.

''Course I will, bird.' Becky patted her arm. 'Don't you worry. Everything will be all right. Now, what shall we have? Need some proper food, you do. Any of that lamb joint left? I'll go and pick some spinach. Jory can shell the peas when he come in. He love doing that. You boil a few potatoes.'

Sarah pulled a face. 'I'd better sweep up the cups first.' After tipping the broken crockery into an empty flowerpot outside, she moved about the kitchen, taking down pans, setting out cutlery, then fetching the potatoes. She kept thinking of what Becky had said, clung to it. *'Tis you got his heart.*

She heard the gate slam and the sound of small running feet. Instantly her spirits lifted as Jory clattered in, beaming, and dropped his canvas bag on the floor.

'All right, Ma? You'd never guess what I been doing!'

Holding him close, she nuzzled his neck. 'No, but I'm longing for you to tell me.' No matter what it cost, no one was going to take her son.

The following day Becky drove the shay past Jericho Farm and down the track to the woods. Around the edge of the clearing dappled sunlight filtered through fresh green leaves of oak, ash and sycamore. Vivid blue dragonflies zipped to and fro. She saw two small, gaily-painted wagons lined up one behind the other. A gentle breeze stirred washing pegged on a line between two trees.

She looked round and then realized that Nessa was probably working down at the mill. But Zack was there. He straightened from stacking cut lengths of wood around a waist-high triangle made of three-foot logs laid on top of each other.

A short distance away was a cone-shaped earth clamp. Beyond it a patch of bare ground strewn with ash and dust marked the site of an earlier clamp. Several bulging sacks lay nearby.

'Morning,' Zack nodded, raising a finger to his cap. Becky noted the gesture and appreciated it.

'Morning.' As she slid off the shay, Zack came forward, his eyes bright and sharp in his leathery face.

'You was saying about your girl wanting to learn how to make *hevva* cake?' Becky said.

'She know how to make it,' Zack said. 'What she want is to learn how to make it as good as yours.'

Becky nodded. Though pride and pleasure briefly warmed her cheeks, a frown still tightened her forehead. 'Tell her to stop by my place end of the week. You can come if you've a mind to. I wouldn't want her feeling bad if I can't understand what she's saying.'

'All right.' He studied her for a moment. 'What's on, maid? You're looking some teasy.'

Becky sighed and shook her head. 'Sarah got trouble. But I won't have no more of it. That dear girl been through enough.'

He nodded, slow and thoughtful. 'You need help, you come to me.'

'Much obliged.' She dipped her head. 'See you Saturday.' Despite telling herself all the way here that she was simply doing a kindness, Becky kept remembering how it had felt to have Zack's work-roughened hand clasping hers. She tried to recall the last time she had danced. It was a long time since she had enjoyed herself so much. In a tone meant to imply that she didn't care one way or the other, she added, 'You can stay for tea if you want.'

He nodded. 'I'll bring a couple of rabbits.'

'You don't have to.'

'I know. You mind yourself now.' He touched his cap brim once more and returned to his stacking.

Heaving herself on to the flatbed of the shay, her legs dangling, Becky flapped the reins. 'Get on, Jenny.' That had gone well. She felt like a girl again. She clicked her tongue and smiled. What was she like?

While hoping for similar success at her next stop, she began to prepare herself for a much more difficult interview.

At the end of the track she turned towards the town and wove through the two-way traffic of carts, vans and wagons. It was mid-morning and the town was busy. She inhaled the sharp tang of fresh dung trodden in to the dust, ale-soaked sawdust, newly baked bread and roasting coffee.

As she rode down the hill towards Commercial Road, the acrid reek of mud, rotting fish and hot tar floated up from the river that lapped around the town quay before it divided in to two creeks. One ran behind the warehouses edging the road between Truro and Falmouth. The other led up beneath the swing bridge to Mr Trenery's yard, where it met the stream flowing down through the woods.

Crossing the road, Becky drew the shay in to an alley beside Horace Tregenza's chandlery warehouse. Tying Jenny's rein to a ring in the wall, she shook out her skirts, adjusted her shawl, straightened her bonnet and marched round to the front.

Two wide sliding doors stood open, and in the warehouse beyond she glimpsed piles of crates, boxes and sacks. Rows of shelves were stacked with wood blocks for hoisting sails, shackles, lamps and lanterns, coils of rope and chains of varying thickness.

A short flight of steps with a handrail led to the offices. There were windows on either side of the door. And as she climbed the steps, she could see men moving about inside.

Straightening her spine, Becky took a deep breath and opened the door. She was doing this for Sarah. Directly in front of her was a wooden counter. Behind it clerks worked at desks, retrieving or replacing ledgers on shelves that lined the walls. One of the clerks came forward.

'May I help you?'

She moistened her lips. 'I want to speak to Mr Tregenza.'

The clerk regarded her with a pitying smirk. 'Mr Tregenza is a very busy man. He don't come to the counter. If you tell me what you want—'

'What I want, young man,' Becky interrupted, 'is for you to go and tell Mr Tregenza that Mrs Rebecca Hitchens want to speak to him urgent. You do that and you'll save us both time.'

'I can't disturb him unless I know what it's about.'

'What it's about is none of your business,' Becky snapped.

'Now either you fetch him like I ask, or you can tell Mr Tregenza I've gone up his house to speak to his wife. Make up your mind because I haven't got all day.'

His face crimson, the clerk raised his hand. 'No need for that. If you'd said it was important. Just wait, all right? I'm going.' He scurried out. Ignoring the sidelong glances from the other men, Becky saw him knock on a door and open it. She heard low murmuring. He returned to the counter, lifted a flap and jerked his head.

'This way.' He led her in to a passage. After tapping on another door, he opened it, stood back to let her pass, then withdrew.

Horace Tregenza stood behind an imposing desk. His black cutaway coat was unbuttoned to reveal a single-breasted waistcoat of patterned lilac silk and dove-grey trousers. A black cravat was tied neatly over his starched collar. He frowned at her.

'I hope what you have to say is important, Mrs Hitchens. I do not take kindly to threats or unnecessary interruptions.'

Becky tilted her chin a little higher. 'No more do I, which is why I'm here. Because I won't stand by and do nothing while your son-in-law causes trouble and grief to my . . . well, she isn't my daughter, but she's as good as.'

'Before we go any further, Mrs Hitchens, you had better be very sure of your facts. You are making a serious accusation.'

'Mr Tregenza, I wouldn't be here wasting your time and mine if I wasn't sure. You want facts? I'll give you facts all right.'

He indicated a chair. 'Please, sit down.' He lowered himself in to a high-backed armchair of oxblood leather and regarded her through hooded eyes.

'Much obliged, I'm sure. But if it's all the same to you, I'll say my piece and go.'

He gestured for her to continue.

She cleared her throat. 'I daresay you've heard of Henry Govier. He owned Talvan quarry till he was killed in a blasting accident just over two year ago. He left it to his daughter Sarah and she run it now. Sarah lost her mother when she was but five year old. I brought her up and I love her like she was my own. That's why I'm here. To stand up for the girl your son-in-law took his pleasure with, then turned his back on.' She raised a hand to forestall any interruption. 'It happened one month before he married your daughter. One month,' she repeated. 'The following March Sarah gave birth to a son.'

Horace Tregenza tapped his fingers on the polished oak. 'Why did she not have the child adopted?'

Becky looked at him as if he had taken leave of his senses. 'Oh, yes? Who by? How many decent families do *you* know would be willing to take in someone's by-blow? As for the foundling homes . . .' She shuddered. 'Not a week goes by without some terrible story about poor little mites beaten and left to starve while their mothers work all hours to pay for their keep. Maybe you would put a child of yours in such a place, but Sarah wouldn't. She've raised Jory by herself and never asked for a penny from the parish.'

'What is your point, Mrs Hitchens?'

'Philip Ansell have come to Sarah's house twice now and upset her awful. And don't you go thinking she asked him, because she didn't. She don't want nothing to do with him. You're his wife's father. You won't want to see your girl made to look a fool, which she will if he isn't stopped. So I'd take it kindly if you was to warn him against coming anywhere near Talvan cottages. We don't want no more trouble.'

'Exactly what kind of trouble?'

'He've told Sarah he want Jory.'

'Philip is laying claim to this young woman's son?'

Becky nodded, distress and anger making her heart pound. 'I can't b'lieve the nerve of it. Seven year ago Mr Ansell – Mr George Ansell, this was – said Sarah didn't have no proof the child was his son's. Like she was some common slut instead of an innocent girl taken in by the lies and promises of a . . .' She caught herself, sucked in a breath. 'Begging your pardon, Mr Tregenza. But if it was your daughter being threatened and upset . . .'

'Quite.' His frown was thunderous and anger had whitened the skin around his nose and mouth.

'Make him stop, Mr Tregenza. I heard about your daughter's loss, and I'm sorry. But that don't give him the right—'

'No, it doesn't.'

'Thank you for your time.' With a nod, she turned to the door. As she closed it behind her, reaction set in and her knees felt as spongy as bread dough. But she was glad she had come, for Horace Tregenza's expression had left her in no doubt that Philip Ansell was in for a nasty shock.

★   ★   ★

A buzz of conversation filled the coffee room of Simmons' Hotel. The rich aroma of freshly roasted coffee mingled with tobacco smoke curling up from the pipes of two ship's captains seated opposite one another and comparing facilities at various ports. Two men in armchairs were reading newspapers. A group of four discussed business over their coffee.

Kinser Landry had guided his nephew to a table for two in an alcove by one of the windows. Tucked out of the way, it allowed them a measure of privacy for their conversation while enabling them to see who entered and left. Both were halfway through their second cup.

Staring at his uncle, Philip felt excitement curl in his belly. 'Are you serious?'

Landry eyed him with disdain. 'Do I look as if I'm joking?'

'No, but—'

'I want Crago removed. Had he not interfered, Talvan quarry would be mine now. Sarah Govier would never have been able to keep it running on her own. All that top-quality granite . . .' He clasped his hands so tightly, the knuckles cracked. 'It should have been mine.' He shook his fist. 'I was that close. Now I must listen to Trenery's boasting. It's Crago's fault. When I think of the way he spoke to me.' Philip watched rage mottle his uncle's face. 'I offered him a partnership. I was willing to negotiate. And what was his response? No one has ever dared to speak to me like that. It's as well for him that I wasn't armed, or I'd have run him through.' He trembled with barely suppressed rage. 'No one humiliates me and gets away with it. He has to go. As it's unlikely he'll go willingly, he must be removed. Permanently.'

Philip's blossoming excitement made his hands tingle. 'Killed?' he whispered. He wanted to be absolutely certain of his uncle's intention.

This time Landry's disdain was tinged with impatience. 'What else would be permanent?'

Philip's thoughts raced. 'But even if he was gone, why would Sarah sell Talvan to you? She knows the quarry had top-quality granite—'

'Which she cannot shift without wagons. It has already been made perfectly clear to the drivers and companies moving my granite that if they work for her, they will lose my custom. None of them can afford that. At the moment Trenery is supplying two wagons. But his subcontractor is about to realize he'd be better off losing that business. Consider this, Philip. With Crago out of the way, Sarah Govier loses her gallant protector. Do you still want her?'

'Oh, yes.' Hunger burned. He had been her first. And he was almost certain there had been no one else. The thought of her living a chaste life all these years sent another lightning bolt of excitement through him.

'So, we must get rid of Crago. Once he's gone, and with the boy as a lever, she'll be yours for the taking.'

Twenty

Sarah opened the door and saw Zack on the path. He held out a letter.

'From Mister,' he said, touching his cap.

'Thank you.' Seeing no sign of Nessa, she deduced that Zack had already taken her round to Becky's. 'I do hope Nessa enjoys herself. Becky has been looking forward to today.' After a moment's hesitation, she added, 'She can sound sharp, but she's got a heart of gold.'

He gave a brief nod. 'I'm leaving 'em to get on while I skin the rabbits. I'm handy by if they want me.' He continued down the path.

Closing the door, Sarah pulled out a chair and sat down. With Becky busy entertaining, and Jory at Noah's helping to make a workbox for Ivy's birthday, she had been trying to decide what to do with her afternoon. There was a pile of sewing and mending, raspberries to be picked and rhubarb to make rhubarb and ginger jam. Her fingers shook slightly as she opened the envelope and removed the folded sheet.

My dear Sarah, she read. *If you are not otherwise engaged this afternoon, I should enjoy showing you what has been done to the house. Do come. Yours ever, James.*

She read the letter once more, her eyes lingering on *Do come* and *Yours ever.* The fruit and mending could wait. At the sink she washed her hands and splashed cool water over her flushed face. Drying herself, she ran upstairs. Quickly unbuttoning her old calico gown, she tossed it across the foot of her bed, unpinned her hair and brushed it thoroughly, then twisted it in to a neat coil on the nape of her neck.

As she looked through the gowns in her wardrobe, her hand hovered over the green check. She had worn it to the bonfire and had a wonderful evening. But to wear it again so soon – no. Instead she lifted out the emerald glazed cotton that had lent her confidence when she visited Mr Trenery.

She fastened the buttons, impatient with fingers that were suddenly and unaccountably awkward. Shaking out the full skirt over her petti-coats, she crossed the double-layered muslin pelerine over her bodice and tied it behind, then put on her bonnet. Walking to the farm meant that she must wear her half-boots. The ground had dried, but the track was rough and rutted.

In the kitchen she read the letter once more, then folded it back in to the envelope and put it in the dresser drawer for safekeeping. Then she went to the larder and took a fresh jar of blackcurrant jam from the shelf as a housewarming gift. Wrapping it in a folded cloth, she lay it in her small wicker basket before leaving the house.

Tumbling over the garden fence, the wild rose was a mass of pink flowers. Honeysuckle wove through the thorny stems, spilling blue-green leaves and deliciously scented flowers of cream and gold.

After a cold, wet winter that had lasted well into April, spring had blossomed in to a warm summer of blue skies and long, sunny days. Pink ragged robin, lacy white chervil, purple woundwort and blue speedwell added splashes of bright colour to the lush grass growing in ditches and along the base of the stone hedge that separated the track from the small fields. Many of these were neglected and overgrown, their hedges buried beneath tangled brambles.

But further down the hill, at Hammill's farm, haymaking had begun. In one field swathe-turners moved steadily along the rows, turning the crop to dry it. In another the hay had already been gathered in, leaving pale green stubble. Small black cattle, some with young calves beside them, drifted like a tide across a meadow. A field of barley rippled in the breeze. Ripening wheat had begun to turn deep gold.

Elm and beech trees offered welcome shade on the approach to the house. As she opened the gate, he emerged from the front door. He must have been watching for her.

'I am so happy to see you.' His gaze was warm and his smile curled around her heart.

'And I you.' It was the truth, despite the painful and disturbing echoing of Philip's words in her head. *Are you absolutely certain James Crago wants you? Is his real interest in Jory?*

Taking her hand, he raised it to his lips and her heart turned over. She forced a smile, pushing unsettling thoughts aside for later. 'Besides, how could I resist such an invitation? Ivy talks of little else.'

Brief bewilderment crossed his features. 'But Mrs Triggs has not seen it.'

Sarah felt herself relax and her smile grow more natural and spontaneous as she waved aside his objection. 'A mere detail. Poor Noah has been quizzed unmercifully about everything you have done here. It has given Ivy enormous pleasure to regale Becky and me with everything she has learned.'

'Oh dear. Will reality measure up? Or will it fall dismally short?' He stood back so that she could enter. 'You decide.'

Stepping inside the spacious hall, she saw a wide, curving staircase painted white, the banister rail shining with varnish that emphasized the rich colour and grain of the wood. Light spilled in through a tall window on the half-landing. 'Oh, it's beautiful!' She clasped the twisted wicker handle of her basket in both hands as she gazed around at gleaming woodwork and sage-green walls.

He showed her a salmon-pink drawing room and a small sitting room painted sea green, then opened a door at the end of a short passage beneath the staircase.

'This is the kitchen. Somewhat overcrowded at the moment.' He indicated the camp bed in the corner and the chest that she assumed contained his clothes. 'But not for much longer.'

Seeing the range, she was instantly captivated. 'Oh! Ivy told us about this.'

'I imagine half the town has heard about it,' his mouth quirked wryly.

She placed her basket on the table. 'Is it easy to use?' She was drawn forward, fascinated by the cooking range of black iron and polished brass.

'Very.' Bending, he lifted a latch and opened a door to reveal a square box containing two removable shelves. 'The oven.' He closed it again. 'These small doors –' he demonstrated, '– can be closed to keep the fire in overnight. The ash pan underneath may be lifted out for ease of emptying. The rings in the hotplate over the fire are removable. If one or more of them is lifted out, the kettle or pan sits directly over the flames and will boil quickly. Left in place they allow a gentle simmer, or can be used to heat a smoothing iron.'

'Goodness.' Thinking of her own open hearth, the hook in the chimney for the big black kettle, the iron baking dome and the triangular brandis she placed over the embers to stand saucepans on, Sarah felt envious.

'I have requested a pattern from the manufacturer in Camborne.'

'You're going to make them?'

'Mr Dunstan will. The blacksmith down in the Praze?'

She nodded. 'I know of him. Jeb buys all the quarry borers from him.'

'Sam Venner has already placed an order. He's my first customer.'

She shook her head, laughing. 'You are going to cause such trouble.'

'I am?'

'When Ivy finds out Alice Venner is having one, Noah won't get a moment's peace.'

As he grinned at her from beneath dark brows, she felt her breath catch. 'Ah, you have seen through my cunning plan.' He cleared his throat, suddenly diffident. 'Can I offer you a drink? Nessa made some nettle beer. It is very refreshing.'

'Thank you.' Reaching into the basket, she took out the jam. 'I – a small housewarming gift. It's blackcurrant.'

He lifted the jar to the light. 'What a beautiful colour. Thank you. Please, sit down. Will you take off your bonnet? While you keep it on you look poised to leave. You do not have to hurry back, do you?'

'No.' Feeling her face grown warm, she loosened the bow and removed her hat, laying it aside on the table while he took glasses from the dresser and crossed to the larder.

'What I have seen is very impressive,' she said, thinking of him alone here each evening, perhaps walking through the house, assessing what progress had been made, what still remained to be done, then returning here to sleep. Her gaze was drawn to the narrow camp bed and the dark grey blankets neatly folded down and tucked in.

He set down the glasses, now half full of a dark, sparkling liquid, and took the chair opposite. He lifted one glass, raising it slightly. 'Your very good health.'

'And yours.' She sipped the drink. It tasted astringent and herby. 'That's delicious.' She shouldn't have been surprised: Nessa would be familiar with old country recipes. She swallowed some more, enjoying its thirst-quenching bite.

Swallowing deeply, Crago lowered his glass, turning it on the table. His eyes met hers. 'I'm so glad you came.' He stood up. 'Would you like to see the rest?' There was a hint of irony in his smile. 'Mrs Triggs will never forgive you if you decline.'

Sarah laughed. 'How well you know her.' She followed him in to the hall and up the staircase.

'The water damage up here meant that every wall and ceiling had to be re-plastered,' he said over his shoulder. 'All the doors and windows are opened each morning to allow fresh air to blow through. This long spell of dry weather has really helped.' On the main landing he indicated a large, empty room. She looked in. 'You may notice,' he added, 'that all the rooms up here have the same soft distemper finish.'

Acutely sensitive to every nuance in his voice and manner, Sarah detected tension and a diffidence that she didn't understand. She tried to think of something to say as he led the way across the landing. 'It's a lovely colour and would give the impression of sunshine even on a dull day.'

He paused in the doorway. 'That was my intention, though it is not intended to be permanent. But I wanted the bare plaster covered until . . . while . . .' he stumbled to a halt. 'People have definite views regarding colour. Do you find that? I'm sure you have preferences.'

'I like green,' she admitted. 'The sage downstairs is lovely.'

'Just green? There must be others that you like?'

She thought for a moment. 'I read recently that it is now considered fashionable for the public rooms in a house, like a drawing room, to be painted a strong red, like crimson. I'm sure it must look very striking. But for a small sitting room or – or a bedroom – softer shades would be more restful. Perhaps pearl, or lilac or peach-blossom pink. Though,' she added quickly, 'it would also depend on the size of the room and the amount of light it received.'

'Not blue?'

'If it was south-facing and sunny, then possibly. But blues can look very cold.'

Shaking his head gently, he smiled. 'I knew I was right to ask you. I have little experience in these matters.'

'I am no expert,' she said quickly. 'But Mr Rundell in Lower Street has a selection of boards in his shop window painted to show the different colours he stocks. I always look in when I pass.' She shrugged. 'My father believed in the merits of plain white lime-wash.'

'You have not been tempted to try a colour?'

'I haven't had the time to think about it. Or the money.'

'Of course you haven't. That was foolish and insensitive. I beg your pardon.'

'Don't. I didn't – I shouldn't have – Oh!' She had followed him in to a large sunny room. 'This is lovely. What a pretty fireplace.' Glazed tiles patterned in sapphire, magenta and white framed the decorative black arch. The same tiles formed a hearth bordered by barley-stick twisted wrought iron. Then she noticed the wardrobe on the inside wall, complete but for the doors. 'Noah's work?'

He nodded. 'He has just completed a matching bedstead. But we moved that next door to allow him space to work.' He crossed to the window and looked out before turning to face her. Was he waiting for her to say something?

'The house is beautiful, James.'

'I'm glad you like it.' He beckoned. 'Come and see the view.'

Reaching his side, she looked out of the tall window and felt her heart soar. Spread out below her was a panorama of small farms and densely wooded valleys. Houses packed the hillsides leading down to the river, which curved in a glistening ribbon past small quays and boatyards to the blue waters of Falmouth harbour.

Their arms brushed. Then his fingers curled lightly around hers. Her heart leaped at his touch. Her skin felt incredibly sensitive, and inside her everything shimmered.

'Stunning, isn't it?' he said softly, then turned her towards him. 'I am truly glad you came, as I had an additional reason for wanting to see you.'

She waited, acutely aware of her high colour, her eyes downcast. Her physical reaction each time he touched her was startling and profound. She found it unsettling, yet yearned for more. Could he tell? What was it that he wanted?

Twenty-One

'I should like to engage an attorney to fight Ansell's claim to Jory.'

Her head flew up. Her throat dried. 'An attorney?' She froze, suddenly terrified. *No. Don't let Philip be right.* 'Why? Why would you do that?' She held his gaze, watched the groove between his brows deepen as he frowned, knew his expression reflected her own. He slid his hands lightly up her arms until they rested on her shoulders.

'What is it? What's wrong, Sarah?'

'Do you remember what you said to me? *No pretence, not between us.*'

His eyes searched hers. 'Of course I remember.'

'Did you mean it?'

Anger narrowed his eyes. 'I'm not in the habit . . .' He stopped, shook his head. When he spoke, it was with quiet sincerity. 'Yes, I meant it. I meant it with all my heart. What has happened that you need to ask?'

She tried to wet her lips but her mouth was dust-dry.

His fingers tightened. 'He came back?'

She nodded. Her voice sounded clogged. 'I was in the garden. I would not allow him through the gate.'

'What happened?'

'He . . . he said . . .' She shuddered, recalling the spite-tipped darts he had hurled at her. 'He said your interest was not in me, but in my son. You want Jory because it is unlikely . . . because you have no family of your own.'

Dropping his hands, he turned away and the room crackled with the dark energy of his anger. He paced from one side to the other, drove a hand through his hair, then whirled round to face her.

'I suppose I must be grateful,' he snarled, 'that he did not accuse me of having an unnatural interest in the boy.'

She gasped as if he had hit her, a hand flying to her mouth.

His face drained of both fury and colour. 'Sarah, forgive me. I should never have . . . I spoke in haste and in anger. But I cannot believe—' A harsh laugh ripped from his throat. 'Yes, I can. He is preying on your worst fears. Because I have the face of a devil, it follows that I must also have the heart of one.'

'No!' Her denial was instant and instinctive. 'You would never harm him, I know that. That is not my fear. But—'

'Ah, yes. The *but*.' Gripping her shoulders, he looked in to her eyes. Anger still shimmered behind the desperation that she believe him, trust him. 'I met Jory because he came to the farm with Noah. Then he began to look for me because he enjoyed helping with Balal. He sought *me* out, Sarah. Not the reverse.'

With the realization of how her accusation must have wounded him, her skin grew damp with anguish and shame. 'I'm so sorry,' she whispered. Yet surely he must understand her need to know the truth?

'Don't.' His voice was rough with suppressed emotion. 'I want no apology. Because I *have* deliberately taken time to get to know him. If Jory did not like or trust me, it was unlikely that you would either. I'm truly fond of the boy. But he will grow up and one day he will leave to make his own life. That is as it should be. Meanwhile, while he is young, I will do everything in my power to ensure your happiness and peace of mind.'

'Why, James? Why would you do that for me?'

She saw his throat work as he swallowed; saw his tongue snake across his lips. 'Because – because Jory's well-being is integral to your happiness.' He shrugged, perspiration gleaming on his forehead and upper lip.

'Oh, James,' she whispered, touched and disappointed. She had hoped for more. Hoped that maybe his feelings matched her own.

'Nor,' he added, 'can I blame you for your suspicions. You have little reason to trust men. Both Ansell and his father behaved shamefully, leaving you to bear the disgrace alone. Then Landry conspired with your ganger to cheat you. Now Ansell is once more attempting to invade your life.'

He drew her hand through his arm. 'Come, we will return to the kitchen. I have something to tell you, and I think you would welcome some tea.'

She glanced up, grateful. 'Indeed I would.'

Seating her at the table, he moved about the kitchen.

'This feels very strange,' she said.

'Being waited on? Or the fact that I know my way around a kitchen?'

'Both.'

He smiled. 'During my years in India I learned to fend for myself. It was either that or starve.'

'But – I thought officers had servants.'

He nodded. 'I did when we were in camp. However, I spent a lot of time on reconnaissance, or behind enemy lines. Sometimes I was alone. On other occasions there might be two or three of us. We travelled light to enable us to move quickly and became adept at foraging and cooking for ourselves.' He poured milk in to the blue-and-white cups, added tea from the pot, then took the chair opposite.

Steadying her cup with both hands, Sarah sipped slowly.

His gaze met hers and the tender concern that she saw made her eyes sting. 'Better?'

'Oh, yes.' The tea was hot, strong and reviving. She raised the cup again, using it to mask her face while she struggled to control emotions that in recent weeks had become increasingly erratic.

She had grown used to dealing with difficulties and challenges, shouldering responsibility. Yes, Becky, her dearest friend, was always available to offer comfort and support. But when it came to decisions, she made them alone.

So much had happened in the past few months to undermine her confidence and self-belief, and neither were now very strong.

With no idea of the changes she would set in motion, she had marched in to the valley and demanded James Crago's help. Did she regret it? No. How could she? But such upheaval was inevitably accompanied by doubt and uncertainty.

He had taken some of that burden from her. On one hand, the relief was wonderful. But on the other, all her instincts urged her to trust him. But she had trusted Philip. She had been young then. Young, naïve and, she realized now, as much in love with the idea of love as with the man himself. She had never really known Philip. He had revealed only as much as he wished her to see.

James was different. He understood so much, often without her having to explain. She was drawn to him: an attraction so potent that it sometimes frightened her. She had not known herself capable of such powerful or conflicting emotions. She knew that she loved him. Yet still she feared committing herself. Terrified that if she did, and he rejected her, she would not have the strength or the will to recover. But if she did not take that leap of faith, if she held back through fear, she did not deserve to love and be loved.

'You . . .' her voice cracked. She tried again, 'You said you had something to tell me?'

He nodded. 'I hope you will not take this amiss, but I have consulted my attorney regarding Ansell's claim on Jory.' He paused, giving her time to absorb what he had said. 'I thought you would wish . . . that it might help you to know the legal position.'

'You did that for me?' Cup rattled on saucer as Sarah set them down.

'It was no trouble,' he said simply. 'I was in town anyway and it took but a few minutes.'

She knew from her own experience following her father's death that he was making light of it. Attorneys were rarely so swiftly or easily reached. Meetings usually required an appointment that might be changed without notice. She leaned forward, apprehensive as she studied his face. 'What did he say?' As he smiled, hope flared bright as a flame.

'He quoted a clause in the New Poor Law. It states that all illegitimate children born after the act was passed in 1834 are the sole responsibility of their mothers until they reach the age of sixteen.' Reaching across the table, he covered her hand with his own. 'Ansell has no legal claim on Jory, Sarah.'

She turned her hand, her fingers gripping his tightly as she swallowed. 'Jory was born in March of that year. Would the act have been law by then?' *Please, please let it be so.* Seeing the answer in his eyes, her own grew hot and gritty. Bitterly disappointed, she tried to smile. 'Thank you so much for trying, James. I really appreciate . . .' Her throat closed and she could not go on.

'I'm so sorry, Sarah. I hoped this might have put an end to it. But if you will allow me, I want to help.'

'And do *what*?' she cried in anguish.

'I'm not sure yet. But know this,' he held her hand between his, 'You are not alone. We will fight this together. Now I will walk you back.'

She would have been happy with that alone. But after closing the gate, he drew her arm through his. Her heart quickened.

'This is a public road,' she murmured in case he might have forgotten.

He looked down at her, his eyes shaded by the brim of his hat, his voice gentle. 'And your point is?'

The farm had been his grandfather's. He had grown up here. Of course he knew. 'Only that if we are seen . . .'

He stopped then, facing her so that her arm fell from his. 'It was not my intention to embarrass you.' She knew he meant it, knew too that his stiffness masked deeper hurt.

'No, you misunderstand! My concern was not for myself. God knows it is too late for my reputation. It was for you. For what might be inferred should we be observed arm in arm.'

'Ah.' His reserve dissolved. 'In that case,' he reached for her hand and tucked it beneath his elbow once more, 'If you are seen to have a . . .' he hesitated, 'protection . . .' as she flinched, masking it with a cough, he pressed her hand, oblivious to the effect or implication of his chosen word, 'you are less likely to suffer unwelcome attention.'

Was that how he saw himself? Her *protector*? Neither stupid nor naïve, she knew well enough what the term signified. And yet . . .

She had believed, *hoped*, that what had begun as a business arrangement and evolved into friendship had changed, deepened. It had seemed to her that she was being courted. But in referring to himself as her protector, he put a very different interpretation on their relationship.

Was it her fault or his that she had expected more, hoped for more? How could she, usually so wary in such matters, have been so mistaken? But was she?

Despite knowing her past, he treated her with courtesy and respect. He had jumped through the flames with her. And after securing her approval, agreed to Jory's plea to be his pa. He had invited her to Jericho Farm to show her the changes and improvements he had made. And though he had kissed her, he had not pressed for more. He could have. The touch of his hands, the pressure of his mouth on hers, had stirred her deeply. He must have known, yet he had been the one to step back.

She knew that he was attracted to her, but that was all she could be certain of. He kept his deepest feelings hidden, leaving her adrift, confused and out of her depth. An ache began to throb at the base of her skull.

She loved him. But she dared not let him see, fearful of embarrassing him or herself by revealing emotions he might not share, might not want.

'Sarah?'

She started, her heart clenching at the tenderness in his voice.

'You are very quiet. Is something wrong?'

Grateful that the brim of her bonnet hid her face, she took a moment to gather herself, then turned and smiled up at him. For both their sakes she must lie. 'No, not at all. I was just thinking about the house. How sad and neglected it looked for all those years. But you have worked a miracle. You must be so pleased with what you have achieved.'

'I am. But it would not have been possible without Jack, Sam, Noah and the others.'

They had reached the crossroads and were within sight of her cottage. He stopped and turned to her, taking her free hand in his. 'Will you forgive me if I leave you here?'

'Of course.' She hid disappointment behind another brilliant smile. 'I really enjoyed seeing everything you've done.'

'It was my pleasure. I'll be away for a couple of days, but I hope to see you when I get back.' His gaze held hers as he raised her hand, his lips brushing her knuckles. At the warmth in his eyes, longing surged through her like a breaking wave and she was helpless against it.

'I should like that.'

He dropped her hand and backed away. 'Goodbye, Sarah.'

'Goodbye, James.' Despite her confusion, she had found comfort and reassurance in his nearness. Alone again she started towards her cottage, but she could not resist glancing over her shoulder. He had turned to watch her. She waved and felt her heart lift as he raised his hand in reply. Then he walked on and disappeared down the track.

Later that evening, with a reluctant Jory at last in bed, Sarah sat outside in the evening sunshine with Becky, a pile of mending on the bench between them.

'A very nice afternoon.' Becky sighed contentedly. 'I thought it would've been harder than what it was. First going off it felt a bit strange, you know, having to—' she made exaggerated gestures of pointing and mixing. 'But she's some quick, dear of her. 'T'wasn't long afore we was laughing fit to split our stays.'

Sarah looked up from the patch she was sewing on to the ripped knee of Jory's trousers. 'I'm so glad.'

'So what's it like, then, the house?'

Sarah's hands stilled. 'Beautiful. The hall and staircase are sage and white. The drawing room is a lovely salmon-pink, and there is a small west-facing sitting room painted sea green. It looks very restful.'

'What about upstairs? Show you that, did he?'

Sarah nodded. 'It's all been re-plastered.'

'Come on, then,' Becky encouraged. 'What about the colours?'

'Primrose distemper.'

'What, the same all through?'

Sarah nodded. 'But it's only temporary.'

'Why have he gone to all that trouble if he's going to change it?'

Sarah shrugged. 'Perhaps just to get it finished.' She set another couple of stitches and then looked up once more, remembering her pleasure at being asked and her uncertainty about how she should respond. 'He asked me which colours I liked.'

Becky's eyes widened. 'He did? Well, now.'

'He even went to the trouble . . .' Sarah's voice wobbled and she drew a breath to try and steady it.

'What, bird? What's wrong?'

Sarah shook her head. 'I'm all right. It's just . . . Becky, he consulted his attorney to find out if Philip really could take Jory away.'

'He did? Well, bless his dear heart for that. What did this here lawyer say?'

'That there is now a law making bastard children the sole responsibility of their mothers until they reach sixteen years of age.'

Relief smoothed the anxiety from Becky's features as she pressed one hand to her pillowy bosom. 'Thank the Lord for that. I wasn't going to say nothing, bird. You been worried enough and I didn't want to go making it worse. But ever since you told me what Philip Ansell threatened, I been fretting something awful. Still, 'tis over now—'

'No, Becky, it isn't.' Sarah shook her head, trying to swallow the painful stiffness in her throat.

'What d'you mean? You just said—'

'The law came into force *after* Jory was born.' Sarah dragged in a breath, forcing out the words. 'If Philip tries to take him, legally I cannot prevent it.'

Twenty-Two

Wearing soft kid slippers that made no sound on the tiled floor of the passage, Margaret Ansell paused outside the kitchen door. The servants would be talking about her, it was foolish to expect otherwise. In her head she could hear their voices: scornful, mocking, condemning a wife unable to fulfil the most basic duty of giving her husband the son he so desperately wanted. She burned with shame and a searing sense of inadequacy. It *wasn't* her fault. It *must be* her fault.

She paused, not to eavesdrop, but to steel herself to face the pity she knew they felt for her.

She did not understand *why*. She had birthed her two daughters without any problems. Why could she not carry a son to term? Losing the first had been a terrible shock. Surely there should have been some warning, some sense of things not right? But she could remember nothing that might have prepared her.

Shaken, bewildered, grieving, she had trusted the doctor's assurance that such things happened, sometimes for a reason, sometimes for no reason at all. And next time all would be well.

Only it wasn't. Not then, and not since. Now she wondered if it ever would be. Could the birth of a live son erase the memory of failure? Of sadness that had darkened to devastating grief? Of the three tiny boys, all perfect save that they had never drawn breath; their lives over before they had even begun. Of the fear that trailed her like a shadow.

Part of her wanted – needed – to keep trying. Philip had taken her miscarriages badly, drinking heavily and absenting himself sometimes for days. At a time when she most needed comfort and reassurance, he spent ever longer out of the house. Soon his behaviour would surely attract notice. There would be talk, it was only a matter of time. Perhaps it had already begun.

She had never objected to admiring comments concerning her gowns and hairstyle, whether made to her face or whispered behind her back. She took pride in being among the first to appear in the latest fashions. But to be the subject of gossip about her marriage or her childbearing ability, that would be intolerable.

She needed to build up her strength as quickly as she could. Indeed, she had come downstairs as much for the exercise as to ask Mrs Carne, her cook-housekeeper, to whip up a nourishing cup of hot milk with egg yolk and brandy.

The doctor's words echoed in her head: no pregnancy for at least a year. Any sooner and the child was not all she risked. She would be gambling with her life, the odds against her.

The doctor did not understand. How could he? If she did not produce the son her husband wanted, what kind of life could she expect? Already Philip regarded her with bitterness and impatience. That would only get worse.

She had known when they married that he did not love her. At the time it had not mattered; she had wanted him. And with the combined efforts of her father and his, she had secured him, convinced that once she had presented him with a family, his fondness would ripen in to something deeper.

He had acquired a wife at ease in polite society and an expert in home management, a wife he could rely on to support him, a wife he could be proud of. She, diligently hiding her relief at escaping the threat of spinsterhood, had netted the envy of her acquaintance and a handsome husband who was the heir to a prosperous business.

If she could only give him a son, these past two years might be put behind them. Once more she would hold her head high, having fulfilled her duty as wife and mother. People would greet her with admiration instead of pity. Philip would look at her with warmth instead of cold resentment. She would be secure: her position in her family and in society unassailable. That surely was worth any risk.

Lifting her head, widening her mouth in a smile, she grasped the doorknob. Then the raucous voice of Lizzie the laundry girl reached her.

'He is, I tell you. They kept it quiet these seven years. Don't ask me how, but 'tis all abroad now.'

'Mr Philip the father of Sarah Govier's boy? I don't believe it.'

'You please yourself. But 'tis true as I'm stood here.'

Head swimming, knees suddenly weak, Margaret gripped the doorframe. Philip had fathered a child – *a boy* – with another woman? He couldn't have, wouldn't have. She refused to believe it. But as the words sank deeper, weighty as rocks, she felt as fragile as a glass bubble. She dared not move, afraid that she would shatter.

'Who says?' Mrs Carne demanded. 'Not Sarah. I remember when she was expecting, people was asking then who the father was. But she never said. Never let on after the boy was born, neither.'

'Well, 'tis all over town now,' Lizzie was impatient. 'They're saying he want to take the boy from her.'

'Never! What do he want to do that for?'

'Why d'you think? Dear life, Mrs Carne, you're some slow today.'

'That's enough of your cheek, my girl. Any more lip from you and you'll feel the flat of my hand.'

'No need for that. I didn't mean nothing by it. But 'tis plain as day what he want. He want a son. And it don't look like he's going to get one with Missus.'

''Tis early days yet. She just need time and a bit of looking after. Anyhow, I can't see Sarah letting the boy go, not without a fight. Dear life, there'll be some gossip, then. It don't bear thinking about.'

'I tell 'ee what, Mrs Carne. If Missus don't know, 't'will be some awful shock for her.'

'*Shock?* A scandal is what it is,' Mrs Carne said. 'Poor Miss Margaret, as if she haven't been through enough. I dunno what Mr Philip is thinking of. Just say he got the boy, what's he going to do with him? Bring him here? Like I say, he must be off his head.' She clicked her tongue. ''Tween you and me, I always thought Miss Margaret deserved better. But she was set on having him. And too used to getting whatever she wanted. Still, she've surely paid for it, the dear of her.'

Supporting herself with one hand, Margaret pressed the other to her breastbone, as if pressure might ease the knifing pain beneath. Her heartbeat pounded in her ears and the flash of heat that had beaded her forehead, neck and upper lip with perspiration ebbed away, leaving her chilled. Her teeth chattered as shivers scuttled like spiders over her skin. Edging away from the door, she crept back up the stairs on legs that trembled.

In the sanctuary of her room she closed her eyes and leaned against the door. The discomforts of pregnancy, even the agony of delivery, had paled in comparison to her anguished despair as, three times, a tiny, lifeless body had been wrapped in a towel and hastily removed from the room. She never saw them again, had no idea what had become of them. No one would tell her. Her mother simply wept. Dr Prout had told her to put it behind her. And Philip – Philip had left her in no doubt that he blamed her.

Mired in grief, she had been too wretched to argue or to question his certainty that it was her fault. Only now did she understand.

She had been willing to risk her life to give him a son. *He already had one.* As dark spots danced before her eyes and perspiration broke out afresh, she stumbled across to the bed and curled up on her side. All this time he had known, and never told her. Over the past two years she had cried an ocean of tears. But now though her eyes burned, they remained dry. She had done with weeping.

'Don't bother, I know the way.' Horace Tregenza's grim tones forbade argument.

Hearing his father-in-law's voice, Philip looked up from the half-written letter as his office door opened and Tregenza strode in. Ernest Scoble followed in his wake, responding to Tregenza's gesture of dismissal with a brief bow and discreet withdrawal.

His mind racing, Philip rose to his feet as the door closed on his chief clerk. 'Good morning, Sir. This is an unexpected—'

'Does he listen?' Tregenza demanded, removing his hat and setting it on the corner of Philip's desk.

'I beg your p—?' Philip floundered.

'Your clerk,' Tregenza said impatiently. 'Does he listen at the door?'

'Certainly not,' Philip snapped, and immediately regretted his tone. His father-in-law had visited the office only a handful of times, and never without warning. Something had happened to bring him here. He braced himself. 'Scoble has been with this company for—'

'Decades,' Tregenza interrupted. 'He probably knows more about your customers than you do.' Waving aside Philip's protest before it could be uttered, he pulled the visitor's chair forward and sat down. Crossing his legs, he rested his elbows on the chair arms and steepled his fingers.

'Do you recall my warning to you?' he enquired pleasantly. 'My request for discretion? My insistence that Margaret was not to be upset?'

His throat suddenly dry, Philip heard himself swallow and feared Tregenza had heard it, too. He moistened his lips. 'Of course.'

'Then what in the name of all that's holy do you think you're doing?'

'What . . .? I don't underst—'

'Making a fool of yourself over the Govier girl.'

The words rocked him like blows. How did Tregenza know? Who had told him? How did *they* know? 'I–I–' he stammered.

'How did I find out? A Mrs Rebecca Hitchens, who described herself as this young woman's adoptive mother, invaded my office, afire with indignation, declaring that Sarah Govier has not invited your attentions and certainly does not wish to receive them. This irate little person informed me that neither she nor Miss Govier has any desire to cause my daughter embarrassment. Can you imagine my feelings, Philip? No, I don't think you can.' His tone was cold and hard. 'Then she announced that, as threats to inform the magistrate have not stopped you turning up where you are not wanted, I must do so. She insists upon it.'

Philip took refuge in bluster. 'She *what*?' He threw up his hands. 'This is ridiculous.'

'What is? That Miss Govier has no desire for your company? Or that her friend found it necessary to come to me and ask – no, demand – that I warn you off?'

Horrified, helpless, Philip stared at his father-in-law. Fear blanked his mind and gripped his throat in a stranglehold as he struggled for words. But Tregenza hadn't finished.

'That alone would be irritation enough, but I fear there is more. According to Mrs Hitchens, you seduced Miss Govier, got her pregnant, then abandoned her.'

'I . . . It wasn't . . . She . . .' Philip croaked.

Tregenza raised a hand to silence him. 'Did you know this young woman was carrying your child when you married Margaret?'

'No! Certainly not!' Perspiration soaked the underarms of his shirt, the waistband of his trousers. It wasn't fair. Indignation bubbled up, boiled over. 'Just because Miss Govier and her meddling friend make wild claims, it does not mean they are true.' He gestured carelessly. 'Men in my position are all too often a target for gossip and rumour.'

'Is that so?' Tregenza's tone was dry as dust. 'Yet I have to ask myself what motive Miss Govier would have for lying? What could she hope to achieve?'

'It's obvious,' Philip sneered. 'Money.'

'But she has never asked for any. According to Mrs Hitchens, Miss Govier has supported herself and her son on her income from Talvan quarry.'

'Revenge, then!' Philip cried in desperation.

'For what?' Tregenza was relentless.

'A woman slighted—'

'Waits seven years before deciding to cause you trouble?' Tregenza shook his head. 'Miss Govier wants nothing from you but your absence. Indeed, Mrs Hitchens' stated reason for visiting me was to request my help in keeping you as far as possible from Talvan quarry and cottages.'

Philip sweated beneath Tregenza's contemptuous gaze. Interfering old busybody! How dare she involve Tregenza? Maybe he had misread Sarah, but seven years ago she had been willing enough. Who could blame him for believing the interest was still there? As for the old besom talking about sparing Margaret – damned impertinence! His wife was no one else's business.

'So,' Tregenza said, 'I must conclude that Mrs Hitchens was telling the truth. That in the months before your marriage to my daughter you were involved with this young woman.'

'It was nothing serious, a mere fling,' Philip was dismissive. 'One afternoon. The sort of dalliance most young men enjoy before settling down to blameless married life.'

'Indeed.' Tregenza's tone was cool. 'So when *did* you learn of her pregnancy?'

Philip looked directly in to his father-in-law's eyes. If he trod carefully, he might yet extricate himself with no harm done. After all his father-in-law's marital record was hardly spotless. In truth what had happened *before* his marriage to Margaret was none of Tregenza's business. His confidence reasserted itself. He would relate events exactly as they had happened, for they had the benefit of being true.

'After Margaret and I returned from our wedding trip,' he said. 'My father told me that during our absence he had received a visit from Henry Govier, who claimed that his daughter was pregnant by me.'

Tregenza's brows lifted slightly, but he remained silent.

'Naturally my father rejected the accusation. Quite correctly he pointed out to Mr Govier that his daughter had no proof that the child was mine. That was the last we heard of it.' A drop of sweat slid, tickling, down his temple. His collar felt as tight as a noose.

Trengenza's face was completely unreadable. 'So you never acknowledged the child?'

Philip shook his head. 'Certainly not. Why would I? As I said—'

'Yes,' Tregenza interrupted. 'I heard what you said.'

'In any case,' Philip continued, 'regardless of any — liaisons — I might have enjoyed while a bachelor, after my marriage my wife's well-being was my first concern.'

'Thoughtful of you.' Tregenza's voice carried no inflection, yet there was something in his eyes that made the words sting like a whiplash.

Philip felt hot colour climb his throat. He did not have to put up with this. Nor would he. 'I believe so,' he snapped. 'Were it not for our recent tragic loss and the others of recent years, I would not be in the position of having to relinquish my marital rights in order to protect my wife's health.'

'So this recent pursuit of Miss Govier . . .?'

'I was simply following your advice.'

'I see.' Tregenza rose to his feet and picked up his hat. 'May I suggest you look elsewhere? For someone more amenable? Good day to you.'

As the door closed behind him, Philip blew out a shaky breath. Stretching his neck, he ran a finger between his damp collar and the moist skin of his throat. He had almost lost his temper, but who could blame him? Still, all things considered, he had acquitted himself well. He needed a drink.

Taking his hat from the peg, he walked briskly down the passage towards the open front door.

'Later,' he said as the chief clerk tried to stop him. 'I have business in town.'

As he walked up the street heading for Simmons' Hotel, he recognized Sarah's child perched on a cart standing outside Hocking's timber warehouse. Curiosity made him pause. A horse whinnied further down the street and the boy looked round.

My son. Surely the boy would remember him? He lifted his hand. Eyes widening in terror, Jory started to scramble down off the cart. An older man in working clothes emerged from the warehouse, followed by two lads carrying several broad planks.

Waving the boy back on to the seat, the man clambered up

beside him. After checking that the boys had loaded the planks and secured the tailgate, he picked up the reins and clicked his tongue at the horse. Watching the cart pull away, Philip followed up the street. He saw the boy glance nervously over his shoulder, then quickly turn his back. A moment later they had rounded the corner and were out of sight.

Angry, bitter and seething with resentment, Philip crossed to the hotel. *What in God's name had Sarah said to the boy?*

Twenty-Three

Crago turned the team of four on to the track leading to the farm.

'Be glad to get down, I will,' Zack muttered beside him. 'This seat have got harder by the mile. My backside have gone to sleep.'

'I lost all feeling at Devoran,' Crago replied. 'Still, we've made good time and the horses have settled well.'

'I got to say I had me doubts,' Zack admitted. 'Two pair from two different farms.' He shook his head. 'But they're all right. Working together a treat. Good job, too. What you going to do about the wagon? 'Tis never strong enough like he is, not for they big stones. Take'n down to one of the blacksmiths in town, will you?'

Crago shook his head. 'It's needed at once and Dunstans are too busy. I know there are other forges but I've had no dealings with them. Besides, if they work for Landry . . .' He shook his head again. 'I won't risk delay or sabotage. I'll take it to Talvan tomorrow. Jeb Mundy has a good blacksmith working in the quarry. We can use Trenery's light wagon to fetch iron girders, rivets and so on. It should be ready to haul stone within a few days.'

'And Landry none the wiser,' Zack cackled. 'I like it.'

They rumbled on a bit further. Crago felt Zack's gaze.

'So what's the rest of it, then? C'mon, boy,' he said as Crago glanced at him. 'I wasn't born yesterday. Even though Landry have scared off the other drivers, you still had one of Mr Trenery's heavy wagons. Now you got this one. What you haven't got – leastways not yet – is a quarry producing enough stone to keep 'em both busy full time. So what's on?'

Crago smiled. 'Not just a pretty face, are you?'

'Don't need no buttering up, neither,' Zack retorted.

'All right.' Though he had thought long and hard and was sure he had made the right decision, Crago took a deep breath. 'I'm going to work the farm. That's why I need the horses.'

Zack puckered his lips, air hissing through his teeth. 'Be some job, that will. They hedges haven't been cut back since—'

'I know. So I'm going to need help. Someone who will manage

the woods and trim the hedges while I tackle the ploughing. By this time next year I want to have crops planted. Potatoes and turnips, maybe wheat and oats.'

'Best start with a few pigs,' Zack said. 'They'll turn the ground over lovely. If I can get part of the woods fenced off by autumn, they can forage for acorns.'

As Crago stared at him, Zack raised his eyebrows. 'What? You said you need help. And Nessa like it here. So I'm minded to stay.'

'I'm grateful, Zack.'

'Don't need no thanks.'

'Well, you've got them anyway. If you'd refused—'

'You'd've been right in the dung heap.' His grin faded. 'What about the mill?'

'I've got a buyer.'

'Told anyone?' They both knew whom he meant.

'Not yet.' Thinking of the paper in his pocket, Crago's doubts flooded back. What had possessed him?

'What you waiting for?' Zack raised his hand, palm out. 'None of my business.'

Drawing the team to a halt in the centre of the yard, Crago jumped down from the wooden bench seat, flexing his back and shoulders to ease the stiffness. He trusted his charcoal burner as much as he trusted anyone. But not even to Zack could he admit his mouth-drying, gut-churning fear. He knew Sarah liked him, knew she trusted him: with both her confidences and her child. But could she love him?

He started unbuckling the straps fastening the long shafts to the harness. He knew he should talk to her, but he didn't know how. For as long as he could remember his world had been one of *doing*. The early death of his parents, a reclusive grandfather, boarding school and then the army, had taught him that survival lay in action. He had buried his emotions deep, safely out of the way.

Anjuli had opened a lock rusty from disuse, awakened tenderness and a desire to protect. He had imagined that was love. He knew differently now. He felt all that for Sarah, but there was more. So much more.

She reached him, touched him in ways that were new and alien. And despite fluency in several languages, he could not find the words to express what he felt.

In the past he had responded to desire in the same way that he reacted to hunger or thirst, an appetite to be satisfied then forgotten until the next time. But she occupied his thoughts every waking moment and haunted his dreams when he slept.

The day she had come to the valley, anger firing her cheeks, her candour and demands had first startled and then amused him. Only as he grew to know her better had he realized the true depth of her courage.

Refusing to hide, she had faced the town gossips. She had rejected being bullied into selling her quarry; refused to be beaten by a cheating ganger. And despite Ansell's betrayal and the grief her situation had cost her, she refused to be ashamed of her son.

Driven by a powerful need to keep her safe, he knew himself capable of killing anyone who harmed her. The thought gave him no pleasure. It was a fact, not a source of pride.

He wanted to tell her what she meant to him, about his hopes for the future, a future he wanted to share with her and Jory. But what if she did not – could not – feel the same?

Sweat broke out on his body as every nerve and muscle tightened in anticipation of pain that would be far worse than anything he had previously experienced. Physical injuries healed and scar tissue lacked sensation.

But words once spoken could not be recalled or erased. There would be no going back. She would be honest with him. Her integrity and her respect for their friendship would permit nothing less, denying him even the bleak comfort of platitudes.

He would wait a little longer, give her more time. Meanwhile, in every way he could think of, he would try to *show* her how important she was to him.

'Mr Crago!' Jory hurtled out of the barn, a grin splitting his small face.

Before he could utter a warning, the boy slowed to a walk and circled round so the horses could see him. 'Cor! Are they yours, Mr Crago?'

'They are.' Crago nodded. 'Run and fetch me four halters from the tack room. Wait.' Jory's eyes were red. 'I'll come as well.'

'I can do it.' Jory backed away.

'I don't doubt it,' Crago retorted in his usual brisk manner, knowing that would reassure. 'But I want water buckets as well. The horses need a drink.'

'I'll fetch them soon as I've brung the halters. You unhitch the wagon.' He raced off across the yard.

Catching Crago's eye, Zack grinned and then shook his head.

Crago unshackled the leading pair from the long shafts and led them across the yard, leaving Zack to deal with the other two.

'What you got them for?' Jory panted, waiting for Crago to replace the full bucket with an empty one before working the pump handle again. Water gushed and foamed.

'To carry stone from Talvan quarry down to Mr Trenery's quay.'

Stripped of its harness, each one of the lead pair was tied to a separate ring on the outside wall, their noses buried in the buckets as they sucked up water. Zack had led the other two inside.

'Are you going to groom them now?' Jory asked. 'Shall I fetch the leather bucket?'

'In a moment.' Crago crouched. 'Come here,' he said softly, relieved when the boy immediately approached. 'Just between you and me,' he kept his voice low, 'Are you in trouble with Noah?'

Jory shook his head. 'No.'

'Have you hurt yourself?'

Jory shook his head again. 'I'm all right, honest. You won't tell Ma?'

Crago laid a gentle hand the boy's shoulder. 'Not if you don't want me to.'

Jory's chin quivered for a moment, then he swallowed. 'Can I go and get the brushes now?'

Crago nodded, rising to his feet. If the boy wasn't ready to talk, it would be counterproductive to press him. 'Yes, but be careful when you come back. The horses aren't used to you yet.'

'If I had some sugar lumps, they would know I was their friend,' Jory wheedled. 'Then I could brush their legs and save you a job.'

'Run rings round you, he will,' Zack grinned as he passed, carrying two buckets of water.

Glancing down at shaggy hooves the size of dinner plates shod in iron, Crago lifted his gaze to Jory's little face. 'If you get trodden on,' he warned, digging in to the pocket of his breeches and dropping four sugar lumps in to a small, dirty hand, 'your mother will be extremely angry. Neither of us would enjoy that.'

'I'll be careful,' Jory promised as the huge mare raised her head from the bucket, water dripping from her whiskery muzzle.

*   *   *

Standing at the rear of the shay, Sarah handed the last of the quarry workers his pay packet and waited while he made his mark in the wages book that lay open on the wooden planks of the flatbed. Handing her the pencil, the worker touched his cap and turned away down the slope, following the others back to work.

Closing the book, she hugged it as she looked down at the activity. The quarry had already increased in size by a third. The blacksmith stood at his anvil, beating and shaping a length of iron.

Recent blasting had heaved out another massive chunk of granite from the new rock face. Two teams of men were boring holes for plugs and feathers to split it in to several blocks. Another two men were using the crab winch to haul smaller pieces within reach of the spider for loading on to Mr Trenery's wagon.

Glancing over her shoulder, she saw Jeb approaching. Becky returned from the quarry edge. Sarah placed the wages book in her basket and took out a jar of blackcurrant and another of gooseberry jam.

'Dear life!' Becky said as she reached the shay. ''Tis some great pit. If my John could see it now, he'd be some pleased, dear of him.'

Sarah offered the jam to her foreman. 'I really appreciate all your hard work, Jeb. This is just a small token of my gratitude.'

'You didn't need to do that,' the foreman mumbled, then tugged the brim of his cap. 'Making good money, we are. Still, I won't say no. My missus love your jam. Much obliged.' About to leave, he turned back. 'Look, I daresay it don't mean nothing. You can tell me I'm seeing trouble where there isn't none . . .'

'We can't say nothing till we know what you're on about,' Becky pointed out. 'C'mon, my 'andsome. Spit it out.'

'Well, I was in the Three Tuns last night with my brother-in-law, and Eddy Rowse was in there mouthing off about some special job he've been hired for.'

'Eddy Rowse? Special job?' Becky rolled her eyes. 'Half the time Eddy don't know which way is up. 'Tis all talk. Known for it, he is.'

'True,' Jeb agreed. 'But, see, he was halfway to drunk.'

'That's nothing new,' Becky muttered.

'She's right, Jeb,' Sarah said.

'With respect, Miss, you're missing the point. Gwyn would never have served Eddy without seeing he had the money to pay.

And to get Eddy swaying like he was last night would take a brave bit of beer.'

Becky's brows climbed. 'So what's this job, then?'

Jeb shrugged. 'Gwyn asked'n but Eddy just winked and said it was a secret.'

Becky snorted in disgust, pursing her lips. 'Eddy haven't done a full day's work in years.'

Jeb nodded. 'That's what I can't figure. Who'd be daft enough to hire him at all, let alone give'n money in advance?'

'Not you,' Becky said. 'You got more sense.'

Jeb shook his head. 'I dunno why I'm fretting. It's just, when he seen me, Eddy jumped like I was a ghost or something. Then he dropped his tankard and bolted out the back door.'

Patting his arm, Becky smiled up at him. 'You shame'n, Jeb. That's what 'tis.'

'Aw, get on.' The foreman's weathered face creased in to a shy grin.

'She's right,' Sarah said over her shoulder, as she hitched herself on to the shay and gathered up the reins. 'Without you, I'd never have been able to hang on to Talvan. None of this,' her gesture encompassed the expanding quarry, 'would be happening.'

'Reck'n Mr Crago had a part in it,' Jeb said, and Sarah's heart quickened.

James. She owed him so much.

'You got that right,' Becky nodded.

Jeb lifted the jam. 'Much obliged, Miss.' Then he stomped away.

Clicking her tongue, Sarah urged the donkey in to a trot.

'Who'd be daft enough to pay Eddy Prowse for work he haven't done yet?' Becky mused.

'Maybe they paid him half in advance, with the other half to come when the job is finished,' Sarah suggested.

'More fool them. They won't see hide nor hair of him now.'

Sarah shivered. Despite the warm sunshine, anxiety feathered like cold breath over her skin.

Becky glanced at her. 'All right, bird?'

Sarah nodded, forcing a smile. 'I'm fine.' But she wasn't. She felt unsettled, nervous. It made no sense. The quarry was more productive than it had ever been. She had the men and machinery she needed. The contract with Mr Trenery guaranteed work and a healthy profit for the foreseeable future. James had promised to find an additional wagon and team. So why did she have this gnawing sense of dread?

Philip closed the front door quietly. After one of the most disconcerting days he had ever endured, it was actually a relief to come home. He started towards his study. He needed a stiff drink and time to gather his thoughts.

He was halfway across the tiled hall when Mrs Carne bustled out of the kitchen.

"Evening, Mr Ansell. Mistress said you was to go in to her as soon as you got home.'

Philip's lips tightened as he fought the quick spurt of temper. 'I will see her shortly.'

'Beg pardon, Sir. But she was most partic'lar. Said I should tell you right away.'

'And now you have,' Philip spoke through gritted teeth. 'Thank you, Mrs Carne.' Margaret was getting above herself. He might have to bite his tongue when dealing with her father, but he had no intention of permitting such impertinence from his wife.

God knows he had made allowance for her endless weeping. Now she was taking advantage. Sending him instructions via the housekeeper was totally unacceptable. Such presumption must be nipped in the bud. He started towards the stairs.

'She isn't up there, Mr Ansell,' Mrs Carne said. 'In the drawing room, she is.' Philip stopped and turned as the housekeeper waddled back to the kitchen.

'The girls?' he called after her.

She paused. 'Gone up their grandma's. Mrs Tregenza come for them this afternoon.' She disappeared, the door swinging shut behind her.

His relief deepened. Though fond of his daughters, tonight he was in no mood for their prattle. Changing direction, he crossed to the drawing room. He had not expected Margaret to leave her bed so soon. Yesterday she had been as pale as candle wax with plum-coloured shadows beneath her eyes.

Doubtless she would enjoy regaling her female acquaintance with details of her suffering. But what of the difficulties *he* faced every day? Did she ever spare a thought for those? Greasy perspiration beaded his forehead as he recoiled from too-vivid memories of the interview that had followed Horace Tregenza's grim-faced arrival.

Squaring his shoulders, he jutted his chin, deliberately stoking anger at being summoned like one of his own staff. Opening the door, he paused. He had expected to see his wife lying on one of the sofas, propped on pillows and clutching a cologne-soaked handkerchief.

Instead, wearing a gown of lilac and pink shot-silk and a frilled cap, she was seated at the walnut bureau, writing.

His forehead tightening, he waited impatiently for her to acknowledge his arrival. But she didn't look up and continued writing.

'Good evening, Margaret.' He spoke sharply, making no effort to hide his irritation. 'I am surprised to see you downstairs.'

Laying down her pen, she turned in the chair, resting one arm along its back as she surveyed him.

'Are you, Philip? Please sit down.'

'You must excuse me. I have had a particularly trying day and require a period of quiet before dinner. First, however, I must tell you I did not appreciate being instructed by Mrs Carne—'

'I wished to speak to you,' she interrupted, astonishing him. Margaret *never* interrupted.

Something had changed. Normally clingy and anxious to please, she was now aloof, distant. In recent years her efforts to ingratiate herself and win his approval had irritated him beyond measure. But this sudden withdrawal disturbed him. Despite the familiarity of her features, he had the impression that he was talking to a stranger.

'I don't care for your tone, Margaret,' he warned.

'Don't you?'

Her blatant lack of concern unsettled him even further. This was not how he had envisaged their conversation. She shouldn't be this way. Flicking his coat-tails aside, he lowered himself in to an armchair.

'As you see, I am sitting. Now perhaps you will do me the courtesy of—'

'How long,' she enquired coolly, 'have you known about your son?' He stopped breathing for a moment, staring at her while his thoughts raced.

'Please don't insult me with denials.' Her tone was weary. 'It is all over the town. I overheard the laundry girl telling Mrs Carne. Would you care to hear her exact words? Philip Ansell is the father of Sarah Govier's boy.'

He moistened his lips. 'And you believe two gossiping women?'

'Shouldn't I? Lizzie was certainly convinced.'

Rising, he took a step forward. 'Margaret—'

'Don't.' She lifted a hand. 'Don't come near me. Just answer my question. How long have you known?'

Blood pounded thickly in his head. First her father, now this. It was too much. He clasped his hands behind his back, then gripped the lapels of his coat as he paced towards the window. 'Really, my dear,' he tossed the words over his shoulder. 'There is no need for such drama. There is no proof the child is mine.'

'Yet she must have had cause to believe that he was. So it follows that you must have lain with her.'

'This is intolerable!' he shouted. 'I will not be questioned in this manner. It's none of your business. I don't wish to hear—'

'You married me,' Margaret was quiet but determined, 'aware that another woman was expecting your child?'

'No! I knew nothing of the kind. How many more times do I have to say it? First your father—' He could have bitten off his tongue.

'My father?'

'It's of no consequence. To answer your question, I only learned of this woman's claim after we came back from our honeymoon.'

'Even if I accept that as truth, you have known for seven years that you might have a son.'

'*Might* have. And even if – just suppose – he is mine, he's not *ours*.'

She tilted her head. 'In that case, why do you want the boy?'

He clenched his teeth. He couldn't tell her he *didn't* want Jory, had never wanted him. Had only threatened to take him in order to force Sarah's hand. Now between them, Sarah and Margaret had backed him in to a corner. He wouldn't have it. How *dare* they?

'Why not?' he shrugged. Guilt, fear and fury spilling out as spite. 'Your efforts to give me a son have been singularly unsuccessful. Why should I deny any longer the son that might be mine?' He waited, expecting her to crumble in to sobs. He would let her suffer for a while, then show some mercy and magnanimity. The last thing he wanted was for her to go crying to her father.

But though every scrap of colour had drained from her face, leaving her ashen with knuckles that gleamed bone-white, her eyes remained dry. Her throat worked as she swallowed. Hoarse with shock, her voice dripped contempt.

'So, what is your plan? Assuming you are able to wrest the boy away from his mother, what then? Am I expected to welcome this little cuckoo in to our nest?' She shook her head. 'Not while I have breath, Philip.' Turning her back on him, she picked up her pen.

Shaken to the core by the disaster he had unleashed, he crossed to the door, telling himself the tremors that gripped him were the result of rage, not fear.

'I will ascribe this unseemly outburst to your weakened health and the effect on your mind of your recent loss. But be warned, Margaret, my patience is at an end. I will not be spoken to in such a manner. I suggest you take time to reflect on the duty a wife owes to her husband.' He swept out, closing the door firmly, then stood listening, expecting to hear her break down in sobs. That would have reassured him. Instead, the silence was far more frightening.

Twenty-Four

''Tis too soon to go worrying.' Becky laid a calming hand on Sarah's arm. 'Could be Noah had to stay on a while to finish a job. He'd never let Jory come home on his own.'

Sarah shook her head. Her stomach writhed like a knot of snakes, and though she kept taking deep breaths, she couldn't get enough air. 'It's after six, Becky. They're never this late.'

'Then like as not Jory is over chatting to Ivy. I know she love to hear what he been doing. I'll go across and see if he's there.'

'I'll come with—'

'No, you stay here.' Becky said. 'What if he was to come in and find the both of us gone? I'll be back d'rectly.' She hurried out.

Stirring the stew that had been ready for an hour, Sarah replaced the lid, moved the pan further from the flames and pulled the big black kettle over to heat water for Jory's bath. There could be any number of reasons for him being late. Any minute now he'd come running in.

She carried the pile of ironing upstairs and put it all away, moving from her room to Jory's and listening for the sound of his running feet on the path.

She heard the click of the latch, then the gate slam, and flew downstairs reaching the front door as Becky panted over the threshold.

'Where is he?' Fear gripped Sarah's throat and squeezed.

'Noah have been home since five,' Becky gasped, one hand pressed to her heaving chest. 'Far as he know, Jory's with Mr Crago. He thought 't'was all arranged. That's how he never come over.'

Sarah shook her head. 'It wasn't. Jory would have told me.' She pushed past.

Becky grabbed her arm. 'Where you going?'

'Jericho Farm. If he comes home while I'm out—'

'I'll keep him here. Don't worry, bird.'

'Too late.' Not caring how it might look, she picked up her skirts and ran, leaping over ruts and stones. After five minutes her lungs were on fire and her throat was dry. But only when the knifing pain in her side grew unbearable did she slow to a fast walk. *Please let him be safe. Let him be with James.* Her heart pounded and her shift clung damply to her skin. As soon as the pain eased, she started running again. By the time she reached the yard, her legs ached and trembled from the exertion and she was sobbing for breath.

The back door stood open. She tried to shout but all that emerged was a croak. The kitchen was empty. She looked frantically around the yard. *The stables!* As she stumbled towards them, Crago came out carrying an empty water bucket.

'Sarah?' Dropping the bucket, he came quickly towards her. 'What is it? What's wrong?'

'Jory?' she rasped, bending forward as her head swam.

'What about him? Has he been hurt?'

Dread broke over her in a suffocating wave. She was drowning in it. 'Isn't he here?'

'No.' Concern drew his brows together. 'Did he not go home with Noah?'

Sarah shook her head. 'Noah thought he was staying on with you.'

'I haven't seen him since about four.' His big hand was warm as it cupped her elbow. 'Did you run all the way?'

She nodded, allowing herself to lean against him for one precious moment, drawing strength from his powerful frame.

'Come inside and—'

'No.' She forced herself upright, away from him. 'I need to find him first. He's never gone missing before. We have a rule. He tells me where he's going, who with, and what time he'll be home. Something's happened—'

'Sarah!'

Like cold water dashed in her face, his sharp tone helped her regain control. 'I'm sorry.'

'He's definitely not with the horses. You search the house. I'll check the hayloft, tack room and the rest of the outbuildings.' He gripped her hand for a moment. 'We will find him, Sarah.'

Scalding tears sprang in to her eyes and his image splintered. She bit hard on her bottom lip to stop it quivering. Another sob wrenched her chest but she swallowed it down. Squeezing her hand, he released it and they separated. As he strode towards the tack room, she raced across to the back door and in to the kitchen.

'Jory?' she shouted, recalling her last visit: James showing her around the house, pointing out the changes and improvements. She peered under the camp bed, looked in the scullery and larder, and then ran into the hall. After searching the ground floor, she sped upstairs.

'Jory, are you there? If you're hiding, come out now. Please, love. Please come out.' Her pleas echoed through the empty house.

She returned to the kitchen as Crago walked in from the yard, shaking his head before she could ask.

'I don't understand. Where is he?' Images of him alone and frightened or lying injured filled her head. Terrified, helpless. She hugged herself and paced.

'Sarah, will you wait here for me?'

'Why? Where are you going?'

'To the woods.'

The gunpowder mill. She felt the blood drain from her face. Suddenly light-headed, she braced against the table.

'I'll be as quick as I can—'

'I'm coming with you.' Shaking her head to clear it, she sucked in a deep breath and straightened up. 'I have to. I can't stay here. He's my son.'

He nodded. 'Show me your feet.'

Quickly she lifted each in turn. 'They're the same boots I wore the first time I came to see you.'

He caught her eye and one corner of his mouth tilted. 'An occasion etched on my soul.' His expression and the shared memory were a brief respite from anxiety. Then he frowned. 'Your hair.'

Swiftly pulling the metal pins out, she dropped them on the table and saw his eyes widen as the thick coil loosened and tumbled down her back.

Abruptly he turned away and changed his riding boots for the soft ones he always wore to the mill.

He slammed the door closed. 'Take my hand,' he ordered as they hurried down the track to the woods. 'It's rough underfoot. The last thing you want is to fall.'

Despite her apprehension, she drew comfort and renewed strength from his firm grasp.

As they reached the clearing, Sarah saw Zack crouched beside the campfire, feeding chopped wood in to the flames. Straightening up, he raised a finger to his lips and gestured for them to back off. With an uncertain look at the man beside her, Sarah waited.

'The boy's here,' Zack said softly, jerking his thumb towards the wagon. 'Safe and well. I wanted to bring'n home, but he wouldn't have it. Something have scared him good and proper but he wouldn't say what 'tis.'

Leaving the two men, Sarah ran to the wagon. 'Jory?'

A small figure appeared in the doorway. 'Ma?' Jumping down the wooden steps, he hurtled towards her, his arms outstretched. 'I knew you'd come.'

Sarah swept him up and swung him round while she fought tears. *He was safe.* 'You little baggage. I've been so worried. Why didn't you come home?'

His arms tightened around her neck and he wrapped his legs around her waist, clinging like a limpet. 'I was 'fraid,' he muttered in to her neck.

'Why?' Sarah asked gently. 'What were you afraid of?' She carried him towards the fire, where Zack and Crago were waiting.

'That man.'

'What man, my love?'

'That man who came to our house and made you sad. I heard you tell Aunty Beck he might take me away and you couldn't stop him.' Sarah's gaze flew to Crago and she hugged Jory closer. But before she could find the words to comfort her son, he went on, 'Then today when me and Uncle Noah was in town for wood, I seen him again. He was across the road looking at me. Then we went back to the farm. But I was 'fraid to come home in case the man might have come to take me away.'

Sarah closed her eyes. 'Oh, sweetheart. I'm so sorry you were frightened.' She desperately wanted to reassure him, tell him his fears were groundless. But how could she?

'Jory?' Gently rubbing Jory's back, Crago rested his free hand on the nape of Sarah's neck.

''Lo, Mr Crago.'

'Jory, no one will take you away. You will never have to leave your mother.'

As Sarah opened her mouth, Crago's hand tightened in unmistakable warning.

'You promise?' Jory's small face was pale, his eyes huge with anxiety and hope.

'I promise,' Crago said.

Sarah bent and set her son down, forcing herself to smile in order to reassure him. 'It's time we were going home. Run along and fetch your croust bag and thank Zack for looking after you.'

As he skipped away across the clearing, Sarah turned on Crago. 'You shouldn't have done that,' she hissed in blazing anger. 'How can you make such a promise? Your attorney told you the new law does not apply to Jory.'

He looked away for a moment. 'This is not . . .' He turned back to her, his expression unreadable. 'If you married me, Ansell would have little chance of making a successful claim.'

Stunned, she stared at him, yearning, aching. She loved him so much. Desperately tempted, she looked away. His offer was generous and she knew it to be sincere, but she could not accept. Not even to protect her son would she marry a man who did not love her.

Philip's seduction and abandonment had shattered her spirit. Keeping Jory had destroyed her reputation. But remaining independent since her father's death, supporting herself and her son by her own efforts, she had gradually reclaimed her self-respect.

Marrying James Crago under these circumstances would be the act of a coward. It would cost her everything she had striven so hard to rebuild. Had he loved her, it would have been different. Had he loved her, she would be the happiest woman in the county. Had he loved her . . .

Behind her, Crago cleared his throat. 'It was not my intention to embarrass you.' He sounded stiff, hoarse. 'If you will excuse me, I must check the drying house. Should you desire an escort home, I'm sure Zack . . .' With a brief bow, he loped away.

Closing her eyes, Sarah heaved a shaky breath. Her throat felt painfully tight. He had not tried to persuade her. Did that not prove she had done the right thing? He didn't love her. If he did, he would have said so.

At least Jory was safe. She should take her son and leave now. Becky would be waiting, anxious for news. She should go, but she couldn't. His proposal had taken her totally by surprise. Yet because she had not instantly fallen on his neck in gratitude, he had simply walked away. That was not fair. What had he expected? Surely, knowing how frightened she had been, he could have allowed her a few moments? Time to frame a reply?

She could not have accepted. But nor could she simply leave, not like this, with so much left unsaid. He had paid her a great compliment. For that, at least, he deserved a response.

'Zack?' She ran towards the wagon. 'Can Jory stay with you a little while longer? I need to speak to James – Mr Crago. He's gone—' she gestured. 'And I forgot to—'

'Go on, maid.' He waved her away. 'Boy'll be fine with me.'

She ran across the clearing and down the thickly wooded slope, trying to avoid tree roots and protruding rocks on the narrow path. Her boot slipped on a patch of mud and she grabbed hold of a sapling, narrowly avoiding a fall that might easily have snapped a bone. She stood for a moment to catch her breath and heard the rushing sound of the stream and the creak of the waterwheel.

Looking down the slope, she saw James's back as he disappeared in to the glazing shed. Then, glimpsing movement, she saw a figure – a man – sidle round from behind the powder mill and slip inside. *Eddy Rowse.*

'James!' she screamed and, without hesitating, plunged down the path. As he appeared in the doorway, she pointed. 'The powder mill! I saw someone—'

'Stay there!' He raced past the corning and pressing sheds, towards the mill.

What was he doing? As her hands flew to her mouth, she heard him shout, 'Nessa!' Then with a thunderous roar that made the ground vibrate, the powder mill exploded.

Flung backward by the shock wave, Sarah found herself lying on the ground, her ears ringing. Scrambling unsteadily to her feet, she clung to a tree, the acrid smell of burnt gunpowder making her cough. Around her dust and leaves hurled skyward by the blast thickened the air as they drifted earthward.

She heard running feet, the cracking of twigs, and saw Zack pounding towards her, with Jory several yards behind.

'Take care of your boy!' he shouted as, white-faced with fear, arms flailing, he skidded and stumbled down the path.

Trembling with shock, dread a metallic taste in her mouth, Sarah caught Jory and looked down the slope, searching. She saw James, his face a bloody mask, trying to sit up. Zack had jumped in to the stream and was splashing towards Nessa, who lay unmoving.

'Ma?' Jory tugged her hand, his voice high-pitched, quavering. 'Is Nessa dead?'

'I don't think so.' Sarah gripped his shoulders and held his frightened gaze. 'Wait here, love.' As he nodded, she hurried down to the debris-strewn bank.

'James?' He had managed to sit up. His head drooped and his arms hung between his bent knees. Kneeling beside him, she gently turned his face and smoothed back his hair. Blood trickled from several cuts and there was a graze along his cheekbone.

'I'm all right,' he muttered, clearly dazed. 'Just need a minute.' Suddenly he stiffened. 'Nessa?'

'In the stream. Zack's with her now. Stay there.' She pressed on his shoulder as he tried to move. 'I'll help him. Don't you move.'

She slithered down in to the stream, gasping at the shock of the cold water. It quickly soaked her skirt and petticoats and they dragged as she waded towards Zack, who was struggling to lift his daughter.

An egg-sized swelling above Nessa's left eyebrow was already turning purple and blood trickled from a cut on her forehead. But her eyes were open and, though pale and shocked, she was holding on to her father and trying to stand.

Supporting Nessa between them, they waded to the bank. Zack clambered up, and with Sarah pushing from below, hauled his daughter out. Then they both collapsed, completely spent.

Sarah tried to scramble up. But her boots slipped on the muddy bank and her sodden clothes weighed her down. Shivering, she could feel panic building but dared not cry for help in case she frightened Jory.

'Here, take my hand.'

James was on his hands and knees, battered and bloody, but reaching down to her. Looking in to his beloved face, she felt her own crumple. Scalding tears poured over her cheeks as she grasped his hand. Then she was on firm ground, heart pounding, limbs trembling with shock and relief.

'The explosion . . . I was so afraid – I thought you might be . . .' She shuddered, her fear still too raw.

'No, I'm all right.' As she reached out to touch him, he eased away. 'I can't . . .' His gaze met hers and the naked pain in his eyes pierced her soul. 'Dry your eyes,' he said softly. 'Jory hates to see you cry.'

With no handkerchief, Sarah wiped her eyes and nose on her wet petticoat.

'Ma?'

Scrambling to her feet, she opened her arms to her son.

'You been crying,' he accused, his lower lip quivering.

'I was frightened in case Mr Crago was hurt, and Nessa,' she said. 'But they are both all right, see?'

'Mr Crago got all blood on his face.'

'Don't worry, Jory. It will wash off.' Sarah heard a bone-deep weariness in his voice.

'James, the man I saw—'

'Dead. Which is fortunate for him. Had you been any closer . . .' He looked away, a muscle jumping in his jaw. 'Take Jory home, Sarah.'

She dug deep for courage. 'Come with us.'

He shook his head.

'Please.' She touched his hand. 'I . . . You need a hot meal and I have a pan of stew ready.'

'Please, Mr Crago?' Jory begged. 'That man won't come if you're there.'

His gaze was shuttered, unreadable. Sarah felt her cheeks burn. 'What you said – I wasn't expecting . . . Then you left before . . .'

He turned his head, his voice an anguished whisper for her ears only. 'Your answer was clear enough, I did not need to hear the words.'

'You are wrong,' she said simply. 'And so was I.'

'Sarah . . .' For an instant his guard dropped and the tangle of hope, fear and yearning she read in his face stopped her breath. What a fool she had been.

'Oh, James—'

Shouts and footsteps crashing down the slope heralded the arrival of others alerted by the explosion.

He got to his feet. 'I can't – I need to . . . The body . . .'

'I understand. Come when you can. If you want to,' she added quickly.

'Do you doubt it? But I might be a while,' he warned.

'It doesn't matter. I'll be waiting.' She smiled, letting him see the love that fear had kept hidden.

Catching her hand, he pressed his lips to her palm and his eyes told her all that she needed to know. Then he looked down at her son. 'Take your mother home. I'll be along as soon as I can.'

*   *   *

It was after six when Philip arrived home. He had remained in the office until five thirty, then after a chat with his father concerning two new clients, walked slowly up the hill, nodding and touching his hat to various acquaintances. One or two had seemed distant but he had been listening so hard that he had barely noticed.

The instructions had been explicit. The explosion must be timed to coincide with end-of-day blasting at the quarries, when huge chunks of granite were heaved out of the rock face ready for the morning. But how to differentiate between those and the destruction of his nemesis? He fancied that he would know. Besides, the news would be all over town by the morning. And he, eating dinner with his wife, would be blameless.

Closing the front door behind him, he lay his hat on the polished mahogany table. He checked his appearance in the mirror, then crossed the hall to the drawing room and opened the door. Expecting to see Margaret, he was surprised to find the room empty.

Mrs Carne met him in the hall. 'I thought I heard you come in. Mistress isn't here. Her mother and father was down earlier. She went back with them.'

'I see. Will she be home for dinner?'

'Shouldn't think so,' the housekeeper shook her head. 'They took a trunk and I dunno how many bags. There's a note.' She pointed to his study. 'Your dinner'll be ready in half an hour.' She started back to the kitchen.

'Mrs Carne,' Philip snapped, waiting until she turned. 'I will tell you when I wish dinner to be served.'

The housekeeper nodded. 'Cora can serve it any time you like, Mr Ansell. I'm just telling you when 't'will be ready.' With a brisk nod, she waddled back in to the kitchen.

Philip frowned after her. He recognized insolence when he heard it. He should have said something. He *had*. But that must wait. Trunks? A note? What was going on?

Squaring his shoulders, he marched across the hall to his study, his heels clicking loudly on the tiles. Propped against the inkwell where he could not miss it was a cream envelope with his name on the front, written not in Margaret's small, neat hand, but in Horace Tregenza's flowing scrawl.

Seated in his leather chair, Philip re-read the letter, which trembled in his vice-like grip.

... Deeply upset to find her husband the subject of lurid gossip, Margaret has decided she would be more comfortable convalescing in her childhood home, where she will have the privacy of our extensive gardens in which to walk and rebuild her strength. Naturally the girls wish to be with their mother. As Margaret's husband and the girls' father, you may, of course, visit whenever you wish . . .

'Oh, yes,' he spat. 'I can just imagine my welcome.' Screwing up the sheet of paper, he hurled it across the room, then seized the whisky decanter and splashed three fingers in to a crystal tumbler. He gulped down, feeling the spirit sear his throat, then winced as it hit his tender stomach. Leaning back, he raised the tumbler in a defiant toast. 'Freedom.'

After dinner, he sprawled in his chair, gazing at the tawny port as he swirled it. Was it true? Was the whole town talking about him? So what if they were? If Eddy Rowse had done his job properly, they'd soon have something far more shocking to pick over.

Draining the port, he pushed himself to his feet and walked unsteadily to the door. Collecting his hat from the hall, he let himself out, slamming the door behind him. On the doorstep he blinked hard, breathed deeply to clear his head and set off up the street.

Turning in to the alley that led behind the Three Tuns, he hammered on a door.

Opening it, Sally Jenkins stood on the threshold wearing a grubby yellow gown with elbow-length sleeves and a neckline cut low to expose the generous swell of her breasts. Drawn up in to a careless knot, frizzy hair framed her painted face with curls and ringlets.

'Well, now.' A knowing smile curved her wide mouth and she rested one hand on her hip. 'Look what the cat dragged in.' She shook her head. 'You got tongues wagging, all right.'

He glared at her. 'I didn't come here for a lecture.'

'No?' she mocked. 'So what did you come for?'

Pushing her back inside, he pressed her roughly against the peeling wall and bit her neck. 'Guess.'

Agile as an eel, she slid free and held out her hand, snapping her fingers against her palm in imperious demand.

'I aren't giving it away, my 'andsome.' Her tone was dry. 'Let's see some money first.'

Twenty-Five

While Becky bathed Jory in front of the fire, Sarah took a bucket of warm water in to the scullery and stripped off her wet, muddy clothes. She was drying her feet when Becky tapped on the door and poked her head in.

'All right, bird? Boy's all done. He've had his tea. I'll take they wet things outside and stream the mud off.' Gathering them up, she bustled out.

Putting on a clean shift, Sarah reached for her blue calico gown. Freshly washed and ironed, it smelled of soap and sunshine.

'Give us that bucket,' Becky ordered. 'Leave the towels in the sink. I'll see to 'em d'rectly. You get your hair dried.'

Understanding the fear behind Becky's bossiness, Sarah put her arms around the older woman. 'It's all right,' she whispered. 'We're safe.'

Becky hugged her hard. 'Dear life,' she whispered. 'When I heard that blast – I knew it wasn't Talvan. I tell 'ee, bird, I never been so scared in all my life.'

'Ma?'

Sarah released Becky, who picked up the bucket and marched briskly outside, her head averted as she quickly wiped her eyes. Sarah quickly turned to her son. 'Yes, love?'

'Can I stay up till Mr Crago comes?' His toffee curls had been brushed, his rosy cheeks shone from Becky's scrubbing and his head was propped on one arm. But his eyelids were drooping.

'No, sweetheart. We don't know how long he's going to be. Come on. Up the stairs with you.' He pulled a face, but slid off the chair. 'Want a carry?' As he lifted his arms, she picked him up and pretended to stagger. 'Dear life, how much stew did you eat?'

'Lots.' His soft giggle warmed her heart. 'Will you ask him to come up and say goodnight?'

She nodded. 'I promise.' His eyes closed. By the time she had tucked the sheet and blanket around him, he was already asleep.

Scooping her damp hair back over her shoulders, she walked downstairs.

Becky stood near the fire clutching a ladle. 'You going to eat now? I had mine with Jory.'

'I'd rather wait until James comes. He—'

'Could be hours. Come on, bird. After all you been through, he wouldn't expect you to wait—'

Hearing the gate latch click, Sarah bolted to her feet. 'Becky . . .'

Patting Sarah's cheek, Becky laid the ladle on a plate. 'Everything's all right.' While Sarah pressed a hand to her fluttering stomach, Becky opened the door.

'Come in, my 'andsome.' She stood back to let him to pass. 'Right, I'm gone. See you tomorrow, bird.' She disappeared, closing the door behind her.

Crago's face was clean. His hair, still wet, was ridged with comb marks and he had changed his clothes. They both spoke at once.

'James—'

'Sarah—'

Then he opened his arms and she walked in to them.

Twenty-Six

Her arm tucked through his, Sarah smiled at her new husband as they walked up the wide staircase. 'How did you do it?'

'Persuade the vicar to come here?' With the evening light streaming through the landing window, she saw mischief dance in his eyes. He shrugged. 'I confided my fear that if it were held in the church, my appearance might turn our wedding into a sideshow for the curious. When I produced the special licence, he agreed there was nothing to prevent him conducting the ceremony here.'

'That was wicked.' She hugged his arm. 'But I'm so glad you did it. I did not want a public spectacle. Today was for us.'

'And Jory, Becky, Ivy and Noah,' he teased.

'And Zack and Nessa,' she reminded.

'Sam, Joe, Jeb and their wives.'

'Miss Nicholls was thrilled that I invited her. She worked day and night to have my dress ready. She and Ivy cried all through the ceremony.'

'I nearly did myself when I watched you enter the drawing room between Becky and Jory,' he admitted. 'I wondered who you would ask to support you. I know Noah and Jeb would have been honoured.'

She shook her head, smiling. 'Jory is my nearest male relative, and Becky has been as dear to me as any mother could be. It may have looked strange, but—'

'It was perfect. You didn't mind Mrs Hitchens taking him back with her tonight?'

'I had no say in it. Becky informed me it was all settled.'

'But you're happy with it?'

She met his gaze, felt her face colour. 'Had she not already arranged it, I would have asked her. I have not been parted from Jory since the day he was born. But tonight . . .'

'*Tonight?*' he prompted. The smile hovering at the corners of his mouth deepened her blush.

'I wanted just for us,' she said simply.

'I'm relieved to hear that.' He opened the bedroom door and stood aside. 'Because it wasn't her idea.'

'Then whose . . .?'

'Mine.'

As she walked in, Sarah gave a tiny gasp. In the fireplace a huge vase of roses and honeysuckle perfumed the air. The bedcover had been turned back and pink and cream rose petals were scattered over the linen sheet and pillows.

'Oh! How lovely!'

He closed the door and turned her towards him. 'As are you. I have always thought you beautiful. Today,' he held her arms wide, then spun her round so her primrose silk gown swirled softly, 'You are a vision.' He caught her, drew her close and rested his forehead against hers. 'And you are mine, now and always. I love you, Sarah. You are my heart.'

She lifted her face to his kiss: a kiss that claimed and cherished. A kiss that melted her limbs and made every nerve end tingle.

He raised his head, carefully removed her hat and tossed it on to a rose velvet armchair. Then he unpinned her hair. As it tumbled in waves down her back, he gathered it in his fists and kissed her again.

She took his face in her hands, using her thumbs to trace the old brutal scars and the newly healed cuts and grazes. 'I love you, James. There aren't enough words to tell you how much.'

As evening fell and the sky darkened, shyness gave way to need and tenderness to passion. The past was forgotten as, with whispers and sighs, laughter and breathless moans, they discovered each other. And eventually, wrapped in each other's arms, they slept.